Binary Witness

Binary Witness

Book 1 in The Amy Lane Mysteries series

by

Rosie Claverton

BINARY WITNESS © Rosie Claverton
ISBN 978-1-9997652-4-8
eISBN 978-1-9997652-5-5

First edition published in 2014 by Carina Press
Second, revised edition published in 2018 by Crime Scene Books

A CIP record of this book is available from the British Library.

Cover image: David Oliver, The Image Bank, Getty Images
Cover design by blacksheep-uk.com
Printed in the UK by Marston Book Services

For Pam, the epitome of grace under pressure – thank you for showing me that all things are possible and raising your son to be my perfect husband.

Acknowledgements

Thank you to my talented editor, Deb Nemeth, for weaving her magic to turn my shabby manuscript into a novel. Thank you to Sarah Williams for giving this book a second life in paperback and continuing to support The Amy Lane Mysteries.

Thank you to Professor Burkhard Schafer of the University of Edinburgh for proving invaluable in my research on digital evidence and forensic computing. All the facts are his, and all the mistakes mine.

Thanks to all my friends and housemates who have lived at various locations in this novel, particularly Nicole who shared my wheelie bin anxiety.

Cardiff, I am so glad I came home to you. Consider this a love letter, hopefully the first of many.

Finally, thank you, Huw – words cannot express how much of this novel I owe to you and your indefatigable support. *Diolch yn fawr, cariad.*

Chapter 1: Reduce, Reuse, Recycle

The soft burble of the television threatened to lull her to sleep, and Kate forced her eyes open. She twirled the end of her messy blonde plait around her finger and tried to find the will to get off the sofa. *Have I Got News for You* had just finished, there was nothing on for half an hour, and if she didn't take the rubbish out before her housemate got back, there'd be hell to pay.

Neither of them could be bothered to get up early on a Monday morning after a weekend of shifts at the club, so Friday night was her opportunity to shove the wheelie bin out front. Kate knew they'd get poisonous looks from their lemon-sucking neighbour for leaving it out all weekend, but she was also the woman who'd complained about their barbecue last month. Kate had no qualms about ruffling her feathers.

With Herculean effort, Kate prised herself off the faux leather couch and stumbled towards the back door. Opening it let in a sharp draught of autumn air, and she drew back her hands into her hoodie sleeves, teeth already chattering. The outside light flickered to life, blinding her after the dim, dingy student living room. She'd add that to her tale of woe for her housemate later.

With one hand, she stuffed the kitchen waste into the overflowing black bin, while the other rummaged among the detritus on the windowsill for the gate key. She eventually found it among the cocktail umbrellas and, waving her arms to get the outside light on, she twisted the key against ancient rust to wrangle the lock open. She shut the back door, but didn't bother with the lock. It would only be for two minutes. What could happen in two minutes?

Pushing the bin like a mam with a pram, Kate manoeuvred the thing through the gate, wincing at something sticky between her palm and the handle. The light clicked off behind her, and she spent a minute or three trying to fit the wheelie bin round a corner too slim for it. Finally, it budged and she shoved it down the narrow alleyway to the street.

She wedged the bin against the windowsill, ignoring the twitching curtains. As long as the foxes didn't get at it, she didn't see the big deal. In October, the bin was more likely to freeze shut than raise a stench.

Kate looked back down the alley.

With the streetlights behind her, it looked ominous. High walls overshadowed the tiny walkway, with no light at the end to guide her through. The anaemic moonlight played off the ivy curtains, casting shadows that looked like men. Leafy green monsters. Kate scowled. It was stupid to be afraid – she'd only just walked down it. There was nothing there. Was there?

She crept down the alley, the darkness pressing in on her. The ivy monsters formed an honour guard as she passed, ready to end her with a branch bayonet at the slightest misstep. She was certain there were eyes on her, watching her, following her every move. Could she hear footsteps…?

Kate turned, twisting round to stare back at the road. Nothing. She took a deep breath, pulled herself together and hurried down the rest of the alley.

Reaching her gate, she stopped on the threshold. The outside light was on.

Suddenly, the feeling of being watched returned. She was sure the light had been off when she'd left. How could it be on now? What movement in the shadows had triggered it again? Kate was acutely aware that she'd left the door unlocked. Anyone could be inside her house.

'God, you're ridiculous,' she told herself and marched through the gate, slamming it shut behind her and snapping closed the lock. She walked determinedly towards the back door. It must've been a cat, or a mouse. How many times had it come on for no good reason? They should get the landlord to look at it.

Closing the back door behind her, Kate locked it and dropped the key on the windowsill. Then she turned to confront the house. The kitchen was a state, overflowing with dishes but empty of intruders, and she could see all the way through the dining area into the living room. There was nowhere a man could hide.

Kate breathed a guilty sigh of relief and returned to her spot on the sofa, but she didn't feel like TV anymore. She had to haul herself to the library in the morning, and she'd have to take the bus if it was raining. Of course, it was always bloody raining, but she'd moved to Wales – what else could she expect?

She turned off the lights, set the box to record *Dr. Quinn, Medicine Woman* (Naomi loved that retro nonsense) and made sure the dead-lock was off so Naomi could actually get in after her shift. Having her housemate howl down the door at 3:00 a.m. did nothing for their relationship with the neighbours.

The house slipped into its midnight state, the faint strains of Maroon 5 coming through one wall accompanied by the rhythmic banging of headboard against plaster. Kate yawned, plodding up the stairs and straight into the bathroom.

From the vantage point of the cracked toilet seat, she stared at the shower curtain. Naomi always pulled it across – to let it dry, she said, something about mould – and Kate hated it there. For a start, it was an ugly curtain, all mutant fish and kids' bathtime phrases on deep plastic blue.

And, secondly, it would make a great hiding place.

Shaking her head, Kate went to wash her hands in the sink, letting the water warm her hands and calm her nerves. It was just that bloody cat outside. That was all. She looked at her face in the mirror, picking at her blemishes.

Then, out of the corner of her eye, she realised: the shower curtain was drawn back.

Chapter 2: I'd Do Anything

'So, what do you want to be?'

Jason stared at the man incredulously. Ever since Jason had walked in and sat down in front of his desk, the nervous little man had grown more anxious, shrinking into his chair and tapping away at his keyboard as though it held the secrets of the universe. Sure, Jason was a big, white guy with a shaved head and a few tats, but he knew how to smile and speak softly. That got you a long way with people.

Still, this 'Martin' – as his neat plastic badge proclaimed – seemed to think Jason was about to pound him into the ground, and yet this didn't stop him asking stupid questions. What was the point of looking like a hard man if it didn't stop people asking you stupid questions?

'I want to be whatever gets me money.' Jason kept his voice even and calm, but that didn't stop Martin from shrivelling further into his chair.

'Er…anything specific you like, though? Something…um…outdoors? Or with animals?'

What did he want to do? His fingers itched to work, to craft something with his hands – make something, do something. And stay the fuck out of prison. Since getting out of lock-up, he'd spent every day in his mam's living room watching daytime TV. He could only take so much of 'My sister stole my girlfriend while I was in prison.' (If Cerys had done that, Jason hoped she'd have the sense to keep it off the television.)

'I like cars,' he said finally. His only escape was Dylan's garage over in Canton and the motors he fixed up. True, most of them weren't entirely legal, but it was good money. He could lose himself in the pure roar of the engine, the beauty of the whole working in harmony. But it was that legal thing that bothered him now. If he got involved in the business, it would draw attention to Dylan, and he couldn't do that to his mate. One of the few he had left.

Martin dutifully typed something on his keyboard that was a lot longer than 'cars' but he probably had some fancy name for it. Jason had no time for faff.

'Well…we have one vacancy,' Martin said, nervously smacking his lips and peering at his screen. 'It's not exactly cars…'

'I'll take it,' Jason said immediately. He couldn't care less what it was, as long as it was work. It had been a heavy blow to his pride just to walk through the doors of the job centre. Everything now was just getting on with business.

Martin blinked at him. 'Don't you want to know what it is?'

'Put my name down and then tell me where I'm going.' He wouldn't give himself any opportunity to turn chicken shit and back away from this now. Then he could go home and tell Mam and Cerys that he had a job now and that was that.

'Report to the Roath Cleaning Company on Monday morning, nine o'clock. They do commercial and domestics and they employ a lot of con…victs.' Martin looked at Jason with a mixture of terror and pity but Jason ignored him. He was used to that look now, got it from his mam's friends and his sister's boyfriends, the ones who thought he was stupid to get caught.

So, cleaning. That wouldn't be so bad. He'd grown to like order and cleanliness during his time inside, taking pride in a job well done. He'd just go to work, get it done, and then he'd have cash to go out with his mates on a Friday night, have a couple, and glare at the young boys from the Valleys down Catherine Street as they stuffed their flapping gobs with chips. He could help Dylan on the weekends and he could buy his mam something decent for Christmas. And, most of all, he'd have his pride.

'Yeah,' he said. 'I can do that.'

'Mam! I'm home!' Jason dumped his holdall on the kitchen floor and flopped down at the kitchen table. He felt tired for the first time in weeks, the pleasant ache of a hard day's work settling into his muscles.

'What the hell are you wearing?'

Jason looked up and scowled. Cerys stood in the doorway, giggling at him from behind her dyed-blonde fringe and freakish false eyelashes.

'That's a lovely shirt that is, Jason,' his mam said, breezing her way in and filling the kettle. Cerys's giggles erupted into sitcom laughter, an exaggerated state where the laugher holds their sides and requires the wall to prop them up. His long-suffering mother, the formidable Gwen Carr, wisely held her tongue.

'Mam, it's pink!' Cerys pointed out between spasms, and Jason directed his scowl at the table instead. It was definitely not pink. He wasn't wearing a pink anything. Apart from the Cardiff Blues away shirt, but that was different.

'It's lilac, Cerys. Don't be rude to your brother. He's got himself a job, thank God, and this is what he has to wear.' Gwen set down his mug in front of him and handed one off to Cerys, before picking up her own. 'Jason's paying his own way now.'

'He's cleaning toilets and washing old ladies' knickers.' Cerys curled one loop of peroxide hair around her finger. 'Any mug could do it.'

'Yeah, then why don't you?' Jason said, aware this conversation was descending into petty sniping.

Cerys sighed dramatically. 'Nobody works these days, Jason. It's a sign of the times. Something about the economy or some shit.'

'Mind your tongue, *bach*.' Gwen leaned up against the kitchen counter, her cracked red hands curling around the mug. 'So, how was your day? Did you meet some nice people? From around Roath Park, was it? Those houses are so lovely.'

With a final roll of her eyes, Cerys left the kitchen, humming as she ran up the stairs.

Jason watched her go and waited for the door to slam at the top of the stairs, before smiling up at his mam. 'I liked it. Was good to do something.'

Gwen smiled, the lines at the corner of her eyes and mouth deepening. 'That's my boy.' She sat down at the table with him and they sat in companionable silence for a few moments, nursing their cups of tea.

'Have you seen this terrible thing in the paper?' Gwen nudged the *South Wales Echo* across the table. 'There's a girl missing – she's a student, she is. Only nineteen, bless her.'

'She's probably run off with the boyfriend. That'll be Cerys next.' He raised his voice so that it carried up the stairs to his sister's ears. A door slammed loudly and he grinned.

Gwen frowned. 'Now, don't talk about your sister that way. She's doing the best she can.'

Jason snorted, earning 'a look' from his mother. 'She's doing what pleases her,' he said, with the newly acquired smugness of the employed. 'You should be more firm with her.'

Gwen grew silent, shifting her mug round and round between rough hands. 'Well, that was always your father's business, wasn't it? I was never one for being firm, *bach*. Drink your tea, now, and I'll see what I've got for dinner.'

She left him at the table while she poked around the freezer.

Would his father be proud of him, the cleaner in pink? The working man. For the past year, Jason had been glad his dad wasn't around to see the state he was in. But now he craved that approval and he was never going to get it, would never know for certain what his dad wanted for him. His mam didn't talk about him often and Cerys was too young to remember. Jason had been ten years old when he'd passed away – bowel cancer. The GP kept telling him he should get tested, sending out letters, but Jason quietly tore them up when his mam wasn't looking.

He didn't want to know how much he was his father's son.

Chapter 3: The Mothership

Jason slammed down the boot of his Nissan Micra and shouldered his bag. He adjusted his scratchy lilac T-shirt, garishly emblazoned with the company logo, and looked up at the house. It was one of a shabby pair of semi-detached houses, holding each other up like drunken sailors, paint peeling on the outside and gutters overflowing. There were two doors, side by side in the centre. The door on the left was boarded up, the windows shuttered with corrugated iron. The one on the right – 12 Canberra Road – had a fancy buzzer box with only one button and a thin screen at the top. The corners of the door were plastered with cobwebs – maybe the remnants of Halloween? He pressed the button, unable to hear the tone through the door, and waited.

Jason glanced down at the request again. The client lived in Australia and was hiring on behalf of her sister. He'd read the list of warnings, about the occupant refusing the previous two cleaners entry. This would be strike three.

After half a minute and no sound of movement from inside, Jason pressed the buzzer again. Immediately, the box beeped and Jason jerked his hand away. A digital display scrolled a message: *WHO ARE YOU?*

Jason was baffled as to why the door buzzer was writing to him. He leaned a little closer. 'Er…I'm Jason Carr. From the Roath Cleaning Company. I've come to clean your house.'

The box beeped again. *I DONT WANT YOU GO AWAY.*

Jason scratched at his chin with his knuckle. 'I don't think I can do that. I'm paid to be here for the next two hours.' Another insistent beep: *DONT CARE GET LOST.*

'Who still says "get lost"?' he muttered to himself.

He got down on his knees, pulling out his duster and starting work on those cobwebs. Halloween or not, it was now November and time they went.

The box beeped again.

Jason clambered to his feet and squinted at the screen: *I SAID GO AWAY.*

Jason stared down the box. 'Look, as I said, I'm paid to be here. If I can't clean the inside, I'll at least clean the door.'

A long pause, before a low buzz came from the box and the door shifted open. Jason pushed it all the way open with a satisfied smile and stepped over the threshold.

To find another door.

Slowly closing the front door behind him, Jason inspected this new barrier. Made of riveted reinforced metal, it looked like it could survive a nuclear holocaust. Abruptly, it jerked apart, revealing a small metal space: a lift.

'Well, this is fucking bizarre.' Was he about to take a trip to Dexter's Laboratory? He stepped inside and turned to face the door, looking for the buttons. Nothing. The metal was blank on both sides.

The doors jerked shut. Jason wasn't claustrophobic, but standing alone in a little metal box... He rubbed his sweaty palm on his jeans, struggling to keep breathing. The lift suddenly surged upwards and he steadied himself. *Get it together, Carr.*

The lift stopped. Behind him, the wall slid away. Jason turned, clutching his bag with a white-knuckle grip, and stepped out.

The air was stale, like the old attic at his nan's house. Beneath his feet, the carpet was dusty and covered in what looked like wood chippings. The hallway opened out to the left to reveal the living room, with decent furniture gone bad, dirty and worn.

'Hello?' Jason ventured farther into the flat and tried to get his heart rate down.

Then he saw her.

The first impression he had was of metal – three flat-screen monitors, surrounded by computer towers and metal boxes, two keyboards, and wires taped haphazardly to the marked grey walls. Before this shrine to technology, a young woman sat in a high-backed office chair, typing on one of the keyboards. She was slight, drowning in loose casual clothes that had seen better days. Her hair was long, thick with grease and tied in a rough ponytail, and her skin was sallow, as if she hadn't seen the sun or a steak for several weeks. She was also steadfastly ignoring him.

'So…um…where do you want me to start?' Jason said with as much cheer as he could muster. Her fingers never slowed on the keys, typing faster than he could keep up with, adding to the random words strung together with symbols on her computer screen. 'Hello? Can you hear me?'

'Do what you like.' The voice was barely audible, a cracked whisper that only just reached him over the clacking keys. She sounded rusty, as if she only spoke twice a week, and he decided he was unlikely to get any further conversation out of her. No wonder her sister was in Australia.

From hovering in the doorway to the living room, he could see the kitchen further back and decided that was as good a place as any to get going. He moved through the living area, stepping over old magazines and newspapers, curled and yellowing. The kitchen was a windowless room, smelling strongly of tomato sauce. Every surface was covered in dirty plates, cups and glasses, with the dishwasher open and bulging. The kitchen bin had overflowed to three bags, one of which was threatening to spill. How could anybody live like this?

It was a bit more than two hours' work, but he was determined to make a dent in the chaos. Jason set the dishwasher going and cleared the counters with good old suds and water. Next, he gathered up the rubbish and hesitated. He hadn't seen any bins outside.

'Chute in the hall,' muttered the woman, without a pause in her typing.

Jason, resigned to only ever talking to the back of her head, approached the two metal boxes in the hall. One was labelled Mail and the other Trash, ink stencilled directly onto the metal. Opening the trash, Jason placed the bags in the chute – who had a rubbish chute in their flat? And where did the rubbish go? Out of sight, out of mind?

Out of curiosity, he opened the mailbox. Inside were half a dozen letters and about two weeks' worth of the *South Wales Echo*. All the front pages carried stories of that missing student, the most interesting thing to happen in Cardiff since the Dark Ages. Jason pulled them out and carried them through to his client. 'Where should I put the mail?'

The woman waved her hand vaguely in the direction of the sofa, continuing to type with the other, and Jason placed the letters on a small end table, removing a couple of mugs. 'Would you like a cup of tea?'

The typing halted. The woman tilted her head to the side. 'I think the milk's gone off.' The typing resumed as if there had never been an interruption.

Convinced this woman was a sandwich short of a picnic, Jason returned to the kitchen and checked the fridge for milk. What greeted him was a hideous laboratory of biological warfare. He shut the fridge and struggled not to gag. 'How do you eat in here?'

'Microwave. Takeaway,' she said, her voice growing in strength with use. She was English, he realised, or possibly American. The accent was difficult to pinpoint and he spent a few minutes attacking the fridge, wondering if she was Australian.

Satisfied that the fridge wouldn't be developing sentience any time soon, Jason glanced at the clock. An hour gone already, and he hadn't even finished the kitchen. She didn't need a cleaner once a week – she needed someone to work on this place every day for a month. He repeated this aloud in her general direction and again the typing stopped. 'You want to come here every day?'

She seemed surprised, but he couldn't tell how she felt about it. He guessed she probably liked to be on her own with her code, but surely she didn't want to live like this? His mam was going to have a fit when he told her the state of the place. 'I think you need it.'

She tapped one key three times, then paused again. 'Okay then. I'll email them.'

Her hands starting flying away again, *tap-tap-tap*, and it seemed the conversation was over. But Jason was persistent and, if he was going to be here every day, he needed to know a little bit more. 'I'm Jason, by the way.'

'Yes, you said.' She was back in her rhythm now, a frenzied beat that reminded him of the bass at a nightclub or the primal roar of the Hakka. Maybe she was one of those reclusive web designers, churning out websites for big corporations. Though, if that were the case, why was she living in a flat like this? She should be in one of those glassy modern things down in the elegant and expensive Cardiff Bay.

'I meant…I don't know your name. Or anything about you.'

He'd expected the typing to stop again, but it just raced on, incessant as the rain. 'Amy Lane. I code. Mostly for fun, sometimes for profit. You should clean.'

Despite the dismissal, Jason smiled. He was finally getting somewhere.

Chapter 4: Show Me the Way to Go Home

It was too bloody cold to be out, even if it was Friday night. And it was pissing it down, like always. Melody shivered and pulled her coat closer around her, heels splashing freezing, dirty water up her calves. Brilliant.

A car dashed past her and she turned her back, shrieking as water soaked through her thin coat, the top button hanging off and causing the thing to gape. Why hadn't she bought a new coat yet? Why hadn't she stayed in with Teresa and the boys? They would all be laughing at her drowned-rat look when she got home.

Yeah, it had been a laugh, and the girls had got her pretty hammered on cocktails. Cocktails were lethal – you drank them down like juice and then they snuck up on you, the bastards. Even after only five – was it six? – she felt ready to totter off the pavement and sink ankle-deep into a proper Cardiff puddle.

Too bad she had a thing due Monday, or she would've stayed out 'til gone three. It was final year and she had to knuckle down now or it would've all been a colossal waste of her dad's money. Or so he kept telling her.

Somehow she kept her feet and staggered down St. Mary's Street, the heart of Cardiff's nightlife, looking for something to soak up the alcohol sloshing in her stomach. Dark deserted shops stood flush against the glare of clubs and bars, boys out front for a fag catcalling as she passed and the street awash with debris from McDonald's. In her drenched state, the smell from Chippie Lane was too great to resist. She dived down Catherine Street to pick up a box of steaming chips, drowning in cheese and gravy. Lush it was and she scoffed the lot in the shelter of the building overhang, gravy dribbling down her chin.

Stumbling back onto St. Mary's, she headed out in search of taxis. Nothing doing. It was obviously too early in the night, nowhere near closing for the nightclubs and past time for the pubs. She knew the rank was around here somewhere and, even if it wasn't, she was mostly home now. She was sure Teresa told her there was a shortcut this way. It had reached the stage of downpour when she couldn't get any wetter, and the rain was just refreshing the water that matted her long blonde hair.

Melody stopped. Where was she? Maybe she'd got turned around. She'd meant to head back towards the student wasteland of Cathays but this was looking more like it went to the Bay. She walked on a bit farther, wandering under a couple of bridges, until she came to a road running alongside a patch of withered autumn grass. She definitely wasn't among the restaurants and bars of the classy Bay either. She couldn't see many buildings at all, in fact, but she thought there might be a couple of hotels in the distance. She'd ask them for directions, or maybe they'd call her a taxi. Few men could resist a girl shivering in their lobby, even if she looked like she was more water than woman. 'A moisten bint'.

But, as luck would have it, she heard a car come up behind her. She turned to stare into the headlights and stuck her arm out, waving frantically to flag down the longed-for taxi and trying not to totter backwards in her six-inchers. The car pulled into the pavement and she yanked open the back door, clambering in and sitting down with a sigh. She was shivering now but it was at least a bit warmer in the car, and it smelled of industrial cleaners and the peculiar scent of an air freshener pretending to be pine.

'Where to?' he said, glancing up at the mirror. He clearly liked the look of her dress. She smiled politely at him and pulled her coat round her. She'd feel like a right tit if it was right round the corner. 'The Colonies,' she said. 'Australia Road.'

'Right,' he said and pulled off. The doors locked.

Melody suddenly realised she couldn't see a metre. Or a badge hanging up front. She couldn't see the driver's face. And she couldn't get out.

'Actually, maybe I'll walk,' she said tentatively, hand going for the door handle.

He ignored her, hands gripping the steering wheel.

'I don't think I have any cash.' Her heart started to race, her hands shaking as she clutched her handbag closer.

'That's okay,' he said.

Melody screamed.

24

Chapter 5: An Inspector Calls

On his way to Amy's, Jason stopped to pick up milk. A man needed a cup of tea to do a proper job. Clutching his groceries, he jogged up to the front door and punched the buzzer. The door opened instantly – crazy woman must have a camera on it – and he stepped back into that little metal box and the war zone at Number 12.

Amy was huddled on the sofa in her dressing gown, a grubby off-white thing that had probably been pretty nice at one time. At first he thought she was asleep but she eventually looked up and to the side, not meeting his eyes. 'Hello.'

'Hi.'

He felt knocked off balance by seeing her away from her computer. She didn't look like a technological whiz now – she must be his age, maybe younger. Maybe as young as Cerys. Her skinny wrist poked out of her dressing gown, sporting a clunky wristwatch that looked like it could communicate with Mars.

'I bought milk.'

Her gaze tracked to the groceries in his hand and he saw that her eyes were green. No, maybe hazel – alive with little brown flecks, hundreds of them, beyond counting. She licked her dry, cracked lips and he realised he was staring.

'I'll make a cup of tea, eh?'

She nodded imperceptibly and he went into the kitchen, set down the bread and biscuits on his clean countertop, and placed the milk in the shining fridge. He was pleased to see she hadn't destroyed the place since last week.

'How do you take it?' he called through, already hunting through the cupboards for sugar. *No such luck*. He fished his sweetener out of his pocket.

'Milk. Sugar if it's there.'

Jason laughed silently at her response. When was the last time she'd even looked in the cupboards? It was odd, how much he gave a damn, because what was she to him? But there was something pathetic about her, like a stray cat that needed a can of Whiskas and a blanket. His mates would have a field day if they saw what a sap he'd turned into.

'You need dishwasher stuff.'

He brought through her tea, chocolate digestive balanced on the rim, and set it on an old newspaper. She demolished the biscuit, still not looking at him, and cradled her mug close. Jason perched on the edge of an old armchair that was in need of a shampoo and sipped his tea. The flat wasn't that bad really, underneath it all. Once it was cleaned up a bit, it would look quite homey.

He made a couple of rounds of toast – after emptying half a loaf of crumbs out of the toaster – and hunted around for something to put on it that didn't consist entirely of mould. He discovered that peanut butter could survive anything, and he spread it thickly on the toast before taking it through to her. Amy had returned to her computer, but nodded when he set down the plate at her elbow. He watched her for a moment, as she picked up the toast without looking, her eyes never leaving the screen and her right hand continuing to dance over the keys. Her hair was wet from the shower, but it was drying to a mousy brown, sticking to her porcelain skin in thick knotted clumps. Little rivulets of water were running down her pale neck and under her dressing gown collar, but she didn't even flinch.

Feeling like an intruder, Jason returned to the kitchen and continued to wage his war on the washing up, until the doorbell rang.

'Expecting someone?'

When she didn't respond, he wandered back into the living room, to see her peering at a pair of grainy faces on one of her monitors. *So the camera's in the buzzer box.* One of the figures held up a police badge to the camera.

'It better be interesting,' she said mysteriously and pressed a button under the desk.

The door opened downstairs and Jason wiped his hands with the tea towel, twisting it taut. Had he somehow broken parole? Were they coming to tell him that the board had changed its mind and he was going back? He couldn't help the nervous sweat that broke out over his back and shoulders, as he took out his anxiety on the poor tea towel.

However, the two plainclothes officers ignored him completely, approaching Amy at her keyboard. 'Toast and peanut butter, eh? Did you scrape off the mould?'

Jason felt himself rile at these officers insinuating that he'd let Amy eat mouldy food. Then his brain caught up and he realised that one, they didn't know he'd made the bloody toast, and two, they knew Amy well enough to comment on the state of her cupboards.

'I have an assistant now,' Amy mumbled, and the lead officer turned to face him, clearly sizing him up.

Jason returned the favour, taking in every inch of a well-built Welshman who had let himself go. His hair was greying but still thick, and the suit he wore was old and creased. He had a couple of inches on Jason, who wasn't used to a man having the advantage of him.

The younger cop was eyeing Jason with interest, better dressed than his partner, and leaner too. Jason looked away, uncomfortable with the scrutiny from the cop's piercing blue gaze.

The lead officer shook his head. 'An assistant, eh? Poor sod. What's your name, son?'

'Jason,' he said, holding out a wary hand to shake.

The policeman shook it with a small smile, obviously taking in the logo on his shirt. He didn't offer a name in return, just took a seat on the chair closest to the computer and stared at Amy. 'How about you fetch us some tea, Jason?'

Realising he was being dismissed, Jason returned to the kitchen and refilled the kettle. However, he kept half an eye on what was going on in the living room. The younger cop handed an envelope to Amy and she tipped the contents over her keyboard. There was a glossy printout that looked like a photograph and Amy held it up.

'Looks real. Where'd you get it?'

'Internet forum,' the young guy replied.

Amy nodded. 'Explains the quality, I guess. The camera's not all that. Though this could be anywhere. Why are you interested?'

'It's the missing girl – Melody Frank.'

Jason nearly dropped the mug. The second missing girl, the one who'd never returned from a night out. She'd only been missing a few days. Why were the police coming to Amy with her photograph?

He dug out a tray and brought through the tea with a small plate of biscuits – proper brain food – and set it down on the end table. The young guy smiled and thanked him, but the older officer just took the mug without a word.

Peering over Amy's shoulder, Jason got a look at the photograph. It was slightly blurry, but he could make out a young blonde woman sleeping, bare shoulders showing above the white sheets of her bed. The shot was close, nothing visible of the rest of the room, except for a wooden headboard. And the girl was Melody Frank.

'See something you like?' Jason jumped as the older cop sneered up at him. 'Get back to your scrubbing.'

'Leave him alone, Bryn,' Amy said, returning to studying the photograph. Jason was glad he'd brought her another cup of tea.

Bryn, however, continued to look at him like he was less than dog shit. 'You stay, you shut up. And if I see this in the papers, I know where to find you, all right?'

Jason simply nodded – he had no desire to get a bad rep with the cops. Not again. He still remembered the shattered look in his mam's eyes at the trial, how she'd fidgeted with the cuffs of her worn black jacket. The one she'd worn to his father's funeral.

Finally, Amy sat back in her chair and sighed. 'I'm not a pathologist – I can't tell you how she died.'

The reaction was instantaneous. Bryn seemed to crumple in on himself, staring at the photograph in disbelief. 'How...how can you tell she's dead?'

Amy pointed at Melody's neck. 'The human body can't sustain that angle. Asleep or drugged, she wouldn't lie like that. She's dead.'

Bryn blew air through his lips. 'I didn't want to believe it. Owain, call the boss and tell him we've got a murder.'

Chapter 6: UPPER CASE, lower case, numbers

Amy's gaze discreetly followed Owain as he left her flat and went outside to make his call, her cameras picking him up in the lift and as he crossed the threshold. Outside. Out of her domain.

She set the photograph to one side, her eyes fixed on the dead girl before she tore them away. She pulled herself together and pulled up her browser. 'Where did you find the picture?'

Bryn flipped open his notebook over his fingers, worn wedding ring outside the shield of soft black leather. His ex-wife must be speaking to him this week. He read out the web address as she typed, and it loaded in seconds.

'Band fan forum. Nu metal.' Generic BB template, basic customisation – poor effort. She could've knocked together a better site in fifteen minutes.

She could feel Jason leaning over her shoulder and tried to control her urge to tense, to move. He was a big guy, intimidating, a skinhead with old-fashioned tattoos wound around both his arms. But he could've been any guy, really. It didn't take much to spook her.

Out of the corner of her eye, she watched him scan the text, tongue slightly protruding from between pink lips. He scratched absently at a smattering of light brown stubble on his chin – he was probably one of those guys who had a five o'clock shadow at midday. His dark brown eyes flickered across the screen faster than she expected. The educational attainment of the prison population wasn't exactly renowned.

'Crash and Yearn? They're more punk pop.'

Bryn looked at him with amusement. 'This is what you bring to the table, boy?'

Jason scowled at him. Amy felt like the referee on some bizarre American wrestling show.

'The original post is down,' Amy said, scanning the forum. 'Not the 'dead naked girl' types. I'll find the archive – you got that before it went dark?'

Her simple yet thorough methodology for profiling and password trawling involved a lot of social networks and a bit of hacker's intuition. The old science fiction trope of advanced technology seeming very like magic unfolded before her audience, and she caught sight of Jason's gormless expression in her monitor reflection as she uncovered the identity of one of the forum's moderators.

To complete the trick, she returned to the band forum and logged in. The forum greeted her as 'flyangeldust' and Amy opened up a set of moderation options, scrolling through them at speed.

'I'll pretend I didn't see you break into that boy's account,' Bryn said mildly.

Amy couldn't resist a smile, the temptation to show off a little and gain another inch of respect in this man's eyes. 'She's a girl. Her name is Fiona and her boyfriend's name is Michael, which is also her password. With a *1* instead of the *i*. Child's play.'

'You just guessed that girl's password?' Jason said. 'In one go?'

She would never make the Magic Circle. 'Her only topic of conversation – him and the band. My next guess would've been their first big single. People need to pick stronger passwords. Cracking them is boring.' Amy rummaged through the moderation queue and located the Trash folder. 'Not one but two posts from your mysterious photographer.'

'Two posts?' Bryn said. 'There's another photograph?'

Amy loaded the picture: another blonde woman, young and sleeping – or dead. The sheets were blue this time and there were faint marks around her neck.

'Kate Anderson,' Bryn said bleakly. 'That's her bedroom. Those could be signs of strangulation, not that we can prove it… What a mess.'

Amy looked up at Bryn. He was frowning, all the lines of his forehead deep as chiselled stone. She had never seen him look so sad. 'You know both these girls?'

Bryn looked at her as if she was completely mad, but Jason got there first. 'The missing students? Kate's been missing for over two weeks and Melody went out Friday night. You don't know about this?'

'I don't watch the news. It's depressing – case in point.' She could imagine enough fears – she didn't need reality to augment them. 'They're not missing anymore.'

'Their bodies are,' Bryn said grimly. 'We didn't even know Kate was killed at home. And we don't know where Melody died – her bed was all pink, and we know she never made it back there. Her friends waited up for her.'

'It could be the killer's home,' Amy said, 'or a hotel. This is your area. I can't believe you've brought me my first murder.'

'You could sound less excited,' Bryn said, but he wore a small smile.

Amy echoed his expression. She would never tire of solving problems for him – this work, police work, made it all seem worth it. For a little while.

From that first knock on her door – which no one had approached for months, years – when she'd refused to let him in, to even acknowledge his existence. He'd waited outside her door for half an hour, talking about CCTV and this old man's shop that had been vandalised, and wouldn't it be great if they could find the bastards who did it?

When he returned, she let him in after seventeen minutes. Then grilled him on how he'd found her in the first place. She learned that grateful mugging victims liked to stick it to the coppers who'd failed them.

The work intrigued her. It was a mental challenge, and it allowed her to forget that she was the one in need of protection. It was the unseen, the victims with thin voices, who benefited most from the evidence obtained from metal eyes. The meagre income from her consulting work also provided some explanation as to how she maintained her flat and kept up her supply of biscuits.

The door buzzed and Amy's eyes flicked up to the monitor. The spike of adrenaline was still ingrained, conditioned, and she felt her heart rate soar before registering it was really Owain and letting him in.

'I can look at these forum posts. They don't log IPs, but I can find something. This man must have more of an internet trail than this. Are the girls linked at all?'

'Not that we know of, but we weren't particularly treating them as linked before,' Bryn said, as Owain came to stand beside him.

'Linked?' Owain asked.

'Amy found a photo of a Kate on the forum. Possibly strangled. We started the day with two missing persons and now we've got two murders. That's bad for statistics, that is.' Bryn scrubbed at his face. 'I'll have to call the local bobbies to deliver the news to their parents.'

Amy had two Facebook screens open, and another window with scrolling computer code: her cross-referencing algorithm was exceptional, but Facebook's bloated servers would only work so fast. 'They had a few mutual friends but that's not surprising. Cardiff isn't a big city and they were both students. It might be worth checking out.'

The printer spat out a list of half a dozen names and Owain bent down to retrieve it. 'You could've emailed it. Saved the trees.'

Amy clicked idly through some more forum posts. She didn't hope to find anything in particular, but she needed to distract herself from the ugly code. 'How did you find this forum?'

'Anonymous caller,' Bryn said.

Amy looked up at him, before her gaze skittered away again. It was too intense, staring for long. He would see her, really see her. Then this would all be over.

'Can you get me the tape?' she said.

Owain shrugged and looked to Bryn. 'I guess. Why?'

Amy rolled her eyes. *Amateurs.* 'Because the caller saw the picture and realised that the girl was missing. Which means she probably lives in Cardiff. A Crash and Yearn fan who lives in Cardiff and happens to visit the forum before the post is taken down? It's a bit of a coincidence.'

'Wait,' Bryn said, 'how do you know it's a woman?'

Amy shrugged. 'Most men would try to peer through the sheet. A woman would look at her face.'

'Bit sexist,' Jason said. Amy just caught his mumble: 'And those sheets were pretty opaque.'

'Well, it was a woman,' Bryn said, 'and we'll get you a copy of the tape.'

'You'd better get going then,' Amy said. 'Some of us have to catch a killer.'

Chapter 7: Man About Town

Jason didn't stay long at Dylan's. The garage was the local area's gossip hall and everyone had something to say about Kate Thomas and Melody Frank. Was someone holding them hostage? What must their parents be going through? What if they were…you know…?

Well, they were 'you know' and Jason knew about it before anybody else. Maybe it was true that ignorance was bliss because he sure as hell didn't want to know this in a crowd of his mates not-knowing. It wasn't his right to tell them neither, so he got out of there and made his way to the next job.

It was a gig at one of the large nightclubs on St. Mary's Street – Koalas, the Australian place. Jason remembered huddling in front of one of their big screens for the Rugby World Cup semi-final, beer in hand at nine o'clock in the morning, and his heart breaking into a hundred pieces as his beloved Wales lost to France. Gutting it was, and the ten pints he'd downed after had done nothing to ease the pain.

Several of the cleaning boys were going to help out at the club after a large party they'd hosted the night before – medical students, apparently. They really knew how to tear a place up and had been banned from several venues across the city, including Cardiff Castle. Something about someone pissing on a three-hundred-year-old tapestry.

Jason showed up a couple of minutes late but the others were right behind him, so they just got a bit of an eye roll from the manager. The mops and brooms were handed out and they got to work. The place appeared like a vaulted cavern when empty. The top floor overlooked the basement below, where most of the action happened, and where the big screens dominated the main wall. It was weird to see them dark and dormant instead of showing rugby or some obscure late-night athletics. Of course, the stickiness of the floor was the same as always, and Jason wished he'd worn his old trainers for this job. This was worse than Amy's for unknown organic substances covering the surfaces.

Jason, as the new boy, got men's toilets, and he was grimly reminded how piss really did get everywhere. The stalls looked like they had been flooded, and he figured it would take a couple of go-overs with the mop before it was anything like usable again. Followed by a week of washing to get the awful stench out of his clothes.

While he was waiting for the floor to dry, he snuck out for a cigarette and bumped into a couple of bar-backs also out for a crafty one. They nodded to each other, a mutual understanding established, and concentrated on their fix.

'You heard anything about Kate?' one heavy guy said, frowning down at his mate sitting astride a keg.

'Nah, nothing. Police are still looking, but they're fucking useless.'

The man threw down his cigarette and tugged anxiously at his goatee. He looked haggard, but he couldn't have been more than thirty. He was Australian, but a hint of South Wales had slipped into his accent. 'It's been two weeks, Dan. How can she still be alive?'

'You can't think like that, Pete,' Dan said, shooting a glance at Jason to see his reaction.

Jason straightened, taking it as an invitation.

'You talking about Kate Thomas?' They both turned to look at him. 'You know her, then?'

Pete stood up, looking like he might be cruising for a fight.

Dan just shrugged. 'Yeah, she worked with us. Was meant to work the Saturday shift but never got here. Naomi thought she must've missed her at home, but she could've gone at any time. Naomi's pretty cut up about it – housemate going missing like that, from right under your nose.'

Pete walked off, clearly not interested in telling a total stranger about his friend's disappearance.

Dan, however, seemed to want to get it off his chest and leaned against the wall next to Jason. 'Pete and her had a thing. Nothing serious, but he's right upset. Down the cop shop every day, he is. But I wouldn't be surprised if they fished her out of the Taff.'

'You think she was pushed, or…?' Jason trailed off, uncomfortable. How did you bring up the idea that this guy's friend had jumped into the river?

'I don't know what to think, mate. All I know is she ain't here no more, is she? And every day she stays missing, it's less likely she's coming home.'

Jason shook his head. 'That's hard, that is. Don't know how you cope with it, like. Had she been here long?'

'Only since the beginning of term. We get a lot of students, y'know. I don't think she was a fresher, though, but she needed a job to get her through the year. She always wanted the extra shifts, just like Naomi. They were pretty skint most of the time.' He pulled at his cropped, gelled hair. 'Fuck, I'm already talking like she's gone.'

Jason turned away until the sniffles beside him had stopped, taking another slow drag of his rollie. He heard the familiar click of a lighter and the shaky exhale of a comfort cigarette.

'They'll find the bastard who did it,' he found himself saying. 'We may talk shit about the Cardiff cops, but they've got eyes everywhere.'

'Hope you're right, mate,' Dan said and threw half his cigarette away, letting it fizzle out in the rain.

Chapter 8: The Body in the Trunk

He couldn't keep her in the suitcase forever.

For a start, the suitcase was staring at him. Accusing him. He needed to Get. Rid. He'd thought he was being smart, keeping her locked away until he was ready to deal with her, but he hadn't expected such accusation.

He waited until sunset, which didn't take long these days, not after the clocks had gone back. It was fate, really, everything coming together like this. It meant that she would finally come back to him. It was destiny, Disney, devilry – like true love should be.

He dragged the suitcase down the stairs and out the front door. Nobody noticed him. Nobody ever noticed him. He was invisible, like a superhero. Crusading for his girlfriend, his Lois Lane, and one day, she'd learn his true identity and they'd be together. Fate.

He heaved at the suitcase, the leather slipping in his sweaty grip as he lifted it. He hadn't realised a person would be so heavy, but he'd learned that lesson the first time. He hadn't brought a suitcase then, because how could he be sure? The pretty blonde girl with the easy smile, so very easy. But then he'd seen her and she was…nothing like *her*, nothing at all. He struck down temptation – but then he had to move her out. He hadn't made that mistake the second time, brought the old suitcase just in case. It never hurt to be prepared.

With the suitcase in the boot, he carefully switched on his lights and his wipers, driving exactly at the speed limit. He would be invisible. There were a few cars heading out of town, but as he got farther away from the city, the traffic died away and it was just him and the Welsh Valleys.

His mum had once taken him on holidays to the Brecon Beacons: hills and lakes, damp and cold, endless walking. Now he welcomed their brooding silence. Dead men tell no tales, and neither do the hills. He quite liked that, actually – it was almost poetry. He'd write it in his blog. He'd write it to her. One day, she would read it, and that could be the key, the way back to her. She was the reason, the one thing that made this whole distasteful thing worthwhile.

She'd be jealous – and then she'd be proud.

He pulled up alongside the lake, dark waters stretching away as far as the eye could see. The alarm beeped as he opened the door, the headlights still blazing fire along the deserted road. Popping open the boot, he hauled out the suitcase and it thudded on the ground. But the clasp held and she stayed contained within. He hesitated on the shore. He didn't want to lose the suitcase – he might need it again.

She tumbled out on the bank, and gravity did the rest, tugging her inexorably towards her final resting place. The ripples spiralled outward and then faded to nothing. It was peaceful here. She'd like it. She could be with the other girl and they could talk and stuff. Yeah, it would be nice for them out here. He didn't want there to be any hard feelings. It wasn't really about them, after all. Just her. Only her.

Slamming the boot, he got back in the car, finally silencing that irritating beep, and drove back home. He had work tomorrow and he should get an early night. It might be another busy weekend.

Monitoring social networks was like watching a car crash, or so she was led to believe. Amy hadn't been in a car in the past ten years and the next ten were looking unlikely.

Facebook had Find Kate and Melody: Have You Seen Her? groups, full of well-networked university students and friends from home. The student population was expert at getting a message out, information flowing over Facebook, Twitter, Tumblr, Reddit, sinking into every crack and crevice of the interverse. Amy looked on, the spider at the centre of the web. Big Sister's Watching You.

The mood would change tomorrow, when the police announced they were dead and likely connected. The national press would prick up their ears and come running, camping outside the Senedd building until the First Minister and the Welsh Assembly declared martial law or whatever it was they wanted. Sniffing out the story.

That would be useful. Journalists could talk their way into anything and then splurged it out in print, on blogs, in 140 characters of BREAKING NEWS. Amy had found the Cardiff Castle robber using a combination of newspaper articles and online dating – but this was an altogether different beast.

She already had so much to absorb. The local press had done their best with Kate, eking out every modicum of interest. Melody was relatively fresh meat and they still had more to find, more to churn out for Amy's eager eyes.

For the moment, however, they didn't know. The IP trace was running itself in circles, and trawling through the rest of the forum had yielded only teenage obsession and a purist's love of the drum solo. Amy kept her eye on the usernames flashing up on the bottom of the screen, the number of anonymous Guests. Did the killer share this forum space with her, idly surfing through the posts? Police wisdom said that murderers liked to lurk at the scene, watch the aftermath, the crowds. Now they could do it from a smartphone.

Amy idly flicked up her sister's Facebook page. There were photographs taken on beaches, in bars, with boys and barbecues. Ten thousand miles away from Amy's life. She checked her watch. It was afternoon in Australia, but she wouldn't bother Lizzie today.

While her mind was wandering, she pulled up a programme and released her technological babies, like genies from a lamp, summoned to do her bidding. A series of transactions appeared on the screen and she scanned them quickly. She had about thirty seconds before the alarm sounded in a tech's office in Switzerland. Oh, they were in Monaco. How nice for them.

Amy severed the connection, yawned, stretched. She had nothing left to do. She sat at her portal, merely an observer, an idle running process waiting to be activated to greater purpose.

Until then, there was the watching.

Chapter 9: Streetlight Serenader

Jason walked home from the club, bag slung over his shoulder and mulling over the day. When he'd left for work that morning, he'd had no idea that he'd be involved in a murder investigation. Of course, 'involved' was too strong a word – he was watching other people investigate a murder. It was like being an extra in *CSI*.

The most surprising thing, of course, was that the unassuming Amy Lane was able to tell a woman was dead from a photograph. He had seen her working at her computer, but this had real-world, practical use.

He'd never thought of computers like that before. Of course, people used them to type up reports or whatever people in offices did. Facebook was fun to waste an hour or two on games or to look up some bird from last night's pull, but Amy used it to work out how people were connected and who might've killed them. Jason decided he'd been born in the wrong decade – he'd have been better in the seventies or eighties, maybe, but then he would have most likely ended up down a mine. The beauty of the music might've made up for it though, and he hummed his own off-key version of 'Comfortably Numb'. He wished his mam had kept his dad's old record player, mourned the boxes of classic LPs gathering dust in the attic, unplayed.

The rain had settled into a mild drizzle and he pulled up the collar of his leather jacket, hunching his shoulders against the chill. His mam would give him another lecture when he got home about how he needed a mac and would catch his death any day now. Jason started to wish he'd brought the car down, but parking in the centre was hell and would've wiped out half his day's wages. Still, he should've brought change for the bus.

Jason made for Bute Street, his home in the former Docklands – the bit that hadn't been overhauled for the shiny new Cardiff Bay. His mind was on dinner and how much tea he could drink before it was ready. But as soon as he stepped back into his territory, he was aware something was wrong. He knew this part of town like it was his family, but now it seemed hostile, threatening. The last edge of dusk was fading away and he put his head down and walked faster. Suddenly, he didn't want to be out alone.

A couple of boys sauntered out from a side street and Jason recognised them, checked them over for weapons, and carried on past. They ran with a gang out of Canton but they weren't bad kids. Jason could say that, because his mam was friends with their mams, and he was sure they'd caused their families fewer tears than he had his.

He was only a hundred yards from home now, but he was seeing more faces by the roadside, the same crew. He didn't know what they were planning but he couldn't help but feel he was part of it somehow.

Then the boy standing in the middle of the road proved it: Damage Jones.

The hood pulled over his cropped brown hair couldn't hide his coal-black eyes, that intense stare that made him the spit of Lewis – a ghost from Jason's past in the form of his best mate's baby brother. Well, not his best mate anymore.

It was no use pretending that he hadn't seen him, making a scene like that in the street, so Jason slowed right down. The pavement ahead was blocked and he had no choice but to step off the kerb, turning his walk into a casual stroll through his turf. Damage was just a kid, nineteen years old and full of himself, the prick. But he also had an axe to grind and Jason had avoided the inevitable confrontation, like any sane boy would.

He'd spent six months lying low, hanging around his mam's and the garage, but not on the streets after dark. He wasn't afraid – Jason Carr weren't afraid of no one – but because he didn't want to break Damage's nose, especially when he owed the kid's brother a debt he couldn't repay.

'Evening, Damage. Throwing me a surprise party? It isn't even my birthday.'

Damage scowled. 'You think you fucking own this street. You're a cock, Jay Bird.'

Jason flinched. No one had called him that for over a year and it stung to hear it out of this little brat's mouth, especially when Lewis was the one who'd given him the damn nickname in the first place. In return, he'd got ten years in prison.

42

'I don't own nothing,' Jason said quietly. 'Let it go, Dai. You don't want to do this.'

He was willing to give the boy a pass, but Damage had all his mates watching him, his little friends manning the pavement for him while he took down the older, jail-hardened veteran of the streets. The quest for glory was too good to walk away from, especially now he'd got Jason just where he wanted him. Jason quickly ran through what he had in his bag and debated how he was going to take down the kid without scarring him with bleach.

He was aware that Damage's mates were closing in, about ten of them, and he could spot a couple of knives. For the first time since prison he wished he still had his switchblade. They were circling him, and he realised he wasn't going to get out of this without busting a few heads and probably cracking a couple of ribs himself. He wished he had his boys at his back, but his boys were never going to have his back again. They were too busy hating him from their cells – the deserter, the traitor.

'Think it through, Dai.'

If he could persuade the kid to take him on one-on-one – yeah, fat chance – he might get away with knocking the boy down and walking away.

'Are your betters going to be happy with you? Drawing attention like this?'

The older guys in this club weren't the forgiving sort. Stuart Williams was their ringleader, a boy who'd worn the scars of a glassing since he was twenty. That was the day he'd earned his place at the top of their little food chain and sent his rival crying to his mother in Splott.

'I've thought it through, Jay Bird,' Damage spat at him. 'My brother says hi.'

He took a swing, which Jason ducked easily. He'd dodge as long as he could, take a couple of blows – he'd burn his last bridge with Lewis if he hit his kid brother.

'Scared, are you, Jay Bird?'

Damage was warming up now, crying out for blood. His mates were a jeering ring of arrogant kids, some as young as fourteen. But Jason shouldn't be surprised – he'd been one of them when he was twelve, feeling the power of walking down the street with your hood up and no one knowing what you might be carrying. He remembered the thrill and knew that these kids knew nothing about consequences. It made them fucking dangerous.

In the distance, Jason could hear sirens. It put everyone on edge and he could sense the ripple of fear that went through the group. The police couldn't be coming for them, could they? Unless one of the mams behind the curtain couldn't watch her boy get into it in the street, but they knew better than to start a fight outside their own front doors.

It started with a shove, Damage pushing him back into another kid, who sent him back the way he came. Child's play. Jason kept his cool, trying to rein in his temper. He was stronger than three of them, but all it would take was one of them to bounce off the pavement the wrong way and he'd get life. Not to mention the Technicolor movie playing over his conscience every day of some kid's brains smeared on the asphalt.

The sirens were getting louder. That made no bloody sense, but Jason didn't have time to worry about it. He ducked another clumsy punch from Damage, but caught the blow to his ribs. Slightly winded, he barely avoided the kick aimed at his knee, before he decided that enough was enough. He had to get out of there before he hurt one of them.

With a swing of his holdall, several bottles of household cleaner collided with Damage's stomach. The boy cried out, doubled over, and Jason took his opportunity to leg it. But one of them snagged his shirt and pulled him down, the tarmac scraping up his back. *Shit. No one comes back from the floor.*

But he saw blue flashing lights and suddenly the kids were scrambling and yelling, hoods up and away, leaving him crashed out on the ground.

Jason sat up slowly, wincing as his body reported in his various scrapes and bruises. An anxious-looking copper came over, one hand on her truncheon and the other on her radio. 'You all right? Did they get anything?'

'Just my pride,' Jason heard himself say, levering himself up and onto his feet. He reclaimed his bag and stood up to meet the police officer's gaze. 'I didn't know them, didn't see any faces, and even if I did—'

'You wouldn't be pressing charges,' the officer finished tiredly. 'You lot don't make it easy on yourselves, you know?'

Jason didn't know exactly who she meant by 'you lot' – young men, Bute boys, ex-cons – but he kept his curiosity to himself.

'Thank you, officer,' Jason said, already making to leave.

'Wait,' she said, 'can we give you a lift home?'

'I'm already home,' Jason said and limped away.

Chapter 10: Exhale

Jason sat at the kitchen table with his head in his hand, the other clutching a bag of frozen peas to his aching ribs. His mam had gone on and on about getting into trouble and the police and avoiding the local boys for the past hour, and his headache was growing steadily louder and angrier. Worse still, Cerys was leaning against the kitchen counter, watching his humiliation – yet not with a crowing smile and arrogant eye, but folded arms and a pensive look. Jason couldn't meet her eyes.

'It's not a big deal,' he said for the thirtieth time, which just set Gwen off on another tirade about how he had no sense of responsibility and didn't he know he could've been killed? This continued for another fifteen minutes, before he got awkwardly to his feet.

'I'm going to bed,' he mumbled and dumped the thawing peas on the table, before shuffling towards the stairs. Cracked ribs were the worst – it hurt to lie and sit and stand, and it hurt to fucking breathe. But if you didn't breathe, you got pneumonia. He'd already been laid up with that in prison and he had no desire for a rerun. He still had nightmares about drowning in the infirmary, too hot to live and too cold to die, the faint laughter of the man who'd socked him ringing in his ears.

Of course, he couldn't sleep, staring at the ceiling and thinking over why Damage had decided to come after him now, why he'd brought the whole gang to watch, and how the hell the cops had known what was happening. He replayed it in his mind, but a more intrusive set of questions broke through the haze. Who killed Kate and Melody? Why did they do it?

His battered phone buzzed once and he glanced over at the bedside table. Painfully, he reached out for it and read the text in the dim light from the street outside. Then read it again. A third time.

Come @ 9. Things to do. You need a stronger password. @

No prizes for guessing who that was from, but how did she get his number? Maybe the cleaning company gave it to her? Then again, with the cryptic comment about his password – which was perfectly acceptable, had numbers and everything – she might just have lifted the number off his email or something.

As he tried to get comfortable in his narrow single bed, Jason closed his eyes and pushed away thoughts of gangs, of prison, his haunted past. Cardiff had two dead students. And he had questions his mind was desperate to answer.

Jason didn't even ring the buzzer before the door opened and he was admitted to the elevator and the flat beyond.

'Amy?' he called, shrugging his holdall off his shoulder with a wince.

She surprised him by appearing in the corridor and pushing the bag back onto the shoulder. Jason yelped.

'I need the tape from Whitchurch police station. I've exhausted my leads.'

Jason looked her over, taking in the slightly manic gaze and dishevelled hair, from where she'd clearly been repeatedly running her fingers through it. Quite possibly all night, from the tremor in her hand and the bruise-deep shadows beneath her eyes.

'Have you slept at all? Or had anything to eat?'

Amy waved her hand impatiently. 'The laptops have nothing on first sweep but they didn't have a firewall between them, so there may be something lurking in the background somewhere. God only knows what they were thinking, letting their tech get into that filthy state.'

She walked back into the living room, muttering to herself, and Jason followed nervously. Three different days, three different Amys. He didn't know which way was up with this girl. He couldn't deny that she was intriguing, that his life was getting interesting in the good way since she'd been around.

'Whose laptops? What are you…?'

He trailed off as he realised two laptops were plugged into her computer terminal, lines and lines of file names scrolling across the black screens. One was pearlescent pink and looked brand new, while the other was covered in stickers of every stripe, bands and logos and smiling kittens, with a series of letters along the top that spelled out Melody.

'These are Kate and Melody's laptops. How did you get these?'

'Bryn fetched them for me, but he can't bring the tape until tomorrow and I need it now. How else am I meant to work this out? There's nothing else to find. There's nothing about them that's interesting or death-worthy. Why are they dead? Who wanted to kill them? None of it makes any sense and I need more data!'

She tugged at her hair again, a clump of it coming away in her hand, and Jason automatically reached to stop her. She jumped away from him, suddenly meeting his gaze with wide, frightened eyes.

Jason stepped back, holding up his hands in surrender. Her eyes darted away, back to her scrolling streams of letters and numbers.

'It's always better without the interface. It just gets in the way of the problems and the answers. The data. The clone is never as good as the original, but Bryn needs evidence like I need code.'

He hadn't heard her talk this much since they'd met, and she was probably running on adrenaline and caffeine, about to crash and burn like a meteor.

'I'll find something to eat,' he said and headed to the kitchen. He was greeted with several plates covered in half-eaten pieces of toast, as if she'd made herself some and then got distracted mid-bite. 'Do you have any bread left?'

He rummaged through the cupboards, finding half a packet of biscuits from his last visit.

'I forgot to order the shopping,' Amy said, standing in the kitchen doorway and tilting her head to one side. 'Sorry.'

'No need for that.'

Jason thrust the biscuits in her direction before kneeling down to unload the dishwasher. He needed to at least start the cleaning process before he darted across town to fetch her tape. He added 'errand boy' to the list of jobs he did for Amy that were nothing to do with cleaning, and considered that Amy might actually think he was her personal assistant.

'So, what have you found out?'

Amy's face lit up and she started waving her hands like a child at the circus. Her hazel eyes were animated, her face expressive. She was captivating, like this. Jason felt he could watch her all day.

'Melody was studying English Literature and Kate studied Ancient History, Melody in third year and Kate in second year. A lot of casual contact online, but I can't identify anyone significant. The phones are both missing but the GPS is dead, useless. Kate's battery's dead by now, but why can't we find Melody? Maybe he buried her already or threw her in the river.'

At mention of the Taff, the conversation with Dan and Pete came back to him and he held up his hand.

'Kate did have someone – guy called Pete. They worked together, had an on-off thing.'

The look Amy gave him was incredulous and pitying and Jason was immediately riled. Nobody looked at him like that, not even those little shits from the night before.

'I told you – she didn't have anyone. There were a couple of Petes, but not particularly high traffic or quality interaction. I looked through all her social networks.'

'Well, maybe they wanted to keep it a secret. Or maybe he's just not into Facebook. He didn't look like a Facebook kinda guy.'

Amy rounded on him and Jason was unable to read the expression on her face, apart from guessing it was somewhere between fury and fear.

'You went looking for one of the suspects in a murder investigation? Why would you do something like that?'

Jason held up a hand, surprised at her vehemence. 'I didn't go looking for no one! I did a job at the club where Kate worked. I got talking to the guys there. Pete was pretty cut up about her death, and one of his mates told me they had a thing for a bit. That's it. No need to go mental over it.'

Amy seized his wrist and dragged him into the living room, pulling up Kate's Facebook profile and searching her friends. Two guys called Pete appeared on screen, one retching into a bucket and the other dressed as a Ninja turtle.

'Which one is he?' she said urgently, pointing at the screen and shaking his arm.

Jason reclaimed his arm, massaging his stinging wrist, and squinting at the screen. 'Neither. He's got a beard and he's older than these guys. Told you – not a Facebook guy.'

Amy flopped into her chair. 'I need that phone. He could be the key to this and he's out of reach!'

'Why don't you go talk to him? He's not hard to find.'

The reaction was instantaneous. Amy's body stiffened, her eyes fixed and staring. 'No. I…no.' She put a hand to her temple, as if struggling to concentrate.

'Come on – I'll come with you. He's a big guy, but he's not scary or nothing.'

Jason leaned down to try to catch her eye, but Amy leapt to her feet, her breath coming hard and fast. Little puffs of air escaped her lips with barely a second between each gasped exhale and desperate inhale. Jason twisted to follow her motion as she darted around the living room, muttering under her breath and pressing the heel of hand into the centre of her chest.

After a few moments, Jason stepped into her path and grabbed her shoulders. 'Amy, stop! What's going on?'

She shuddered to a stop and took a decent breath. Then another. She seemed to calm, the tension leaving her body and the high colour in her cheeks fading, but the unnatural energy about her had dissipated. Jason guided her over to the sofa, afraid that her legs were about to give out.

She sat heavily, still struggling to bring her breathing under control. Jason started looking round for an inhaler, but her fingers snagged his sleeve and he was essentially tethered to the couch. He sat beside her and her breathing eased, as if him looming over her had been adding to her stress.

'What was that about?' he said after a moment.

She shook her head, unable to look at him but also unable to let go of his sleeve. It should've been weird, but everything about Amy was weird and Jason left his favourite Superdry hoodie in her possession.

'Nothing,' Amy said, in a strange quiet voice. 'Don't…don't go to the police station. It can wait for tomorrow. I don't need it today.'

'It's no problem for me to go.' But her grip tightened on his sleeve and he backtracked hurriedly. 'But you're right. Can probably wait, eh? I'll just…clean up here, all right?'

'Right,' she said and slowly released his sleeve.

With an awkward pat to her shoulder, Jason got to his feet and went to make them both a cup of tea. He had no idea what that was but knew he didn't want to see it again. It was as if she'd had some kind of attack and lost control of her body and mind. Maybe it was some kind of seizure?

Stirring the sweeteners into their tea, Jason struggled to put it all together. Amy wasn't like his other clients. Of course, the little old ladies loved to chat but he had the feeling that they didn't need him quite as much as Amy did. Her flat was a disaster, but it went deeper than that. She needed someone to hold her life together – she didn't seem to be able to fend for herself at all.

Amy was more of a mystery than a serial killer in Cardiff town.

Chapter 11: A Night in Pictures

'So, what's next?' Jason said, gulping down his scalding tea without flinching.

Amy shrugged, staring at the surface of her tea as if she could divine the answers to the murders in the murky brown liquid.

'I need more information. I need to manually trawl their email and browsing histories if the automatic searches fail.'

'I could go back to the club,' Jason offered. 'See what I can stir up. There's always the uni – someone might know something about what happened before they died.'

Amy carried on as if she hadn't even heard him. 'We need to establish a timeline. We know Kate was at home, but only because of the photograph. What about Melody? What was she doing right before she died and at what point did she go missing?'

'The news reports say she was on a night out.'

Jason headed for Amy's odd corridor mailbox. How did mail even get up to the first floor? He couldn't see Amy going downstairs to fetch it just to dump it in a metal crate in the hallway.

Jason fished out the paper and opened it to page three, where there was a comparison of the two dead girls. He knew today's *Echo* had a summary of the cases, because his mam had been tutting over it at breakfast between sending him baleful glances and asking him about his aching ribs.

'They say she was wearing a blue dress. Her friends said she left them about midnight to get a cab home. No one saw her after that.'

Amy threw up her hands, tea slopping over the side of her mug. 'Someone must've seen her! CCTV must've got her – the city centre's covered in cameras. Why can't they find her?'

She muttered about 'amateurs' and headed over to her computer, her tea dregs clutched to her chest.

'They're still reviewing the footage, but they can't even find her leaving the club. It was raining pretty hard, so the pictures are crap.'

If Jason repeated what the BBC said, he might sound like he knew what he was talking about. But Amy didn't appear to be paying any attention and was instead flicking through a set of photographs. Jason went to lean over her shoulder and realised she was looking through a Facebook album.

Facebook, from his limited experience of it, was a gossip market. Photographs of nights out, bitching on people's Walls, and suddenly everyone knew exactly who was sleeping with which sister and which one gave the best head. Jason had fallen foul of the Facebook rumour mill a couple of times, but knew that he might not have much to be self-righteous about. He hadn't known she was a mate's cousin when he had her up against the wall in that club. The fallout from that had made him more careful where he put it about – and who was watching.

Suddenly, Melody appeared, sporting a powder blue dress and a wide smile. Jason shivered – it was weird to see the girl looking out at him like that, unaware that she'd be dead in just a few hours' time.

'Her friend uploaded them yesterday. It looks chronological, which saves me having to locate the timestamp after Facebook's mangled it.' Amy sat back in her chair, with an expectant smile. 'Tell me what you see.'

Jason leaned forward and looked at the photograph. Three girls, hanging off each other, pissed but happy with it. Melody in the middle, skinny, dark blonde hair, blue dress. The other two were brunettes, one plump and wearing purple, while the other clutched an empty shot glass and was decked out in red. They were having a good time.

'Three girls on a night out. A good night out.'

Amy gestured impatiently at the screen. 'Look at Melody. What do you see?'

Jason looked again. Her hair was a bit stringy, as if she'd slicked it with hair gel, and her dress was darker at the top around the neck. She was listing to one side, a sure sign she'd had one too many. He'd bet she was wearing stilettos – she looked like that kind of girl.

'She looks tipsy. And her hair's wet.'

Amy clicked her fingers. 'Her hair's wet! Why's that?'

Jason hesitated, struggling to put together the pieces. 'Because… it was raining?'

'Why isn't her dress wet?' Amy pointed at the dress with a well-chewed pen. 'It can't have dried much quicker than her hair, but it's not even damp. Except—'

'—at the top!' Jason reached out to touch her neckline, where it was now obvious that the darker patch of the dress formed a perfect V. 'She was wearing something over the dress. That's why no one can bloody find her – they're looking for a girl in a blue dress, but she left in a coat.'

'A gold star for you,' Amy said with a small smile, 'but get your hands off my monitor.'

As Jason set to work on the living room, Amy went on a photo hunt. She tried to explain to him what she was doing, but while he had many good points, living a digital life wasn't one of them.

'It's quite simple,' she said, for the third time. 'I'm seeing which people from Cardiff have uploaded photos to Facebook, Instagram, Tumblr or Flickr in the past week and whether any of them are from Friday night, particularly this club. Some people tag, but most don't, so a lot of it's manual. My plan is track this stag party dressed as crayons.'

'Stag crayons?' Jason said blankly.

Amy pointed to the ludicrous six-foot men in clashing colours with pointy hats. Jason nodded as if in understanding and Amy released him to do the housework while she ran her search, with the odd procrastinating Google to verify the accuracy of the branding on the crayon costumes and how to create wax-effect makeup. It might come in useful.

'Did you know that your carpet's green?' Jason said, once he'd turned off the vacuum. 'You have a good fireplace behind this box mountain.'

'That's nice.' Amy was wading through a set of pictures where not one of the subjects was in focus. Tedious, and headache-inducing.

'It might still work. My mate's a sweep Bridgend-way. Maybe he could clean it out for you?'

'I don't want decades-old soot raining down on AEON, or a fire beside my delicate systems. I think it's best left alone – well alone.'

'Ewan?' Jason asked and Amy stroked the side of her monitor.

'AEON. My first assistant.' She patted her keyboard. 'I've been evolving her for over ten years. I made my first hack with her running Windows 98.'

She sensed that Jason was rolling his eyes, but chose to ignore him. He could never hope to understand the bond between a girl and her computer. Particularly this girl and this computer, the dynamic duo who could visit every corner of the earth together and plot Amy and Lizzie's daring escape to a better life.

The pictures started blurring together after a couple of hours, her eyes aching from a night of data harvesting, but the steady stream of mugs that appeared at her elbow revived her. Every now and then, she'd glance over at Jason, watching him take out the wine bottles and old newspapers, diligently filling her accumulated green recycling bags.

And when she turned back, there it was. The moment of eureka.

'I've got it!' Amy's cheeks ached with the force of her grin.

Jason rushed to the monitor and stared at the picture, a phone-above-the-head dance-floor shot, fifty or so bodies caught mid-dance. 'What am I meant to be looking at?' he asked.

Amy pointed at the top right-hand corner, by the entrance to the stairwell.

Jason squinted and grinned. 'That's a girl in a black coat.'

'That's Melody Frank. With her ponytail and black coat, she looks like a different woman. She'll be on all the cameras now.'

Jason clapped Amy on the shoulder. 'You're brilliant.'

Amy felt her cheeks heat, as Jason's eyes softened. It was different from Bryn's praise, rare and gruff. This was affectionate, natural. She wasn't sure how she felt about it. But she found she wasn't afraid now, that she didn't flinch from his hand on her shoulder. She couldn't remember the last time she'd felt free from fear.

Jason removed his hand. 'I've gotta be off. I'll be here at nine tomorrow, yeah?'

Just like that, the moment fled. 'You're going?'

'I have a job in Canton. You should get some kip before you crash.'

She felt her head nod but the warmth did not return, and it was with a strange sense of emptiness that she watched him pack up his things and leave.

Chapter 12: Somebody Told Me

The best way to interview nightclub staff was to turn up as they were opening, flash the badge at the bouncer and loudly declare that you wanted to see the manager. Bryn found that guaranteed him a cosy back room and time with every staff member he wanted. Jean Moore, manager of Koalas and proud Australian ex-pat, wanted him the hell out of her club – preferably before it got too busy for her to spare even one staff member for his interrogation. Suddenly, with the boss on their back, the staff became delightfully willing to speak with him, knowing it got them in Jean's good books – and out from under her watchful eye for ten minutes.

At this moment, Bryn had precisely nothing. They were random killings, unrelated murders. The victims had a handful of common friends, all women or bent as a threepenny bit, and Bryn had no doubt that this was a sexual crime. If he had a body, he could damn well prove it too. As it was, he had to rely on Amy's mood and willingness to get up in the mornings. Though, as much as he distrusted her new ex-con assistant, he seemed to be doing her some good and Bryn might just get a whole piece of work out of her. Murder was a bit of a step up from phone scams and overseas money trails, but she was pulling her weight like a trooper and he was oddly proud of her for the breaks they'd got so far.

Amy figured the Pete guy for Kate's boyfriend, so Bryn would save him for last, make him sweat. He went for Naomi first, the vic's house-mate. The last time he'd spoken to her, she'd been in shock, babbling on about the rubbish being taken out, and that meant Kate had been home that night, that she must've been kidnapped. Bryn hadn't made head nor tail of it but listened patiently while she blew her nose a lot and worked her way through three cups of tea.

She looked more together now, made up and hair ironed out flat, and she sat calmly across from him. 'I saw on the news. I told you, didn't I? Where's he taken her?'

Bryn hid his wince in his notebook. 'We don't know. We think he probably followed her for several days before he…made his move. We need to know what he knew – and if there was anyone hanging around, anyone—'

'It's a nightclub,' Naomi said bluntly. 'There are always creeps and weirdos hanging about, guys in costume, beards and hats. The same guy could come in here every night with a different fucking mask and a general loser attitude – and we'd never recognise him. Know what I'm saying? He could watch her from the balcony and she'd never even know he was there.' She inspected her thumb, a bright blue plaster over the nail. Her other nails were all bitten to the quick, the skin picked raw. 'Though I guess the bouncers might clock him. They're good at picking out trouble.'

'What about home?'

'It was just a place we crashed. We never spent enough time there to notice stuff, never got to know the neighbours. I only really saw Kate at work – we were never in that house.'

Bryn filed that information away. Unlikely then that the guy saw her at home. Must be work or university, with access to her address or following her home.

'You noticed anything…after?'

'I left that place. Staying with friends up Gabalfa way.' Naomi looked away, a fine tremor running through her body. 'I don't feel safe in that house. Knowing he just got in there. She wouldn't have let him in, I know she wouldn't. She wouldn't answer the door to the gas man in the middle of the day! He must've broken in. Landlord will never get anyone to live there now.'

Bryn had already interrogated the landlord, a Turkish bloke who spent more time abroad than in Cardiff and had the convenient alibi of being in the States when Kate had disappeared.

'Thank you for your time, Naomi. I'll let you know if we need to ask further questions.'

'Let me know when you find him,' she countered and left without meeting his eye.

Bryn didn't know if it was fear that made her anxious – or was it guilt? Did she have something to hide, a boyfriend whose eye might have wandered? Something to bear in mind.

He just didn't have enough facts. Kate Thomas had died at home, but without reference samples, the hair and fingerprints in her bedroom could be the killer's or they could be from a boy she'd shagged the week before. Bryn took a gulp of his ice water and concentrated on the task at hand. There had to be a lead here.

The bouncers did keep an eye on regular troublemakers, but they didn't have anything for him apart from posturing and attitude, the typical response of security guys with a chip on their shoulder about proper coppers. They did describe a few guys who gave the girls hassle, but they'd all been barred now and they had no idea where he could find them. Bryn asked them to tell him if any of them tried to get back in, but he didn't hold out much hope for cooperation from that lot of overeager amateurs. He'd be more likely to find his suspect bleeding in an alleyway.

The barmaids knew Kate to say hi to, but nothing more. She'd only been there for a few weeks, like the rest of them, and they didn't do a lot of socialising. Most of them thought she'd been seeing Pete, but none of them seemed overly bothered about it. Bryn didn't pick up much in the way of jealousy but they didn't think he was a bad bloke either.

Bryn interviewed the bar-backs next, saving Pete until last. They got on well as mates, agreed that Kate was a looker but that she was definitely Pete's bit of stuff. Dan, calling himself Pete's best mate, told him that Kate had been Pete's regular shag for a month or so, but there wasn't much to it.

'You don't think it was Pete, do you?' Dan said. 'It can't have been him anyway – he was working that night. He swapped with me so I could catch this gig at the Union.'

Bryn digested that information, annoyed that his prime suspect had an alibi.

'Don't go upsetting him, yeah?' Dan said anxiously. 'He's missing his bird, her being dead and all. He might...well, he might do something stupid, yeah?'

Bryn figured out exactly what 'something stupid' might be as soon as Pete burst through the door and, instead of taking a seat, paced angrily around the room, hands clenching and unclenching as he circled.

'You've been talking trash about me,' he spat.

Bryn kept his cool and kept his seat, hands relaxed in his lap. 'I'm trying to find out who killed Kate Thomas,' he said quietly.

Pete subsided, blowing air through his lips.

'She was my girl,' he said, struggling to bring his temper under control. 'Yet you're asking all my mates if they'd do her? What's that about?'

'Jealousy is a powerful motive, son. I need to know if there was anyone who'd kill Kate rather than see her with you.' Bryn tried to be honest with the boy, hoping he'd take it like a man and realise that he was only trying to help.

But Pete just continued to pace, his frustration mounting. 'But they're my mates! How can you think that? And what about the other bird—Mel? She's nothing to do with here, is she? It's some serial killer, isn't it? Just picking off random girls.'

Pete clenched his teeth, snorting like a bull about to charge.

Bryn didn't feel threatened but he did a quick inventory of breakables and bludgeoning objects around the room.

'It's hardly ever random,' Bryn said. 'Even serial killers start with people they know. Did Kate have any friends you didn't like? She get on with her family?'

Pete gave a hollow little laugh. 'How should I know? I was just sleeping with her. We didn't do none of that couple stuff. She just wanted some fun, I'm a fun guy, that was all there was to it. I don't even know if she had any family.'

'What about drugs?' Bryn asked bluntly.

'Bit of weed, bit of MCAT at a party – who doesn't? Nothing Class A, nothing regular. Definitely no smack.'

Bryn was always surprised at how easy it was to get kids to admit to drug use, particularly if you were direct about it. They'd found nothing in her house to suggest drug use and, while they had no body to confirm it, her lecturers hadn't noticed any problems with her work. It was always the schools and colleges who were first to cotton on, way ahead of the parents.

'Thank you, Pete. We'll be in touch.' If he was involved, Bryn wanted him to know there was a watch on him.

'Find her, yeah?' he said, before shutting the door quietly behind him.

Bryn sat back in his chair and sighed, not an inch closer to discovering who killed Kate and Melody. His principle suspect had an alibi and there were no other leads to follow. What the hell could he do now?

Missing Persons was badgering him day and night to add another of their runaways to his list of potential victims, but they didn't fit the profile: slender blonde students in their early twenties. Then again, two didn't make a pattern, just a trend, and his nights were sleepless with the thought that there was another missing girl out there, another body not found that might be the key to stopping this bastard dead. Yet he hoped there wasn't another, that he wouldn't have to look at the photo of another girl dead on white sheets.

Students were starting to panic. They'd had an increase in phone calls about people lurking in alleys or on street corners, but they were just the usual brand of pervert or thug, nothing to link them to Kate or Melody. Bryn had banned his daughters from the clubs, much to their disgust, told them to be home by ten and call before they left their friends' houses. At least he knew where they were now. If he had his way, he'd lock them all up until they were thirty.

The press hadn't cottoned on to a unified nickname for the killer yet, but South Wales Strangler was gaining popularity, with Cardiff Ripper a close second. There were a horde of journalists outside police HQ, like a pack of wolves waiting for the next taste of fresh meat.

The city was holding its breath – waiting for another murder.

Chapter 13: Can't Erase the Past

Jason was ten minutes early to make up for running out on Amy the day before, and he'd managed to push back his one o'clock to two. He was going to brave the bathroom today, and tidy up a bit before Bryn and Owain dropped by with the tape.

Kate and Melody had been all over the evening news. Jason watched it with Gwen and Cerys, silently reviewing what the police knew and were willing to share. They were finally using the word *murder*, mentioning the photographs but not showing them. Jason barely took his eyes off Cerys, pale beneath her makeup, and the way his mam's hands tightened on her mug, suddenly looking so much older. No, they didn't need to see the photographs.

The words *elite taskforce* were used and Jason struggled to hide the smile on his lips, at odds with the grim news. 'Elite taskforce teaboy' would look good on his CV. At the end of the BBC Wales report, they showed the picture from the club – a blown-up, slightly blurred image of Melody in her black coat. Testament to the hours of work Amy put in and Jason's ability to keep her in tea.

Jason rang the doorbell – but the door didn't open. He held down the button, waiting for a message to appear. But there was no response. After waiting another minute, he turned towards his car and the lock-picks concealed in the dashboard.

He was stopped dead by an unmarked police car pulling up outside the flat. Something about police vehicles made them so bloody obvious, even when they weren't dressed up. It probably had something to do with the grim men behind the wheel.

Bryn came up the steps and stared at the door, Owain rummaging in the boot as his silly floppy hair was caught by the wind.

'She not answering? Shit, I hoped we'd have more days than this.' The statement made no sense, but Bryn just leaned past him and held down the buzzer. 'Amy, Amy, quite contrary, how does your fungus grow?'

The box beeped and a message flashed up: *Voice imprint recognised.*
The door opened of its own accord and Bryn stepped past him and
into the opening lift, which was crammed full of shopping bags, sitting in ever-increasing puddles. The three men carefully picked their
way across the grocery minefield before the doors closed, and they
stood stock-still in the half dark, as if caught in the middle of a game
of musical statues. The lift doors finally opened and Bryn waded out,
Jason following.

Bryn scanned the living room with a sigh. 'She'll have crashed out.
That's that then.'

Jason wasn't entirely sure what was going on but 'crashed out'
sounded ominous. 'I'll look for her.'

'Good luck with that,' Bryn called after him.

But the cop didn't show any signs of leaving, so Jason walked down
the corridor, exploring the rooms at the back where he'd yet to go. The
first door on the left was the bathroom and it was just as horrible as
he'd imagined, infested with mould and towels that stank of damp.
Jason pushed open the window, allowing some air into the fetid room,
before closing the door firmly behind him and trying the other room.

Heavy blackout curtains hung across the one wall of floor-length
windows, shrouding the room in darkness. The room smelled of
stale sweat and the musk of a woman, a scent he vaguely identified
with Amy. In the centre of the king-sized bed, a small shape huddled
beneath the blankets, shivering.

'Amy?'

The trembling ceased, but the lump in the covers made no move
to reply.

Jason closed the door behind him and sat on the edge on the bed.
'Come on, Amy – Bryn and Owain are here. We've got work to do,
remember?'

'Fuck off.'

Jason swallowed down the wholly inappropriate urge to laugh.
'Amy, you have to get up. World-famous detective, remember?'

'M'not. Get lost.' Still, the huddle stretched out and a tangled mess
of mousy brown hair appeared above the covers, accompanied by a
pair of glaring eyes.

'Good morning,' Jason said cheerfully. 'Jump in the shower and I'll find some breakfast, yeah?'

Amy reached up and ran a hand through her hair. 'Shopping came, but I didn't answer. Might be in the lift.'

'Yeah, I noticed.' Jason didn't hold out much hope that anything fresh or frozen had survived overnight in the stuffy lift. 'See you in twenty minutes, okay?'

He waited for a grunt of agreement before exiting the room, striding back down the corridor to see Bryn and Owain talking together on the sofa.

'She's in the shower. Can I get you something to drink?'

'In the shower?' Bryn said incredulously. 'Have you seen that thing?'

Jason heard two doors slam down the corridor, and then a muffled barrage of swearing as Amy encountered her now-freezing bathroom. Smiling to himself, Jason went to investigate the mass of sodden carrier bags. He discovered, to his surprise, that the milk and cheese had survived, though the frozen microwave meals were all beyond salvage. He carried the dripping carrier bags into the kitchen, hiding his wince from the amused faces of Cardiff's finest – fucking ribs. He put away the few remaining edible items from Amy's shopping and pinched a chocolate digestive.

'I looked you up, boy.'

Jason glanced up to see Bryn in the doorway, arms folded. He wasn't surprised – cops didn't get a haircut without doing a background check on their barber. Jason turned to the kettle and filled it for four, plucking clean mugs from the tree. He would let him say his piece but he wouldn't rise to it. He wasn't proud of his past, but he'd be damned if he let some cop trash him for it.

'Six months at Her Majesty's Pleasure – in Usk, was it?' Bryn picked up Amy's new coffee jar, tossing it from hand to hand. 'At first, I thought you were a nonce. But clearly you're just a bit soft.'

Jason had heard it all before – it was amazing how cutting the words *vulnerable prisoner* could be. His transfer across South Wales from the hardline HMP Swansea to Usk out in the wilds of Monmouthshire had earned plenty of jeers from his fellow inmates, but he was too busy nursing his broken ribs to care. It was almost funny how those verbal blows were always preceded by a physical battering. Funny if you were a masochist.

Jason gritted his teeth and poured water from the kettle. 'Tea or coffee, officer?'

'Coffee. Black, no sugar. And it's Detective Hesketh.'

Jason mashed his tea bag against the side of the mug as if it personally held responsibility for his anger.

Bryn leaned up against the counter beside the sink and held up his hand, counting off on his fingers. 'Taking without consent – from a frail elderly woman. Dangerous driving. Resisting arrest. Oh, and assault on a police officer.' He tutted. 'You've been a naughty boy, Mr. Carr. Now you're working with a lot of frail elderly women, aren't you? Are you going to take a swing at our boy Owain?'

'I served my time,' Jason said tightly, setting his mug down hard enough to make the draining board ring. 'I'm starting again. If you have a problem with me, you can talk to my probation officer. I'd give you her number, but I know you already have it.'

Bryn chuckled. 'Of course I do. I spoke to her as soon as I read your file. She seems to think you're a nice boy who got mixed up with the wrong crowd. Crowd who are now all in prison – for armed robbery.'

Jason froze, holding two mugs in midair. 'I haven't spoken to any of them for a year or more.'

Bryn smiled like a shark. 'Of course not. Because you got picked up a whole seven days before they got caught at that gold exchange. I hear they lacked a decent getaway driver.'

Jason swallowed down his fear. He knew – how the fuck did he know? And what did it mean? He could go down for conspiracy, and if Bryn found the gun… 'I didn't hear that,' he said, mouth dry.

Bryn leaned in, his mouth against Jason's ear as he whispered, 'Oh, I did. And I'm telling you – you put a foot wrong, and I will send you back to your little friends down in Swansea. Am I clear?'

'Fucking crystal.' Jason stepped back, carrying the mugs through to the living room and slamming them down on the table, the scalding liquid spilling over.

Bryn smirked as he sat down and took possession of one of the mugs.

Jason returned to the kitchen, retreating to his sanctuary of order in Amy's chaos, as far away as he could get from the police officers who could send him down for ten years.

Chapter 14: Dial 'M'

She'd never had a man in her bedroom before. The internet had led her to believe it would go differently.

Amy could find no reason to get out of bed that morning. Yesterday, when Jason left her, the case had grown dull, lifeless. She had found Melody – now what? The corners of darkness folded in on her and she was alone with the black hole in her chest. So she went to bed and she stayed there, and she would stay until the black eased a little, just enough for her to believe the day wasn't going to be utter shite.

Then Jason had turned up and hauled her out of bed like a lazy child refusing school – exactly what her parents, her grandmother had failed to do. She should protest, complain that this was not in his job description, and fuck his sense of duty. But she had already asked him to exceed that job description days past and she couldn't redraw the lines now.

So she nodded to Bryn and Owain and made an attempt at a smile. Bryn handed her a cassette tape and Amy scowled at it – God, what decade was this?

Amy hauled her ancient tape deck out from a pile of discarded bubble wrap, knocking it against a collection of empty wine bottles before setting it on the edge of her crowded desk. She loaded the tape and connected the thing to a hub crowded with connections and wires, patting AEON to assure her that the nasty nineties tech would be out of her way soon.

She installed herself in front of AEON, calling up an audio programme she'd cobbled together to identify instruments on metal tracks (definitively disproving the theory that 'Stairway to Heaven' played backwards contained Satanic chanting – and securing her reputation in the conspiracy theory reddit).

She flinched as Bryn leaned over her shoulder, and fought down the urge to snap at him to back off, because this man was her friend, or the closest thing she had. Some days, Bryn gave her a reason to get out of bed.

'Grub's up.'

Amy glanced at the mug that had appeared at her elbow, feeling Jason's presence at her back, and gestured for him to balance the plate of toast and peanut butter on top of the cassette player.

'When you said *tape*,' she muttered, 'I was expecting something from this century.'

Jason laughed and Amy caught Bryn's grimace in the monitor reflection. He was leaning on the back of Amy's chair and trying to subtly edge Jason away.

But Jason just squatted down beside Amy's chair, looking up at the screen with genuine interest. 'This is the police tape?'

'Mmm.' Amy tweaked the programme to adjust for the horrible audio quality it was about to receive. 'Silence in the library.'

No one moved. She hit Record and pressed the Play button on the tape deck. The machine whirred to life, and the scratchy hiss of cassette background noise filled the room.

'*Whitchurch Police Station. Sergeant Parry speaking.*'

The man's voice was surprisingly clear, but a rush of sound answered him, the buzz of several different voices in the background.

A woman's voice spoke hesitantly, quietly. '*I think I have information. About the missing girls.*' She sounded young – and scared. The accent was unusual, something a bit...Spanish, maybe? Amy had to strain to make out her words at all.

'*What sort of information? Can you tell me your name, miss?*' The sergeant's voice was soothing, but the woman didn't want to be calmed.

'*It's on the internet. Write it down.*' She read back the address of the forum, one letter at a time, taking him to the specific post. Her voice shook on each one, a quavering treble that quietened whenever the ever-shifting crowd around her rose to crescendo.

'*And what's there, miss? What are we looking for?*'

A long silence from the caller, as the crowd behind her hushed, as if in anticipation. Slowly, the world filtered back in and she took a deep, shaking breath. '*I think it's Melody Frank. It...it looks like the pictures on the news. Please, find her. He's...*' She stopped, an alarm ringing out behind her. '*I've got to go!*' The phone line went dead.

Everything was still. The tape played on, its eerie static crackling across the room. Amy reached out and hit Stop before pausing the computer recording. Its cheerful *bing* broke the frozen atmosphere in the room, but it did not bring her peace. She hid her disquiet, throwing herself into the mix, separating out the sound waves on her screen, moving them to individual channels and adjusting the volume controls.

'There's an algorithm to block the static. That's half the battle.' With one click, the messy scrawl vanished, leaving a few distinct lines. 'I can get a clear signal on her voice – we should be able to match it. What's her address?'

'We were hoping you could tell us,' Bryn said. 'The phone call was from a blocked number. Trace has it coming from the Heath.'

Amy smiled. 'I presume you mean the hospital and not the surrounding area, its railway stations or the area of grass they call a park.'

'The University Hospital of Wales. Switchboard, if you want precise.'

'Can you make that background stuff louder?' Jason pointed at some of the smaller lines, his finger not quite grazing the monitor.

Amy resisted the urge to bat his grease-stained hands away from AEON, concentrating on his words. She started clipping and adjusting the smaller lines, moving them to a new channel to examine. 'Why? That's what's interfering with the signal.'

'Maybe it'll tell us where she is. Like that alarm? That could be one of their…y'know, emergency things. Where they all run to shock the guy.'

Bryn snorted, but Amy was nodding along, plucking up the large wave sound at the end of the recording and adding it to her collection. 'The crash bell. Could be. Would need a comparison sample.' All that ER-watching was finally paying off.

Jason climbed to his feet and nudged the side of her chair. 'Now eat your toast. It's getting cold.'

Amy dutifully picked up her toast, still playing around with the sounds, and munched thoughtfully. 'Why call from the hospital?'

'She doesn't want to be identified,' Owain answered from the sofa, biscuit in hand. 'It could be anyone – doctor, nurse, cleaner, porter, patient. The place is its own village.'

Amy started playing the various tracks. Some were too quiet to be heard clearly, but there were five distinct voices on the tape, three women and two men. Only the odd word could be made out, but it

71

seemed to be two conversations, one about a failed celebrity marriage and the other about rugby. 'Mundane. Nothing identifiable at all.'

'It could be a waiting room or a café,' Jason said.

Amy just shrugged. Without anything concrete, it was all just guesswork. She played the alarm, a high-pitched beeping that echoed around the living room.

'That would move you in a hurry,' Bryn said, slurping down his tea.

Amy tapped impatiently on her mouse and picked up her second round of toast. 'It's useless without a reference. It could be anything – crash bell, fire alarm, doorbell? Useless.'

Jason suddenly leaned forward and gestured to the middle of the main monitor. 'Go back on her – just before the alarm goes off.'

Amy looked up at him curiously, before doing as he asked, playing the recording again. '*—pictures on the news. Please, find her. He's…*'

'There!' Jason looked round at them triumphantly, only to be greeted with blank faces. 'Don't you get it?'

'No, boy, we don't get it,' Bryn said, his tone cutting. 'Want to share with the class?'

'She said 'he'! Who's she talking about?' Jason gestured at the screen. 'It doesn't make sense with what she's said. Unless…'

Owain grimaced. 'Unless she knows him.'

Amy struggled to process that information. 'Then why hasn't she come forward?'

'She's scared, isn't she? You can hear it in her voice. Maybe the hospital was the only place she could call from. Maybe he put her there.'

Jason sounded like he knew what he was talking about, the woman's tremor echoed in his own words. It was only then that Amy remembered he'd been to prison, that he was a rough man with a criminal record whom she'd invited into her home, but it didn't occur to her that she should be afraid. That those large, clumsy hands that carefully spread peanut butter on every inch of her toast could pound a man into the ground was failing to register on her usually hypervigilant radar.

'Or I was right and the picture was put up on that forum for her. He was sending her a message.' Amy bit her lip, looking nervously up at Jason.

He placed a hand on her shoulder and she looked back to her monitor but didn't move away. His palm was warm through the thin cotton of her T-shirt. She didn't want to move away.

'What kind of message?' Owain said, voice concerned. "You're next'?'

'We don't even know if it is a message.' Bryn moved away from Amy's chair to pace the room. 'We don't know who this woman is. She could be a victim, sure, but she could be Myra Hindley. We need to find her.'

Even with her fascination with the macabre, Amy had struggled to read about the Moors Murderers. The idea that a second Brady and Hindley could be gathering momentum in Cardiff chilled her.

'Ain't that what you do best, Detective – catch crooks?' Jason's voice was all innocence, but Amy sensed something between him and Bryn, something sour that she was only just noticing. What had passed between them in the time it took her to shower?

'Oh, we'll find her, son. Don't you worry about that.'

Chapter 15: Big Brother's Watching You

When he sat down at his computer, his hands were shaking.

The girls were all over the news. Someone had found out they were dead, but he didn't know how. They were calling it murder. Murder! They didn't understand, none of them did. At least she would understand. He could tell her. She'd understand it was all for her.

The old laptop started slowly, but he coaxed it to life, talking to it like his old mum had talked to plants. To help them grow. He'd talked to the girls, but they hadn't wanted to chat, just stared at him. Their pretty pictures would have to talk for them.

He logged on with his good password, with all the letters and numbers, random to anyone else but his shibboleth to the real world. Here, he could be free. Here, he didn't have to be with people who didn't understand.

He knew places, good places where they taught you things. That sometimes loving someone meant that other people got hurt. That was part of life, they said. The way to drive a woman mad, they said, was to make her jealous. Summon the green-eyed monster from the depths and she would come to you, beg you to take her. His friends were mentors to his superhero, spurring him on to greater heights, greater devotions.

He opened up his blog and he wrote to her. She was his muse, his inspiration, his prize. Without her, he wouldn't have the strength to make these sacrifices, but he had to unleash the monster. He had to make her realise that she loved him.

That meant he needed to find a new girlfriend. Slim, blonde, perfect. Nothing like his love, but that flawless skin and shining hair that was splashed all over the covers of magazines, top shelf, quality. Her skin would glow in the flash and there she would be captured, ready to tantalise, to enrage.

He smiled to himself, the fear fading, as he wrote, confessed:

My love, I need you. Please care for me as I do you. Don't you understand? There needs to be more between us, oh so much more. Not with him. I've seen you with him everywhere and it hurts me, freebird. I know you don't want to hurt me. These girls mean nothing to me, just a good time. If you say the word, I will come to you and we can be together. That's how it's meant to be. Meant to be, freebird.

I love you.

Amy found her.

She almost missed her, chivalrously shielded beneath a bouncer's umbrella, but the coat's loose button was unmistakeable. Melody and her distinctive coat then headed down the street towards the Hilton, and walked beyond the camera's meagre range.

Amy slumped in her chair, clearing her parched throat and tapping the rim of her long-empty wine glass. She needed something to drink. She'd get up in a minute.

She picked up the feed from the hotel across the street and fast-forwarded to the correct timestamp. Once she'd found her, it was impossible to lose her – the camera never lied.

She laughed to herself, a croaking gulp. It was funny, how she could make the camera lie in a matter of minutes. Fabricate a girlfriend in an instant so the judge would grant a divorce. She could go to prison for that, but the woman's black eye had been turning yellow round the edges and she looked so tired. Amy had done that one for free.

There – Melody, trotting down the street on her spindly heels, slightly unsteady but practised. She hurried on past the camera and Amy flagged that segment for her timeline, before skipping ahead to the next.

Melody's route followed the walls of the castle, past the statue of the intense Aneurin Bevan and down St. Mary's Street. She was practically alone on the street, too late for latecomers and too early for closing. She was wrapped tight against the wind and rain, swaying like a willow tree. She carried herself with a relaxed, confident air, ironic for her gallows walk.

Amy shifted her shoulders, drawing herself up in her chair. She took a deep breath, forced her shoulders down and lifted her nose, contemplating her reflection in the monitor. No, not even close.

At the end of the street, Melody stopped. Amy's focus returned, waiting. What had caught her eye? Amy tried to find the reverse angle, but the nearest camera didn't cover her line of sight. Melody walked back down the street and down one of the side streets. Here, there were plenty of cameras and Amy had a good view of Melody stuffing her face with chips. Amy's stomach rumbled. She checked her watch – 01:09. When had she last eaten? Jason had made her toast this morning, hadn't he? She'd find food in a bit.

Melody tottered back onto the main street and wandered back – wait, was that the nightclub where Kate worked? Kangaroos, Wallaby, some kind of Australian mammal. Amy captured a still and saved it, before continuing to play the footage. Where was she headed?

The cameras grew sparser away from the city centre and Amy struggled to follow her. Melody crossed roads haphazardly before finally disappearing under the Brains bridge towards the Bay. Amy frantically searched her camera database, but the next set she had was in the Bay proper or much farther along the Taff.

Amy stabbed the keys angrily. So, she was walking towards Bute Street – Jason's territory. Where was she going? Was there a specific person she was looking to meet, a boyfriend maybe? Or was she just lost? She had no data. Just speculation.

Amy got up from the chair, pinning her blanket to her like a cloak, and collapsed in a heap on the sofa. Speculation was boring. She needed something to analyse. She closed her eyes, bored to death. Sleep was something to do.

At 23:49, she heard a noise. An odd little noise – *scratch scratch scratch* like the first hesitant skips of a dying hard drive. The glow of AEON's monitor was the only light, but she had already imagined him: an intruder, a murderer, a rapist.

Amy was frozen, unable to move from her spot on the sofa. What was it? *Where* was it? She had to know, she had to compute – to file it under safe or deadly in her head.

The noise was coming from next door.

Amy was torn between relief and the desperate urge to call Jason. Next door was safe, wired with half a dozen sensor wires and cameras lying dormant that could be activated on her word. Her grandmother's house had been her first project.

It had been Lizzie's idea, hiding in plain sight from Social Services and anyone else who wanted to drag Amy into the light. Their parents were gone, drinking cocktails in some semi-legal speakeasy in Dubai. And their grandmother… There was nothing left of her, not really. The threads of her mind had all unravelled and the woman who stared accusingly at them was not their grandmother anymore. When they took her into hospital, it was the beginning of the end.

Hacking their parents' bank account was the most difficult work she had ever done, but it was the piece of which she was most proud. Five million quid – gone, in an instant. And then slowly filtering into the account of Amy and Elizabeth Lane. Money was all just code, in the end.

She left them just enough for the plane ticket home, but they never came. From their transactions, she gathered they camped out in the Middle East until Daddy's next pay cheque or the insurance company coughed up. After that, it hurt to watch anymore and she stopped obsessing over their pennies and moved on to building her and Lizzie a new life.

And so she'd bought the house next door. Preparing herself for moving even that distance had taken a whole morning of deep breathing, a handful of little blue pills, and Lizzie's hand pressed firmly into the small of her back as she stepped over the threshold.

Lizzie had boarded up their grandmother's house and attended the cremation alone. Amy kept the urn on the mantelpiece of that sad little house, among the dust and the memories. And the things that went *scratch* in the night.

She sank back into her blanket nest and closed her eyes. But sleep was distant, and she spent hours listening to the mice playing in the spaces where she used to live.

Chapter 16: Our House

As he parked on Melody's street, Jason felt a tad uneasy. Did he have the balls for this?

He'd already done a bit of legwork for Amy, talking with Pete and Dan mostly by accident. But eavesdropping on a couple of bar-backs was a world away from knocking on somebody's door and interrogating them about their dead friend.

Did he want to risk going back to prison? Fuck no. He'd thought he was a tough man, swaggering down the street with his boys. If prison had taught him one thing, it was that he'd been nothing but a child before lock-up.

Yet, if he was out here and did nothing, what was the point of it all? Two girls were dead and he could help out. He could talk to these students and the girls' friends. He was more their age, had more in common. They might be willing to tell him things that the cops wouldn't understand. Then he could take it all to Amy, so she could solve this thing. Be a real member of the elite taskforce, a real asset to her.

Maybe he would have to take a risk to do that. If that meant bending the law, playing the cop, or finding his way back around the street, he could do that. He could do that if it meant no one else had to die.

The morning had turned up jack shit, kicking around the docks, looking for information on the river and the barrage. He felt more at home in this world, moving into spaces where the cops would be recognised and resisted. But most of the guys had been secretive, distrustful of a boy from Bute, and the rest had been foreign and unable – or unwilling – to talk. So he'd decided to try a different tack, and Melody's former housemates were as good a place as any to start.

With a deep breath, Jason got out the car and started down the street. Number 22 with the blue door – but the door was open and there were a pile of boxes and carrier bags on the pavement. A couple of lads were sitting on the wall outside with beer in hand, as a knock-out brunette in a T-shirt dress and leggings stumbled out with her arms full of kitchenware.

'Little help, guys?'

The guys in question just laughed and she poked her tongue out at them. But her high-heeled Converse slid on the edge of the kerb and her saucepans went flying.

Jason seized his chance. 'Here, let me get those.'

He gathered up the scattered pans and held them out to her.

She glanced down at her full arms. 'Um…'

'Just show me where you need them,' he said, catching the guys nudging each other out of the corner of his eye.

The girl nodded her head towards a car a few feet away, boot open and half-filled with cardboard boxes. Jason obediently followed and watched her shove the kettle and toastie maker in the gaps between boxes, before taking the saucepans off him one at a time and balancing them among the scented candles and stuffed toys.

'I know it's a bit of a mess,' she said, as the last saucepan found a home on top of a lampshade, 'but I'm not going too far with it.'

Jason held up his now-empty hands. 'I'm not judging. Moving?'

The girl flicked an errant strand of chestnut hair out of her eyes. 'Yeah, the house has…memories, I guess. I'm moving into a flat over in Roath. The nice end, not the dodgy end.'

'Roath's nice,' he said, struggling to keep the conversation going. 'By the park?'

'By the rec. It's not much, but it's my own, y'know?'

She started walking back towards the house and he strolled alongside her, affecting his best 'listening' face.

The guys on the wall kept a steady eye on him and, as they approached, one said loudly, 'Oi, Teresa! We're going down the pub. You can manage here, right?'

'Ryan, I've got a ton more stuff!' she said, throwing up her hands.

Ryan looked pointedly at Jason. 'Get your new man to help you then.'

'He's not my…' Teresa looked over at Jason, cheeks heating with embarrassment. 'Ignore them. They're my idiot housemates – soon to be ex-housemates.'

But she didn't look pleased about that, her lip jutting out and quivering, and Jason guessed that the memories she'd mentioned were of good times past with these boys – and with Melody.

'Of course you don't have to help,' she continued. 'You were obviously headed somewhere and it was great of you to catch the pots.'

With the guys heading off down the street, Jason shrugged. 'I've nowhere to be for an hour. If you need a hand...'

He left the offer open, realising it was odd for a stranger to offer assistance clearing out a house, but he sensed that she liked him, her eyes drawn to the way his T-shirt stretched over his biceps.

'Yeah,' she said, 'I could use a good pair of arms.'

With her room tidied away into boxes and loaded into the car, Teresa boiled some water in a milk pan to make them both tea.

'The guys will never get round to buying a kettle,' she said, carefully pouring the water into mugs. 'Mel was always—' She stopped herself, took a breath, and continued. 'Melody was the organised one.'

Jason tried not to react to what she was saying, stirring sugar into his tea. 'Was Melody an old housemate?' he said, voice carefully neutral.

Teresa sat in the chair across from him, suddenly fragile with her long fingers wrapped around the chipped china mug. 'She's...she's the girl. On the news. The one who died.'

Her eyes were pained – and green-hazel, like Amy's. She carried the same haunted look about her, wearing her hurt like a shroud.

'I'm sorry. God, that's so fucked up. The pictures...'

She smiled tearfully. 'She was a good friend. I want to remember her like she was...not like that picture of her. She's too still to be Melody.'

She looked away and Jason felt like a tosser for making her cry like that, unsuspecting of his motives in seeking her out. But that was what he was here for – to help catch Melody's killer.

'Have the police found any leads?' he asked, sure that was a reasonable question from a concerned stranger.

Teresa shook her head, taking a sip of tea. 'Nothing. They think it's related to that other girl, but they're not sure. She didn't know her – I don't know her, neither do John or Ryan.'

'It must be worse, not knowing what happened.'

He felt genuinely bad for Teresa. It must be awful to have your friend die, but to have them murdered and not know who did it, not have a body and a funeral? He couldn't imagine how that must feel.

'She was just out with some people from the bakery.'

Teresa gestured with her hand as if trying to work through what happened, but with a tone that suggested she'd already replayed this in her head many times.

'She wasn't going to stay out, because she had a piece of coursework due in Monday. She said she'd be home by midnight, but she always said that.'

Teresa smiled through her tears.

'Melody loved to party. So, we just went to bed, and the next day she still wasn't back. We called her phone and the friends she was with, but they said she left them at twelve. That's when we called the police. With that other girl being missing, they got serious about it straightaway. Then her dad came round here, shouting and calling us things, telling us we shouldn't have let her go out alone.'

Teresa shook with the memory and Jason felt helpless. She looked up at him, swiping viciously at her eyes and running mascara.

'God, I'm sorry,' she said, reaching for the kitchen roll to dab at her eyes. 'You've helped me out and I've just blubbed all over you.'

'It's all right, Teresa,' he said softly. 'Anything you need.'

'I'll make it up to you. I'm having a little flat-warming thing tomorrow – you should come. Bring…your girlfriend.'

Jason recognised a water-testing exercise when he saw one. 'I don't really have anyone, but I would love to come. I'd like to…get to know you.'

She smiled at him and wrote down her number and her new address, pressed it into his hand with a shy smile.

Teresa waved him off at the door and Jason got back into his car, the little piece of paper safely folded into his jeans pocket.

If this was being a detective, he could definitely live with that.

Chapter 17: Sunday Morning Coming Down

It had been a miserable Saturday.

Amy huddled on the sofa as the light of Sunday morning filtered through the gaps in her blackout curtains. Despite managing for years without Jason, she now found the flat oddly cold, and the tea remained unmade. She hadn't had anyone in the house except Bryn and Owain for almost five years now, and they only came when they needed something. She had never called them, never reached out. This was business. She tried not to kid herself that it was anything else.

Before that, there had been Lizzie. Her big sister had always taken care of her, since before their parents abandoned them, but Lizzie had to follow her dreams – and her dreams took her to Australia.

Amy guessed she had Lizzie to thank for Jason's appearance at her flat. Her sister worried about her, whether she was eating and keeping the place tidy. That was what sisters did. Amy, in turn, worried about whether Lizzie had picked up a long-haired loser boyfriend of the kind found on *Neighbours* or whether she was going to die from the bite of an exotic snake.

Amy had always tried to get Lizzie to stay in and Lizzie attempted to drag Amy outside, and that struggle had persisted even as Lizzie took her taxi to the airport and Amy couldn't cross the threshold to wave goodbye.

Amy's imagination conjured up one thousand ways to die in Australia. It was a rational fear – anything could happen to her on the other side of the world. Of course, anything could happen outside their front door, as these murders proved. Amy stood by her decision to stay where it was safe, and she had lost her sister because of her conviction. Some days, she wished she could be the kind of girl who followed her sister across the world, but she couldn't even follow her out the front door.

Usually, when she had something to investigate, Amy didn't have time to feel sorry for herself. It was all caffeine and chocolate, a rush of adrenaline until she collapsed in a heap, physically and mentally drained, or she got caught by a black mood and couldn't shift from her bed. Or a panic attack got hold of her and ruined the whole day, but she mostly had those under control. She had nothing to panic about if she didn't open the front door. The house was safe and there were sensors and cameras on every potential entry point. She'd wired them herself.

AEON chirruped happily. Amy prised herself off the sofa to see what her beloved computer had found. The data from the supposedly secure transaction site had returned – she now had a list of everyone who had bought tickets for the last Crash and Yearn gig in Cardiff. Settling into her office chair, Amy filtered the results into her custom database and cross-referenced it with employee data from the Heath Hospital by name and address fields. It was impossible to be sure who had made that call, but this would at least give them a sensible place to start.

Coupled with the information about the alarm, they might be able to narrow down their list to a handful of people, perhaps even one or two, and that was as good as a neon sign pointing down at the woman in Amy's book.

However, the search would take a couple of hours to run, and until then there was nothing to do except bemoan the fact that it was Sunday morning and Jason wouldn't be over for another 27.5 hours.

Amy sighed. 'Screw you, Sunday,' she declared to the empty flat.

AEON beeped in agreement.

She wasn't returning his calls.

He tried to ring her every day but most of the time they wouldn't put him through, told him that they didn't let just any call through. He tried to tell them he was her lover, but they hung up on him nine times out of ten. When he did get through, the men on the other end would tell him she wasn't there and she didn't want to speak to him. The women would promise to give her a message, but the whores always lied. If they'd passed on his messages, she would've called him back.

But she must've got his other messages, even though the stupid moderators had taken them down. He knew she always liked to check the forum at that time, had watched her username pop up at the bottom of the page, revelling in the sense that they were together in that moment, occupying the same warm space.

He just had to be patient. He didn't want to chase this new girl, but she wasn't leaving him any choice. If she wasn't jealous enough to come back to him, she'd need more persuading.

She left him no option but to pursue the girl. She brought this on herself. It was her fault that he had to be so cruel to her, to drive her mad with envy. She was to blame for those two beautiful girls at the bottom of the lake. She'd driven him to it.

She had to return his calls, or she had to face the consequences.

Chapter 18: Mama Told Me Not to Come

Teresa texted to say that people were coming for nine, so Jason turned up at ten with a bottle of Australian red in his hands and sporting his favourite leather jacket.

His mam had insisted on the wine, but she hadn't talked him into the paisley shirt Cerys had bought him for his birthday. While Cerys had decent taste, she seemed to want to bring out his inner indie kid, and he had no interest in wearing skinny jeans and a bowler hat.

Jason felt unaccountably nervous when he rang the doorbell. They were just students and they were older than Cerys, growing out of that compulsive need to be edgy and different all the damn time. They still thought themselves cool and independent, so he'd already decided to keep quiet about the fact that he lived with his mother and worked as a minimum-wage cleaner. In a year or two, these kids would be lawyers and teachers – he wouldn't let them think that they were smarter than him.

He was buzzed straight up and he pushed open the door, stepping into a grubby hallway with flaking plaster and the same ugly terracotta tile that seemed to be universal in all student houses in Cardiff. Jason shut the door behind him and took the stairs two at a time until he got to the second floor and flat 9C.

The door was open and the sound of poorly played *Guitar Hero* carried into the corridor. He knocked gently on the door as he stepped in, to see Teresa on the sofa with John, as Ryan murdered the lead guitar on 'Killer Queen'.

Teresa jumped up to greet him, took the bottle out of his hand and went over to the tiny kitchen area in the living room.

'So glad you could make it.' She poured two generous glasses for them before pressing one into his hand.

'I'm glad you invited me.'

Teresa giggled, clinking her glass against his. She took his hand and led him to the sofa, from which John had tactfully moved to instruct Ryan in the finer points of wielding his digital guitar.

'Busy day?' Teresa said, taking social refuge in idle chitchat.

'Sunday lunch with my mam and sister. Nothing much.'

'So you're a local boy then,' Teresa said knowingly.

Jason tensed, suddenly feeling defensive. He hated the way out-of-towners did that, looked down on you for sticking with your roots and your family. Sure, people could go away to uni or move to other parts, but he saw nothing wrong with staying in town or coming home again. It didn't make him dependent or fragile – it just made sense.

'Born and raised,' was what he said, plastering on a smile. 'My dad was from Liverpool.'

Teresa made an interested noise and Jason plastered on a polite smile, regretting coming to this thing at all. These weren't his people, not really, and he had been stupid to think this was a good place to be just because a pretty girl had made him a cup of tea.

'I don't go home much,' Teresa said. 'My parents live in Oxford, but I've never been a homebird. When my brother goes to uni next year, they'll be lost.'

Now it was Jason's turn to nod appropriately, but he was saved from death by small talk when the doorbell rang. John buzzed the guest up and soon the tiny flat was filled with a gang of boys and girls, bearing party food and drinks.

Jason lost Teresa in the crowd but made his way to the food, where a young woman was carefully arranging cupcakes with white icing and silver baubles on top.

'They're pretty. Did you make them?'

The girl turned and shyly held one out to him. 'No. I mean, yes, I did, but at work. We get to take home the leftovers.'

'You work at a bakery?' Jason took the proffered cake, wondering why that sounded familiar. Was there something in the case about a bakery?

'Just a small one in town. I…uh…I worked with Mel there.'

Of course, Teresa had mentioned Melody had been out with folk from the bakery. Maybe this girl, even… 'It must be sad, not seeing her there.'

'It was funny, 'cause she'd only been there a few weeks, but we hit it off, y'know? I'd come round and we'd chat and have coffee. That's how I got to know Teresa and the boys.'

Just then, Jason's phone buzzed and he fished it out of his jeans pocket. A text from Amy: *Woman at UHW ID down to 7. Easy. @* He frowned, trying to make sense of it. Seven what?

'Sorry about that.' But when he looked up, the girl was gone, having ditched him for more attentive company.

Jason hid his scowl. How was he meant to investigate if the woman he was gathering intel for kept distracting him via text? The life of a modern detective was difficult. Sherlock Holmes never had to deal with this shit.

He sipped the red vinegar in his glass and scanned the room for people to talk with. These kids looked like they were sixteen – he wasn't that old, was he? A few excited yells from the direction of the TV drew his attention, and Jason decided to play to his strengths and head for the games console.

After watching a couple of average performances, he stepped up and angled for the plastic axe. John gave it up to him with a shrug and Jason secured the strap over his shoulder.

'You played before?' Ryan asked him.

'A few times.'

Three minutes later, with a new high score on 'Iron Man', Jason was kicking back in the kitchen, celebratory beer in hand.

'You've got to show me how to do that,' Ryan said eagerly.

Jason told him confidently it was all about rhythm when really it was more about hours in your mate's garage between motors.

The boys weren't so keen to talk about Melody and it was several minutes of conversation about their courses and Dylan's garage before John brought up Teresa's move.

'She said she wanted to get away,' he said, without complaint or anger. 'I get it, I do – that house is too full of Mel. I don't know if we'll stay long.'

'I don't think we'll get anyone to live there, to be honest. The landlord's thinking about selling the place but he won't get much for it. Even though she didn't…' Ryan trailed off, realising just what he was about to say.

'It's not the same as that Kate girl,' he said instead and everyone knew what he meant. There may not have been a dead body in the house, but it still held the curse.

'I wish we knew where she was,' John said feelingly. 'She didn't like to be cold. I hope she isn't somewhere cold.'

It didn't make sense, and yet Jason felt that it did, that there had been a great deal of affection between them and they cared about her resting place. He felt like an intruder at a wake.

'How long had you lived together?' he asked.

Ryan started counting on his fingers. 'It was September last, so... fourteen months? But she'd been in halls with Teresa before that, and we lived in the flat below, so we'd known her over two years really.'

'Were you two...?' Jason left the implication hanging.

John laughed it off. 'Melody wouldn't give him the time of day. Besides, she wasn't one to be tied down. A free spirit, our Mel.'

'What are you three talking about?' Teresa said, coming back for more wine. 'You're having a good time, right?'

'The best, Terry.' John raised his beer. 'Your man Jason's an ace at *Guitar Hero*.'

This time, she didn't deny he was 'her man' and Jason thought that might mean something, though he wasn't entirely sure what.

'I'm not that good,' he deflected modestly, and suffered a minute of Ryan's enthusiastic praise.

Eventually, Teresa saved him. 'Come on, Jason, I'll give you the tour.'

Jason caught Ryan and John's exchanged looks as Teresa dragged him off – the girl's friends obviously had more clue what she was up to than he did.

'So, you've seen the living room-kitchen combo. The bathroom is tiny. In fact, there's not even a bath, so that makes it a shower room, right?' She opened the door to said cupboard-like room, then shut it again. 'At the end of the corridor, there's a storage closet and then this is my room.'

She led him by the hand into her bedroom. The walls were white, the carpet cream, but she'd hung pictures on the walls, prints of water lilies by that famous artist bloke and a poster of a cat hanging off a tree branch. When she closed the door behind them, Jason realised he'd been extremely stupid and, when she kissed him, everything fell into place.

She was drunk but enthusiastic, and he let her kiss him for a minute before pulling away. 'Won't your friends notice you're gone?'

Teresa waved off his objections. 'They won't mind. It's busy in there – they won't even notice.'

It seemed a reasonable argument to him and, in the face of overwhelming logic and a woman pulling him towards her bed, Jason found himself powerless to resist.

Chapter 19: Despair Has Its Own Calms

The alarm went off on his phone at half-seven, like always, but this morning, there was a soft moan next to him and Jason realised he wasn't in his own bed.

He silenced the alarm and got up, politely but firmly removing Teresa's searching fingers from his arm and heading for the shower. After a quick rinse, he shoved on yesterday's clothes and, arm caught once more by the delightfully naked and still mostly drunk Teresa, gave her a quick parting kiss before legging it down the stairs and out into the crisp Monday morning.

He had to get home and get dressed for work before heading out to Amy's. If he walked quickly, he might even have time to grab a bacon butty. He was glad he'd opted for low-key, so that his walk of shame that morning wasn't particularly obvious. He'd had a good time and, if this morning's limpet-like clinging was anything to go by, Teresa would quite like to see him again. Unfortunately, he hadn't found out much about Melody – dead housemates didn't make for great pillow talk.

Of course, his mother was already up when he got home. Gwen shot him a reproachful look as he tried to creep through the kitchen door. 'What kind of one o'clock is this, hmm? Were you drunk last night?'

'No!'

Sure, he'd had a couple and he'd got his wine and beer the wrong way round, but other than that, it had been a pretty clear night. Crystal clear – he remembered every detail: the silver bauble cupcakes, his top score on *Guitar Hero*, the scent of ripe berries on Teresa's hair as she kissed his neck…

'Oh, I see,' Gwen said, with a mother's intuition. 'Did you have a nice time? Was your hostess very…welcoming?'

Jason shuddered. There were some things you just did not discuss with your mam, and one-night stands were one of them. 'She's a nice girl. I'm gonna be late.'

She waved him off, and he hurried upstairs to change and get round to Amy's for nine. He'd meant to pick up some fruit before going round there, but that would have to wait until tomorrow. Amy wouldn't die of her vitamin deficiency in twenty-four hours.

Ten minutes later, he was out the door and in the car, but was soon bogged down in city centre rush hour traffic. Drumming his fingers impatiently against the steering wheel, Jason debated texting ahead to let Amy know he would be late, but he wasn't handy enough with the phone to subtly text while looking like he was paying full attention to the road for any passing cop.

It was twenty past nine before he finally got to Amy's, running up to the front door to find it opening before him. She'd been waiting for him – damn.

'Sorry I'm late,' he called through, as he headed into the living room. 'I was—'

'Stuck in traffic. Yes, I know.' Amy was up and dressed, sitting at her computer in a baggy black T-shirt with a vintage Iron Man in silver. 'You didn't reply to my text.'

'How did you know about the traffic?'

He hadn't replied to her text, true, but then he hadn't really understood what it meant. However, in Amy's world, not replying to a text was probably like refusing to answer her calls or putting her through to voicemail.

'I told you – centre's crawling with cameras. When you didn't come at nine, I went looking for you.' Her words were sharp, reproachful. Jason winced. 'As I told you last night, I've narrowed the woman at the hospital down to seven possibilities – if she's an employee and a Crash and Yearn fan. There are too many ifs, but that can't be helped.'

Suddenly, the text made sense – 7 was the number of women. He couldn't be expected to decipher that with wine in hand. 'What are you going to do now?'

'You should go looking for her.'

Jason bristled at the way she ordered him around like she was his military commander. He was meant to be the cleaner, not her personal slave. Besides, this was Bryn and Owain's job, and they got paid a hell of a lot more than him.

'Get Bryn to do it.' He collected the stray mugs that told him she'd been subsisting on coffee all weekend. 'I've got work to do making this place habitable.'

'I'm paying you. Why won't you just do what I want? You're late and now you want to get out of a job—'

'You're not paying me. Your sister is, and she's paying me to clean your flat. You can't just order me to fetch and carry for you. That's not what I'm here for.'

'You didn't complain before. Why are you now so stubborn? Did you find something better to do?'

'If you want to find this woman so badly, why don't you find her yourself?'

Jason was deliberately baiting her now. His head was starting to ache and he was not in the mood to fight with Amy about what he did and didn't want to do for her. This case had taken over his life already. He'd spent most of his weekend trying to find out stuff for her, and now she was acting like he was slacking off just because he was a bit late? He'd been staying late every day to help her out, and this was the thanks he got?

'Maybe I don't want to.' Amy turned back to her keyboard with a huff.

Jason stalked over to her and turned her chair around, hesitating at the flicker of fear in her eyes.

'I get it – you don't want to go outside. What's so scary about outside, Amy? Would a little sunlight kill you? You're not a bloody vampire.'

With that, he threw open the curtains, allowing the light to stream into the room through the grubby windowpane.

Amy shielded her eyes as if it burned her, whimpering softly at the onslaught of sunlight. 'Don't, please, just…put them back…'

Ignoring her pleas, Jason found a key on the windowsill and thrust it into the rusted window lock. 'Something wrong with fresh air? Do you good. Sun and fresh air and outside.'

'No, don't open it!' she cried out, grabbing for his sleeve. 'I don't want it—'

Jason wrenched open the window and a cold gust of air swept into the stuffy room, the bite of encroaching winter in its ice. He turned back to Amy to find her shuddering in her chair, curled in on herself and gasping for breath.

'Amy…?'

Her breathing showed no sign of slowing, as she huddled in her ball of terror like a startled hedgehog. Jason quickly slammed the window and drew the curtains, returning the room to its usual state. But she did not calm, tension radiating from every fibre of her being.

Jason knelt in front of her, unsure of what to do, his own heart hammering at his impotence. 'Tell me what you need. Amy, you have to tell me how to help you.'

'Not going out, not going out, not going out.' The litany that passed her lips was like a prayer, fervent and unanswered. Her breathing quickened further and she clutched her chest as though she was having a heart attack.

Jason grabbed hold of her shoulders. 'Amy! Snap out of it!'

Amy cried out, shaking now, tears spilling over.

Jason was terrified and started rubbing her shoulders rhythmically. 'It's okay, it's okay – you don't have to go. I'm here. I won't let anything happen to you. You're going to be all right.'

She reached out, clutching at his T-shirt, and Jason wrapped his arms around her, soothingly rubbing her back and drawing her close to him. He bent close to listen to her feverish ramblings, but could only pick up fragments: '…hurts…please…don't let me die…'

'You're not going to die. I'm right here. Breathe.'

She was clinging to him as if he were a life buoy, her only hope of survival, and he wasn't sure how long he held her, as her cries subsided and her breathing slowly returned to normal.

'Are you okay?' he said, unwilling to release her until he knew she was going to be all right.

'I'm not going out.' Her words were muffled against his shoulder, and he ran a gentle hand over her hair.

'You're not going out,' he agreed, shaken to his core by what had just happened. 'I won't make you do anything you don't want to do.'

'Will you stay?' She looked straight at him with pleading, red-rimmed eyes.

'For as long as I can,' he promised, and that seemed to be enough.

Chapter 20: If I Had a Hammer

Jason was cleaning the skirting boards, a task that Amy wholly failed to grasp the relevance of, when the doorbell rang.

Bryn and Owain's faces flickered up on the monitor and Amy buzzed them up. She hadn't moved from her position on the sofa, where Jason had found her that morning, but she could work just as effectively from her iPad.

If she ignored yesterday's events, it was as if they never happened. The whole day had been a write-off, as she'd retreated to her bedroom and Jason had let her go. He was apologetic today, even brought doughnuts for breakfast, and a tiny part of Amy was glad he was contrite. She'd thought she was going to die. She had no way to rationalise that sense of dread.

Full of raspberry jam and tea, she was curled up in her dressing gown when Bryn and Owain entered the room. 'Please tell me you have something,' Bryn said.

Not good.

'I sent you the names…' she started, but Bryn waved that off.

'Dead end. None of the girls know anything.'

Amy set her shoulders at that, indignant. 'That's impossible. I cross-referenced all the available data—'

'They don't know anything, Amy,' Bryn repeated and Amy subsided. 'What else have you got?'

Amy gestured helplessly at AEON. 'Nothing. I've got nothing. The CCTV footage of Melody goes dark before she disappears, I'm no closer to finding the alarm in the hospital – and now you're telling me it might not even matter.' A black cloud was already settling over her. It wasn't worth getting up today for more of this shit.

'Then we'll have to look at everything again,' Jason suddenly piped up, and Amy looked towards him.

'Everything?' she echoed.

'Fresh eyes, adding what we know now to our looking.'

Bryn snorted, but Owain was nodding along. 'It's probably past time for a review, Amy. I could give you two a hand—'

'We have witness statements to type up,' Bryn said, deflating Owain's enthusiasm. 'Not that they'll do any good. You'll call me, when you have something? Bloody papers are baying outside the door every day and night, and Mr. Frank has got hold of my mobile number.'

'No rest for the wicked,' Jason said cheerfully, and Bryn glowered at him on his way out.

Amy wondered what had gotten in to Jason today. He was surprisingly chipper. Maybe he'd seen that girl again. The one whose house he'd snuck out of when he should've been heading to hers.

With Bryn and Owain gone, Amy set about doing exactly what Jason suggested – starting at the very beginning. That meant the forum photographs. While her cleaner popped out for a cigarette – filthy habit, she must stop that – she began combing over the images, trying to spot any clues she might have missed before.

'You will die of lung cancer,' she declared, as the lift spat Jason out in cloud of foul cigarette smoke.

'It's a nice headboard, that.' Jason leaned in to study Melody's picture, finger tracing over the fluted edges and the hint of brass inlay at the top of it. 'I know someone what makes these. If it's special work, he'll know about it.'

Amy swiftly located the envelope containing the police original under a cluster of mugs and handed it off to Jason. 'You said something about the wicked,' she said innocently.

'Cow.'

He affectionately ruffled her hair before heading for the door. And Amy realised she hadn't even flinched.

Jason rested back against the oak cabinet, hands folded into his armpits against the chill that permeated the workshop. The air was thick with floating shavings and the rich scent of wood oil.

Russell held Melody's picture in his calloused hands, face twisted with pity. 'Poor child. But, to answer you, no – not one of mine, but I do know it.'

Russell disappeared into the back and Jason paced to keep warm, his breath misting before him. The days had turned cold, ice on the cars and crystals on the wet leaves. No doubt the Accident & Emergency department at the Heath was doing a swift trade in banged knees and broken hips. Jason wondered if Bryn and Owain had gone back to the hospital. He didn't envy them – the place was a crowd at a rugby match, changing by the minute and the most unreliable of witnesses.

'Here, this looks like it.'

Russell emerged from his tiny office, carrying a large order book with scribbled names and measurements in pencil. On the open page was a rough square torn from a magazine with a picture of a smiling couple in a hotel room, the same sculpted headboard at the top. 'Some lady brought it to me, wanting a copy. That any use to you?'

'Do you have a number for her?' Jason said, already pulling out his phone.

Russell hesitated. 'You know I can't do that, mate. Can't go selling people's details on, can I?'

Jason held his temper. 'You're not selling, Russ. You're helping catch a killer!'

But Russell pulled the order book back, his hostile stare telling Jason that he'd best be on his way. Reluctantly, Jason took back his photograph, placing Melody back, modestly covered by the envelope before leaving Russell to his propriety and his stinking morals.

Jason stomped out into the early morning drizzle, breaking the thin ice on the pavement's puddles. He'd known Russell since he was a lad. The bloke had been mates with Jason's dad, but prison changed the way people looked at you. People were afraid of him now, what he might do. Stole a car off an old lady, punched a copper. At least Lewis and the boys had gone away for a victimless crime. Nobody got hurt robbing gold. That was how the neighbourhood saw it.

He got to the car – and stopped. There were flyers on the back window. But this was the middle of an industrial estate, not another car in sight. Who would be leafleting out here?

His hand went to the switchblade in his back pocket. If his mam found out he was carrying it, she'd go spare, but he wasn't going to be caught unprotected again. It was a deterrent, he told himself. Just to warn them off.

Walking slowly round the car, he pretended to study the gaudy paper squares, while keeping his eyes and ears sharp for movement around him. But a sudden yank at his ankle pulled him to the ground, the air knocked out of him. Fucker was under the car!

Fighting to draw breath, Jason kicked out at the kid beneath his car, but two heavy men crashed down on him, driving his shoulders into the ground and gripping his arms like a vice.

'I hear you've been messing with my boys.' Stuart Williams walked into his eye line, shaking his cigarette to sprinkle ash over Jason's coat.

'They…attacked me,' Jason bit out, still not able to get his breath.

Stuart looked away, exposing the web of raised scars curving around his left eye and over his sharp cheekbone.

'Damage has an anger for you, because of how you left his brother in prison, see. But then the cops show up like they're on speed-dial, and it got us to wondering how you did so little time.'

Shit, they think I'm a grass. 'I never—'

'Save it. We figure the cops have eyes on you, round our way. But out here – who's gonna see?' Stuart placed his boot in the centre of Jason's chest. Jason gasped. 'So, tell us what they know.'

Jason would never tell Stuart anything, even if he had something to spill. He would laugh if he could draw breath, his lungs starting to burn.

A crack whipped through the air and Stuart yelped, ducking behind the car. Were the Cardiff gangs carrying guns now? Jason was suddenly afraid. He knew beatings and he knew knives, but he'd never been shot before and he was in no hurry to try it.

'Let that boy go and get out.' *Russell.*

Jason tried to raise his head to see what was going on, but he was still pinned.

Stuart slowly straightened, then threw his hands up in surrender. 'Look, old man, this ain't none of your business—'

'I'll stick my nose where I like,' Russell said sharply. 'Unless you want a bolt through your arm, I'd get gone.'

One of the lads holding him down clambered to his feet, paled at what he saw and tugged at Stuart's arm. Stuart shook him off, snarling. 'Fine, we're leaving. But we won't forget this, old man. Watch yourself – and your little fag too.'

Spitting on Jason's jeans, Stuart grabbed his boys and cleared out. Jason got to his feet and reflected that this was getting to be a habit. Road rash was a bitch.

Jason looked over his car to see Russell hovering outside his workshop, a large adze in one hand and a bolt gun in the other.

'Russ—'

'Don't bring trouble to my door again,' the man snapped and retreated back into his shop.

Jason tore the leaflets from his window screen and threw them into an icy puddle, sick of the whole rotten town.

Chapter 21: Voulez Vous Couchez?

'Morning,' Jason said.

Amy grunted in his direction, as emo nu metal raged around her. It was too early for small talk and she had a hangover from cheap red wine.

'Have you eaten today?'

Amy shrugged, gripped by the fast-forwarded CCTV footage on her monitors as her stomach rolled nauseatingly. It was a few minutes before fresh coffee and toast landed by her elbow, and she devoured it like a zombie at a brains market.

However, Jason was still keen to attempt conversation. 'I've got a clue to the headboard.'

A sharp jab at the keyboard stopped the footage on a gang of goth kids, as Amy licked her fingers clean of jam and tried to flick out tooth-lodged seeds with her tongue. 'A clue?'

'My mate showed me this photo, ripped from a magazine, like. It's from a hotel, but he doesn't know which one…' Jason trailed off, sounding uncertain of himself.

Amy glanced up at him – he was standing awkwardly too, like he was consumed with self-doubt. Or he'd fallen off his damned unin-sured motorbike.

'A hotel makes sense. Anything else?'

Jason massaged his temples, as if that would help the memory flow faster. 'A nice hotel. One that business folk stay in. There was this… purple stripe at the bottom of the duvet cover.'

'Purple stripe.' Amy pulled up her browser, fingers flashing across the keys, a series of anonymous hotel rooms scrolling across the screen. 'Not great branding…ah!'

The flickering halted, landing on a laughing couple frozen in their artificial mirth. Jason lunged for it. 'That's it!'

'Hmm…big chain. They've got six hotels in the Cardiff area alone.' Amy stabbed at the keys, and the printer ejected a sheet with six addresses. 'Shouldn't take more than an afternoon, less if you take the

103

bike instead of the Micra.' She paused. 'Oh, the bike doesn't have tax. Never mind.'

Jason was silent for a long moment. 'How do you know about my bike?'

Oh...shit. Amy shrank inside her blanket and picked up her tea. *Well, there was just no explaining this, was there? Fuckity-fuck – what a moron, Amy.*

She didn't want to be afraid of him, but that outburst with the window... She hadn't had a panic attack like that for years. That was the price of letting an unknown quantity into the sanctuary of her home. Yet she hadn't pushed him away. She hadn't fired him, like she should've done, like any sane person would've done. But then she wasn't quite sane, was she?

But Jason wasn't angry. 'You don't have to tell me. Just—'

'Dylan ordered parts for a 1940s Harley-Davidson motorcycle totalling two hundred and forty pounds,' Amy said, the words tumbling forth. 'You withdrew two hundred and forty pounds the next day. You pay tax for a white X-reg Nissan Micra but not for a motorbike. Neither your mother nor your sister drive. Therefore, it has to be your bike, but it's not on the road. Well, it's not meant to be.'

'I'm still fixing it up,' Jason said, and she saw that he was smiling, the last remnants of fear ebbing away. 'Doesn't matter. But that's a little creepy, yeah? You can just ask me things instead of...finding them out. Through ninjas or whatever.'

'Google know everything about you,' she said, deadpan. 'There's a chip in your brain and it feeds information directly to the web. I've cracked their secret code. I am master of the internet.'

'Oh, good to know. Erase that bit where I remember my twenty-first, and try not to look at what's at the bottom of my wardrobe.'

'Nothing I haven't seen before.' It was so easy to joke with him. Lame jokes that weren't funny, but she was out of practice.

Jason just shook his head and picked up the list of addresses from the printer. 'You want me to go here now?' he said, flapping the sheet.

'Later is fine.'

He nodded, jamming his thumb towards the back of the flat. 'I'm going to fight monsters fungal and filthy in your bathroom.'

Amy lapsed back into silence, the work calling to her, and the images flickered to life again.

When Jason emerged from the bathroom an hour later, he felt like he needed a turn in the newly scrubbed shower. He padded barefoot into the living room, shoes in hand and jeans turned up to the knees. 'There isn't enough bleach in the world for your flat. But I have conquered it – I am master of the bathroom.'

When there was no response from the pile of blankets, he dumped his shoes and crept forward. Amy was asleep, slumped to the side in her chair, the CCTV images still flashing wildly on screen. Jason found the button to pause it and then looked back at her.

She looked uncomfortable, neck at an odd angle against the chair back, so he slipped an arm around her back and the other under her knees. The effort stretched the scabs across his shoulders, but he was a hard man, tough, like. She didn't stir as he carried her down the corridor to her room and set her on her bed, spreading the blankets carefully over her.

She snuggled her face into the pillow, pulling the covers up over her shoulder, and Jason smiled, shutting the door quietly behind him and returning the room to darkness.

He lifted the list of hotels from the printer – best get going on this, before the evidence got swept under a cheap mass-produced rug. Picking the first hotel on the list, he looked up the route on his phone as he struggled to settle into the driver's seat of the Micra. There was no way to get comfortable when your shoulders looked like you'd been scrammed by a sabre-tooth tiger.

On the drive over, Jason started to have doubts. He had absolutely no authority to march in there and demand the names of their guests or their CCTV footage. In fact, he had nothing except a criminal record and a smile. But he had been a blagger since he had learned to talk and so he pulled his leather jacket on over his uniform shirt, slung his bag over his shoulder and walked up to the front desk.

'Afternoon,' he said. 'My friend's already checked in. Lane, Amy Lane. Can you call her and let her know I'm here?'

The perky receptionist beamed at him. 'Of course, sir. Who should I say is waiting?'

'Detective Bryn Hesketh,' he said, without missing a beat. 'Tell her we need to get going right away – this case won't solve itself.'

The woman looked him over again, perhaps a new appreciation growing in her eyes. 'Detective? Are you...' She lowered her voice. 'Is it about those missing girls?'

Jason looked to both sides and leaned forward conspiratorially. 'Between you and me, love, it is. That's why I'm here.'

The receptionist's mouth formed a perfect O. 'Here?' she squeaked.

'I know it's shocking, but we think he may have brought one of the girls to a hotel.' He put on his best concerned face, stealing a look at the badge pinned to her impressive chest. 'You weren't working on the fourth, were you, Mandy?'

Her eyes were wide. 'I was! Was that...when he did it?' She looked distressed and Jason was suddenly afraid she was going to start bawling. 'But I was only here 'til nine. That's when Mikey took over – it was likely after nine, right?'

'And is Mikey working today?'

'No, he's off for a couple of days – his dad's not well, see.' She looked troubled by this fact, but then her face brightened. 'But we have the cameras. We keep the tapes for a whole month – it'll be on there, won't it?'

Jason smiled. 'It will. How about you send them over to Central Police Station – mark it with my name, eh? Let me write it down so it gets right to me.' He wrote the detective's name in his best cop scrawl on the hotel paper, followed by his own mobile number, and the girl snatched it up with a shy smile. *Nice one, Carr.*

But then the frown was back. 'Oh, Detective, I can't find your friend's name. In fact, we don't have a room under that name at all.'

Jason cursed under his breath. 'Damn it, must've missed her. Still, not a total loss, was it?' He beamed at her and she glowed. Still got it. 'You'll send over that tape, won't you? We know he can't have got far and this place is in the hot zone.'

Mandy nodded seriously and promised him that she would send them over right away, once the duty manager signed off on it, and then she'd call him as soon as it was done.

Jason thanked her sincerely, with another devastating smile, and walked out of the hotel. One down, five to go.

Chapter 22: Closed Circuit

Bryn marched into the living room and shook a handful of packages in Jason's direction. 'Is this you? Because I don't remember talking to any hotel managers about CCTV footage and yet here are all these gifts. Oh, and they're addressed to me, with such notes as *lovely to meet you and drop by any time*. Explain to me how I met these people when I don't even know where the damn hotels are!'

Amy looked at him curiously as Jason affected his most innocent smile. 'They must've been confused when I said I worked with you.'

Bryn exploded. 'You don't work with me! You don't even work for me! You work for her—' he jabbed a finger in Amy's direction, '—and that entitles you to get hotels to send me videotapes and complimentary restaurant vouchers?'

So that was where Jason had gone yesterday. Amy had woken up in her bedroom, confused as to how she'd magically flown there, with a sparkling bathroom and a total lack of housekeeper. Cleaner. Whatever.

She defused the situation by shifting from the couch, taking the packages off Bryn and sitting at her computer terminal. She shook out the envelopes, providing a haul of four CDs and two actual videotapes. Disgusting.

'I can still process these – just. Everyone should be on flash memory. There's no excuse.'

Jason went to make a fresh pot of tea. Amy belatedly remembered that she still hadn't bought sugar and wondered if she should just tell Jason to stock the cupboards. He seemed to know what he was doing.

When he returned, Amy had rigged up the ancient VCR and was already fast-forwarding through the first hotel's footage. 'This one is closest to her last-known location.'

But the reception area was quiet, only two or three businessmen and one middle-aged couple between midnight and morning, and then it was on to the next hotel.

The second hotel was busier, but there were still no young women fitting Melody's type. When the third and fourth hotels were also busts, Amy pouted to herself but kept working. Maybe the headboard was actually a common design supplied to hotels. Maybe they'd have to further widen the net, but they had made so many assumptions already.

It was the fifth hotel where they had their breakthrough.

'I've got her,' Amy said quietly, and the three men crowded round the back of her chair. She froze the picture as a couple entered the lobby, backs to the camera over the main door. Melody's clothes were now unmistakeable to them, the dress that barely reached past her short coat and her high stilettos, which dragged on the ground. She was unconscious, or already dead.

Her murderer was disturbingly normal. Average height, slightly lean, he wore a waterproof jacket, jeans and a baseball cap, all in dark colours. There was nothing remarkable about him. And they couldn't see his face. Amy took a still, and pressed Play.

He paused a second in the lobby and then took them through the door to the right of the screen. Melody's head lolled forward – and, for an instant, there was a glimpse of his face. Half his jaw and nose, a hint of a mouth, but it was there. Amy rewound and stopped the tape, and they all looked at the man who killed Kate Thomas and Melody Frank.

They were so close to him now.

He was on the national news.

He felt a slight thrill at the thought. Now she would have to notice. How could she help but see what he'd laid before her, when the whole country knew it?

But the report also worried him. They'd found the hotel he'd used for the girl, and there was a picture they'd blown up to show his face – it looked nothing like him. He'd have to change his plan, go back to what worked before, away from prying eyes. He couldn't afford to fail, to fail her.

He carefully checked his tools – the camera, charged and memory cleaned; the nitrile gloves, vivid in blue sterility; and his suitcase. It was old battered leather, his mother's travelling trunk, but the bag of lavender from her dresser masked the smell of the girl who had slept in it for two days before her journey to the lake. Soon, it would carry another passenger.

Why didn't she stop him? That was what he didn't understand. She should've come to him by now, begged him to return to her. But she remained elusive and distant. He gave her plenty of opportunity – there was the forum, his blog, email. He'd made sure she knew how to reach him, had written them all out very carefully for her, placed the little folded note in her hand while *he* wasn't looking. She'd smiled at him, and his entire world had exploded into colour in that dark, dingy room full of kids pretending they were too old for this place.

He shook his head, scattering the happy memories, and focusing on the future. If he didn't make it count now, she would never come back to him. He had to make sure she really knew what she was missing. He would prove his love to her, drive her wild with jealousy, until she begged him to take her back.

He wrote:

My heart bleeds for you, but it still beats for you. When will you realise that this isn't a game? You can stop me, freebird. Just say the word. You're everything to me. I'm waiting for you, freebird, to run back to me and be free.

Chapter 23: Don't Wait Up

Gina was tired and ready for her bed. Her king-sized bed was squeezed into her room with hardly any space to get out of it either side, but was still the most amazing bed ever. She would sink into it, wrap the duvet around her shoulders and persuade Laurie to bring her a cup of camomile tea.

Twelve hours straight at the library was knackering. Still, the bloody essay was done and she could now return to the joyous chaos of the house. They had barely cleared up from the party last Friday night and there weren't many ways to get week-old tomato juice out of the carpet.

She walked along the back of the Union, smelling the distinctive scent of marijuana floating in the air. Her first-year halls had stank of it, and she remembered that bloody awful day when she'd eaten the inviting chocolate cupcake at Hayley's party and spent the rest of the night off her head. Messing with chocolate was sick and wrong.

As she passed under the bridge, a shiver went down her spine, the feeling of being watched settling between her shoulder blades. Gina looked around – nothing. The whole road was deserted, and she shook her head and walked on. This stupid serial killer was making her jumpy.

It wasn't that she was bothered about being out alone at night, even with those two missing students – she lived a five-minute walk from uni and she wasn't going to let a little thing like the dark put her off pulling a late one in the library.

The rain had tailed off into a misting drizzle, barely rain at all, but she quickened her steps. Almost home. The slightly haunted feeling hadn't left her and the hedgerows menaced, every dark corner a hiding place, every shadow a man with a length of rope…

Her heart was loud in her ears and her breath caught in her throat. Fuck, she was better than this. She deserved to feel safe in her own town, damn it, and this wasn't fair. *Bastard.*

Gina fumbled for her key outside the front door, trying to find the right one under the flickering light of the one broken streetlamp on her road. Of course it would be outside their house. She would ring the Council on Monday, get it fixed. Do something to stop this feeling of dread lodged in her stomach.

Finally, she found the key and wiggled it in the lock, forcing the door open. They really needed to get that fixed and she added it to the list. She took off her knit cap and shook out her dark curls, setting down her messenger bag by the door.

She heard a noise coming from upstairs. It was a *scrape-scrape-scrape* sound, like wood against plaster. Laurie couldn't be putting up shelves at this hour, so what was it? Gina shrugged off her coat and hung it off the banister, trying to place the sound – then froze. It was the headboard knocking against the wall.

'Laurie?' she called, and the noise stopped. Who the fuck was upstairs with her girlfriend?

Running footsteps sounded across the landing, and Gina started up the stairs as a man in black ran into their bathroom and slammed the door. Gina tried to shoulder it open but he'd bolted it. She heard the window swing out and the clatter as he jumped onto the shed roof and away into the garden.

The house was quiet. Gina turned, looking at their bedroom door, her heart starting to beat double-time in her chest. She thought: *I can't believe she'd cheat on me.* She thought: *Who was that man?* She thought: *I can't hear her breathing.*

The bedroom door was ajar and Gina walked in, as if in a dream. And there was Laurie, sprawled naked on their bed, open eyes fixed on the ceiling, and a trail of blood dripping down her leg.

And all Gina could think was: *He was here. The Cardiff Ripper was in my house.*

Chapter 24: Cry Me a River

Jason started awake at one o'clock in the morning, his phone blaring at him. He groaned and reached blindly for it, hearing Cerys complain loudly from the room next door.

'What?' he answered, irritably.

To his surprise, Amy's voice came down the line, sounding very far away.

'Jason, I've been texting you. You need to get to the crime scene and take pictures. There's a body.'

He sat up instantly, rubbing the sleep from his eyes and trying to take in Amy's instructions.

'Any camera will do,' she was saying, 'but I want the photos as soon as you're done.'

The line went dead. Jason took the phone away from his ear and stared at it. How was he meant to know where this body was, exactly? If he walked into Cardiff centre, would his Spidey Sense start tingling and lead him to the latest victim?

Then he realised he had six new messages. The address, sent through twice, ten minutes apart; a message telling him to get out of bed, another telling him to drag himself from the pub; and then two that just said *Call me*. Amy must be desperate if she was resorting to using old-fashioned telephony to get what she wanted.

Jason, on the other hand, wasn't sure old-fashioned blagging was going to get him very far on this one. He wasn't a police officer – in fact, he was an ex-con, and Bryn hated him at the best of times. Turning up at a fresh crime scene in the middle of the night was only going to fan the flames of disharmony between them. But what Amy wanted Amy got – she had already sent another text asking him to bring her the victim's laptop. Jason threw on yesterday's T-shirt and jeans before sloping off down the stairs.

'Jason?' Gwen called from her bedroom door.

He looked up, waving a hand at his mam.

'I've just got to do a favour for a friend. I'll be back in no time.'

Gwen's face hardened. Jason hadn't seen her look like that since his court date. 'A favour? At this time?'

'Mam, you have to trust me,' he pleaded.

She didn't say a word, just shut the door and left him to make his way down the stairs.

As Jason's brain started firing on all cylinders, the last vestiges of sleep fading away, the significance of Amy's call began to sink in. There was another crime scene. There was a body. He had killed again.

As he pulled on his trainers, a quiet despair settled in his chest. They had failed to find him in time, and now Jason had to take pictures of the consequences. Part of him protested – he wasn't a cop, he could just go back to bed and hear about this on the morning news, like everyone else. But now he had the urge to know, the need to seek the truth. He wanted justice for these girls, and he wanted to see this piece of shit in a high-security prison, where every bruiser who wanted to hurt something knew his cell number.

Armed only with Cerys's camera, Jason stepped out into the cool of a Cardiff night, pushing down his feelings of failure, and concentrated on the righteous fire burning in his chest. They were going to get him now. There was no alternative.

He drove to the address in Cathays, the heating on full blast in the Micra – not that it made much difference. His fingers were turning blue as he gripped the steering wheel, driving through the student back streets until he saw the flashing blue lights strobing over the gathered crowd.

He parked on a nearby street, beside a gutter overflowing with rain-soaked chips. Gathering Cerys's digital camera close to his chest, he headed for the police line, craning his neck for a glimpse of Bryn. He was honestly the last person Jason wanted to see at two o'clock in the morning, and he imagined he was skirting the bottom of Bryn's list too.

He approached the nearest officer. 'I'm Jason Carr and I need to speak with Detective Hesketh. He's, uh...expecting me.'

The guy looked at him sceptically, but went inside. Jason hopped from foot to foot, trying to keep warm. He wished he'd brought gloves or a scarf or a daft woolly hat, because the cold was seeping into his brain and it was hard to think. *Dead girl. Photographs. Amy.*

The police officer returned, but headed to the other side of the cordon and ignored Jason's attempts to catch his eye. Great, he was going to be stuck here all night.

Jason figured he'd give it another ten minutes before asking again, because leaving without the photographs wasn't an option. Three women were dead and Amy was the only person actually discovering things about the girls' deaths. So Jason would make her toast or bring her photographs in the early hours, if that was what would help. He looked round the crowd of morbidly interested onlookers, feeling apart from them. He was a man on a mission.

He also felt a touch guilty. Despite his efforts over the weekend, he hadn't found out anything useful about Melody. He'd written down the few facts he had discovered and left them on Amy's desk, tactfully not telling her how he'd come by them. He didn't think Bryn would approve of him sleeping with the victim's housemate.

But then he had brought in the CCTV from the headboard lead – that had all been him, and they now had their first glimpse of the killer. Except that had done fuck-all to stop him, hadn't it? Jason's grip tightened on the camera.

An ambulance was parked at the end of the street, just within the bounds of the police cordon, and Jason could see the back doors were open. At first, he thought they were here for the body, but from his vantage, he could see a pair of legs hanging below the line of the door, a red blanket trailing in a puddle. Perhaps it was someone who knew the victim? Maybe they could tell him something important.

Abandoning his post by the front door, he worked his way through the sparse crowd, the people who would be interviewed by the news crews later and, yes, he could already see a photographer and a BBC Wales van parking up. Bad news travelled fast.

At this end of the cordon, there were no police officers – at least none paying attention – and Jason easily slipped under the tape and towards the back of the ambulance. He stuffed the camera in his pocket and straightened out his jacket before rounding the open door.

A woman sat on the back step, clutching the blanket and shaking. It looked like she was trying to send a text, but her fingers were jittering off the keys and her cheeks were wet with tears. She looked up as he approached and hastily wiped her eyes, her bottom lip trembling.

'H-have you moved her out yet?'

'Not yet,' Jason said softly, and sat beside her in the back of the ambulance. 'I know this must be difficult for you, miss, so many people asking questions, but can you tell me what happened?'

The woman's expression was suddenly fierce. 'I'll tell you. I want you to catch him. H-he killed Laurie.'

Her eyes filled with tears again and she buried her face in her blanket. Jason put an awkward arm around her shoulder and she curled into him, shuddering with her sobs.

'M-my name is Gina Matthews. Laurie's my...' She trailed off, shook her head. 'I came home from uni – I think it was nine-thirty, and I th-thought I heard something. It sounded like...like the bed moving.' She gasped, choked with tears. 'I thought she was cheating on me.'

Jason rubbed circles into her back, making vague shushing sounds as Gina released her sorrow and her guilt. He could do nothing but wait, holding her against his shoulder, as her tears slowly subsided. She stayed there, shivering with cold and shock, and wiped her nose on the edge of the blanket.

'I saw him,' she said.

Jason started. 'What did he look like?'

If she'd seen him, got a good look at his face, they might be able to find him in less than a day, his whole damn face in every paper, on every channel, on the internet. They'd have him in their sights.

But Gina shook her head, her cheek rubbing against the lapel of his jacket.

'Just the back of his head. He had dark hair and he was wearing black. Not very tall and not fat. God, I'm useless.'

She scrubbed her eyes with the heel of her hand and moved away from Jason, drawing the blanket closer. Her voice grew flat and she looked very far away.

'And then I found her. He had...raped her. There was blood, but she...she was still warm.' She looked back to Jason. 'She looked terrified. And I wasn't there.'

Jason tried to remember the questions they always asked on cop shows, the ones that would get useful information for Amy. 'Did she have any enemies? Did anyone want to hurt her?'

'Everyone loved Laurie. It was always me that caused trouble. She was always out with friends from her course and everyone at that Aussie club loved her. She started doing shifts there – not 'cause we needed the money, but because she loved the place.'

The Aussie club… 'Wait – you mean Koalas? Laurie worked there?'

Jason couldn't help the thrill that rose in his chest. The nightclub was the key. Two of the victims worked there, and now he was sure they'd find a link to Melody. They had a body, they had a witness description – maybe Amy wouldn't even need the photographs to figure this one out.

'Was there anyone Laurie had a problem with at work? Any of the guys giving her hassle?'

Gina thought about it for a moment, then frowned. 'There was this one guy, had a problem with her being a dyke. He made no secret about it too, was fucking rude when I was there last night.'

Jason leaned forward. 'What was his name?'

He held his breath, as she raided her memory, so intent that he completely missed the approaching footsteps.

'Um…Dan? I think it was Dan.'

'Well, this is cosy.'

Jason looked up to see Bryn and Owain staring down at him, Bryn looking perturbed and Owain honestly stunned. Bryn folded his arms and shook his head as if he were dealing with a particularly disobedient child.

'Come with me, boy.'

Chapter 25: Dead Men Tell Tales

Giving Gina a pat on the shoulder and thanking her for her time, Jason followed the detectives, waiting for the bollocking that was surely due.

Bryn leaned close, breath stale with cigarettes and cheap coffee. 'So, she tell you anything?'

Jason blinked, but wouldn't let go of this opportunity to be useful. 'Laurie worked at Koalas, same club as Kate. There was a guy there who had a problem with her…girlfriend, name of Dan. I met him – seemed like a good bloke, but who can tell, eh?'

Owain frantically typed everything Jason said into his phone, as Bryn looked at him appraisingly.

'No, you never can. Come on – Amy's been texting me all night. Take your pictures and get them over to her before she burns a hole in my phone.'

For one horrifying moment, Jason thought she might actually be able to do that, then dismissed it as ridiculous. However, his hand unconsciously went to his pocket and removed his phone, only to find another three texts.

Done yet?

You coming over?

You dead?

He sent back *No soon no* as Bryn led him across the police cordon and into a white tent that had been set up in front of the door. An efficient woman with a clipboard looked at Jason as though he were the living embodiment of contamination.

'Overalls, boots and gloves.' It was obviously a well-rehearsed phrase and she intended to enforce her rules to the letter. 'And this… officer will have to sign in and remain under escort at all times.'

Bryn gestured to a set of white overalls that were neatly bagged and tied behind the woman. 'Could I just have those back?'

'New entrance, new set.'

The woman's robotic demeanour was terrifying. Jason hurriedly scribbled his name on the clipboard and shifted into his overalls,

119

keeping the camera in his hand until he could slip it into the overall pocket. The woman looked pointedly at the device but said nothing. The boots were more like flimsy shower caps, which barely fitted over his trainers, and the gloves were too tight and restricted his fingers. He could already feel sweat gathering on his palms under the latex.

Owain had excused himself, but Bryn was dressed in the same sterile white getup. Jason hoped he didn't look half as ridiculous as the detective, beer belly warping the suit to turn him into a plastic polar bear.

'Let's get inside.'

Jason followed Bryn across the threshold, not sure what to expect. But the place was quite nice inside, wooden floors and everything in matching black and white. There were framed photographs of Gina and Laurie, and one of those Andy Warhol-style prints of the two of them in four different psychedelic poses. The place was fairly neat, with a few books scattered round, but nothing much in the way of clutter or mess. Two large bin bags sat by the back door, overflowing with paper plates and plastic cups. They certainly hadn't been robbed or searched, at least not obviously. Jason turned on Cerys's camera and lined up a few shots, including the ghastly Warhol replica. He turned to find Bryn waiting expectantly on the stairs.

'She's not looking for interior design. Get up here.'

The top floor was crowded, with several police officers and crime scene techs at work, all ghosts in the same anonymous white overalls. Two were in the bathroom, carefully lifting footprints from the tile floor and the windowsill. Jason took a snap.

Bryn walked into the front bedroom and Jason followed without thinking. And froze.

Nothing could prepare him for this. Laurie was lying in the centre of the bed, legs dangling over the bottom, spread. She was naked except for the heart pendant around her neck and the rust-red blood drying on her thighs. The sheet was tangled on the floor, as if it had been cast off in a hurry.

Her eyes were staring at him. They were frosted over, like winter glass, and he knew instantly that she was dead. Her skin was mottled, pale and purple, and a man with a camera leant over, snapping pictures.

Jason couldn't imagine how Gina felt, walking into the bedroom and seeing this. He swallowed down the bile rising in his throat and took pictures: one of Laurie, and then pictures of the room, the bookcase, the sheet on the floor. But he couldn't bring himself to take more of the victim, like she was some posing centrefold. It felt wrong.

'Who is this, Hesketh? And why does he have a camera at my crime scene?' The man examining Laurie turned and folded his arms, glaring at Jason over his glasses. 'If he's a journalist—'

'He's Amy's assistant,' Bryn said.

The man's scowl deepened.

'When are you going to stop running to that introverted child to solve your problems, Detective? And now you're letting her 'assistant' take pictures of a murder victim. Next, they'll be all over MySpace.'

'Rob,' Bryn said tiredly, 'just tell me when and how she died. We need to get her to the mortuary before the press all come out to play.'

Rob snorted. 'Oh, just when and how, nothing much then. Work it all out in my head and then give you a ten-minute window and the exact object that caused her skull to explode, that's all.'

'He hit her over the head?' As soon as he'd asked, he saw the blood matting her hair and the red stain above her head where she might've been dragged down the bed.

Rob sighed, as if it were beneath him to answer questions posed by Amy Lane's assistant. 'Yes. And, as it happens, I can identify the object.'

He reached for a large plastic evidence bag containing a worn hockey stick, blood coating the head and spatter up the shaft. 'Hockey stick. Different method again to the other victims. A weapon of opportunity, I believe – the victim has a number of trophies for university hockey.'

'That's what they have in common: weapons of opportunity. As if he doesn't really want to kill them when he plans it.' Bryn paced as he expounded his theory, his plastic gloves making shapes in the air like a mime artist. 'Anything else?'

'She put up a fight – defensive marks on her hands and forearms, and I've scraped blood out from under her nails. Sexual assault kit positive, left his DNA and everything, but the nature of the trauma sustained indicates that it was post-mortem.'

Jason felt like he was going to be sick. 'He raped her after he killed her?'

Even Rob looked faintly ill. 'Blunt but accurate. She's only just going into rigor and the temperature here's pretty steady, so I can use liver temp to get a fairly accurate time of death – between eight and ten.'

'Gina came back at half-nine and scared him off,' Jason said. 'She said Laurie was still warm when she found her.'

A look of horror crossed Rob's face. 'She touched the body? Please tell me she didn't do something so incredibly stupid.'

'She said she was warm,' Jason repeated, anger building in his chest at how callous this Rob bloke was. 'She was in shock, mate – her girlfriend just died.'

'No excuse for contamination,' Rob said flatly. 'Does she want us to catch him or not? Moronic.'

Bryn, clearly sensing that Jason was about to take a swing at the medical examiner, took him by the arm and led him out of the bedroom and back into the hallway.

'Dr. Pritchard is a knob, but he's good at what he does. You got the pictures?'

Jason nodded curtly, and put the camera in the pocket of the overalls. 'She wants Laurie's laptop too. I saw it downstairs.'

'We'll bag it up for you.' Bryn clapped Jason on the shoulder. 'You did well for your first dead one, son. Now get out of here.'

Jason slipped away from Bryn's hold and tried not to throw up. 'First dead one' – fuck, he hoped there wasn't another.

Chapter 26: A Body of Evidence

'You took your time,' Amy said, as Jason handed her the camera and placed the laptop on the coffee table.

'Sorry,' he said, looking dazed and far away.

Amy wondered if she should ask, but she wasn't sure she wanted to know why he was so distracted.

'You want me to start it up?'

'Check there's nothing plugged in.' Amy turned the camera over in her hands until she found the connection point. 'USB sticks, external hard drives, modems. Check the bottom too. He didn't erase the others, but he might be getting wiser if he thinks we're coming for him.'

Jason dutifully checked the laptop, sweeping his hands over the sides and base as if it were the body of a motor. Amy watched him open it up and push the start button, checking the inside for anything remarkable. The only mark was a dark discolouration to the right of the touchpad. He ran his finger over it questioningly.

'Where she rested her wrist.' She also traced the stain, her fingers brushing against his. She had to ask. 'Did you...see her?'

He hesitated, and she saw the answer in his eyes. 'Yes. It's pretty grim.'

She nodded, digesting his words, and touched his arm before walking back to her computer terminal and the images that were appearing on her monitors. It seemed natural to touch him, to give physical comfort. If that was what he needed, she could do that.

Jason came to stand by her shoulder. 'I got some pictures of the crowd. Owain said I should.'

'Some killers like to watch,' Amy said absently, starting to flick through the images. And then there was the body, remote and sanitised on the monitor, the horror of the scene muted by pixels. 'How did she die?'

'He hit her over the head with a hockey stick. The doctor thinks that killed her.' His voice sounded detached, almost cold, and Amy didn't like it.

'The coroner's photos will tell us more. You did well. This will give me the information to access her accounts.'

'It will?' Jason looked up at the photographs, his brow furrowed. 'I didn't find a list of passwords.'

Amy looked at him in horror. 'Tell me you don't write down your passwords.'

'No.' Jason was defensive, a shade of his usual self coming out from behind whatever walls he'd thrown up to deal with seeing Laurie. 'I only have the one.'

She closed her eyes, an internal groan echoing inside her head. 'Your one password is B-zero-N, J-zero-V-one? Kill me now.'

'How did you know that?' he said, voice an octave too high for dogs to hear.

Amy shrugged. 'They're listed as the first of your favourite bands on Facebook and your profile picture, at least two years out of date, is of you in a Bon Jovi T-shirt. It's not rocket science.'

'But I did capitals and numbers. Like you're meant to!'

She found his temper rather endearing. 'I'll change it for you. Your sister's birthday – full four-digit year – and your mother's maiden name, with the second letter capitalised. That will do for now. We'll work on a stronger password after we find this man.'

Amy put Jason's password woes to one side and started sorting the photographs while tracking down Laurie's various social networks.

'She was well-connected – Facebook, Twitter, El-jay, Foursquare, Tumblr, Pinterest. There should be a lot of information we can find here.'

'What are you looking for?' Jason asked. She ignored him for the moment, putting in several password combinations, all of which failed. 'She's got a decent password, has she? Not her favourite band or her dog or something?'

'Yes,' Amy said sulkily. 'I may have to resort to a cracker.' She tapped on her mouse, pausing to think. 'To answer your question, a killer like this will focus on one victim at a time. He won't have a stack lined up. We can assume he found Laurie recently – after he killed Melody. If we can find Laurie's pattern of behaviour, we can see who she connected with in the past two weeks.'

'Makes sense. What about Gina? She was important to Laurie.'

'I tried her name, date of birth, and their anniversary. What else do couples do?'

Amy was out of her depth. It wasn't that she didn't understand the acts of romance – she'd read a lot of fan fiction, after all. No, it was the in-between times that puzzled her. Did they just talk? She had always preferred silence to conversation. It was one of the things that had driven her sister out of the house.

Jason hovered his hand over the mouse. 'Can I?'

Amy hesitated, before pushing her chair back from the desk.

He went back to the pictures, bringing up a series from the living room. 'Maybe they had a favourite song, or could be the first film they saw at the cinema. A favourite café.'

The room was filled with photographs, and Amy marvelled at how much of their life was on display. The last photo of her was the one her sister took before she left for Australia – Amy hadn't wanted to look at it, afraid of what she might see.

'Hey, is that Venice?' Jason asked, disturbing her thoughts.

It was a shot of the couple in the prow of a pointed boat, water behind them and houses rising up either side. Amy reclaimed her mouse and opened up Foursquare, scrolling through Laurie's activity.

'Venice. April 2012. Two-week tour of Italy with Gina. She wrote glowing reviews of everywhere she went – including the gondola rides.'

Amy typed a password – Venice2012 – and the accounts opened up before her, letting her into Laurie's world. She sank into the chair with a sigh and immersed herself in the information, jumping from account to account and back to the pictures, a sense of contentment filling her as the pieces came together. She added information to a calendar as she went, timelining Laurie's activities for the past three weeks, filling out all the corners of her life. She would know everything about Laurie's last days. That was how she would find him.

She heard Jason yawn behind her and glanced at the taskbar. 05:15.

'Coffee,' she said, and Jason obediently shuffled to the kitchen. She should probably feel guilty for ordering him around, but she was in the data. He had to understand she couldn't leave it half-done.

Amy took a plate from him wordlessly and stuffed a slice of cake into her mouth whole. She heard the distinctive *ba-bing* of Microsoft Windows lurching to life, and turned to see Jason on Laurie's laptop.

'She was looking at holidays in Austria. And—oh.' Jason looked up at her, slightly sheepish. 'Forgot to say, Laurie worked at the same nightclub as Kate. Can we link Melody to it too?'

Amy's mind sparked with possibility. 'Yes, she walked past it on her way home the night she was murdered. Someone from the club could easily have followed her. I'll review the footage again after…this.'

Her brain was thrumming with the effort of holding together several sources of information and coalescing them into one timeline of Laurie's last days. She couldn't afford to be distracted.

But Jason kept talking anyway. 'Laurie was trying to book some days off in January to go away with Gina.' He tapped loudly on the mouse. 'But her boss said no – turns out Dan had booked the same dates. Gina said he had a problem with Laurie.'

'He was harassing her on Facebook too.' Amy brought up a long list of unread messages in Laurie's inbox. 'A mix of hate mail and sexual fantasy. Seems someone had a crush.'

Jason made a noise in his throat, almost a growl of frustrated anger. 'Do we have enough to go after him?'

'Not nearly enough. Bryn can talk to him, though, shake him up. He's good at that.'

She heard Jason's suppressed snort, and wondered how best to keep him out of trouble – with the general public, and with Bryn.

'We need to link him to Melody's death,' she added.

'Crime of opportunity? Like his weapons?'

She could feel the heat of Jason's anger from where she sat. She nudged the cake plate towards him, but he didn't take it.

'The others were planned, attacked at their homes. Dan would have known where Kate and Laurie lived from their employment records. Melody is different.'

Amy paused, insight rushing to the front of her mind. 'We released the CCTV picture. He got scared. He went back to the way that worked for him, with Kate. He was interrupted with Laurie – he didn't have time to get away.' She sighed, frustrated. 'He's made so many mistakes. Why haven't we caught him?'

'We've got him,' Jason said. 'We just need to prove it. We need to get his DNA.'

Amy looked up at him, her mind leaping to the fastest way to justice – and the quickest way to get Jason hurt. 'You've met him. You've been to the club.'

Jason smiled like a shark, and she knew it was a lost cause.

'I've got him.'

Chapter 27: Baby, Don't Hurt Me

Jason went through his Saturday shift in a haze, torn between cloying exhaustion and blinding anger. He wanted this murder to stick to Dan, didn't want him getting another girl before they got to him. He was surprised at how the ball of rage was forming in his chest, simmering there throughout the day. His shrink on the inside had told him his anger would be the death of him and he'd worked hard to hold it back, but he tasted righteousness in his fury now. The man would pay.

He sent the persistent calls from Teresa through to voicemail – he was too tired to be charming. Woodenly polite to the clients, he made instinctive chitchat, but his mind was focused on that evening. On his plan to snare Dan.

His boss, Derek, had pushed his Amy time back to three o'clock. 'Punctuality's important,' he'd said cryptically, but Jason knew he had been pushing his limits, turning up at client appointments a few minutes late, out of breath and dishevelled. He couldn't afford to lose this job, not when they were so close to finding the killer.

Amy was where he'd left her – at the computer terminal in her dressing gown – but she actually turned to look at him as he entered. 'You look terrible.'

Jason scrubbed a hand over his face. His stubble was turning into a beard. Cerys would finally turn him into a scraggly indie kid.

'I'm not used to running on empty.' He yawned behind his hand. 'We should order the week's shopping or you'll have nothing to eat on Monday.'

'Sit down.' Amy gestured to the sofa. 'I'll tell you what I've found.'

Jason did as he was told and sat on the sofa.

Amy faced him, pressing her fingertips together in a steeple. 'He posted another picture.'

The image flashed up on the screen, and Jason leaned forward. Laurie was laid out on the bed, the sheet covering her modestly, but the picture was taken from above, taking in the whole of her body at the foot of her bed. The others had been from the side, the classic sleeping woman, but this photograph was almost predatory. Jason shivered.

'He's escalating,' Amy said quietly. 'I think this was his first sexual assault. The way this picture was taken – you can tell what happened next.'

'He pulled off the sheet. He dragged her down the bed.' His voice was hollow, and he swallowed against his rising gorge. 'He raped her.'

'He's still sending messages. They're not for us. They're for someone else.'

Amy drummed on her mouse impatiently, as though she expected the answers to blossom across the screen.

'The woman in the hospital,' Jason said grimly. 'I can't believe the interviews turned up nothing.'

Amy shrugged – they had to take Bryn at his word that there was no lead there. Jason might be expert at finding the word on the street, but he wouldn't be able to cajole information out of the professional types at the hospital.

'What about the alarm we heard on the call?' Jason leaned back against the sofa, struggling to keep his eyes open.

'I've narrowed it down to a manufacturer.' The clacking of her keys carried across the living room. 'I need to find which of those machines have been purchased by Cardiff and Vale UHB.'

'You will,' Jason said, listing against the arm of the sofa. 'You find everything.'

'I'll wake you,' he heard Amy say from across the room.

I'm not asleep, he wanted to say, but the words never left his lips.

He woke on Amy's sofa at seven o'clock with three missed calls from his mother and a terrible crick in his neck. He shifted himself upright, mumbled his apologies to Amy and went home to change.

Gwen made her displeasure known in the quiet, abused tone of the disappointed mother, one that was far worse than any amount of shouting.

'You should have called. We were worried.'

Jason glanced across at Cerys, who didn't look remotely bothered, but he kept his mouth shut on that point.

'I'm not staying,' he said instead. 'I'm going out – to town.'

Gwen pursed her lips. 'Got paid, did you? Can't say I'm surprised. I expected you to start all that again sooner or later.'

Jason resented her implication that he got drunk as soon as he had a bit of cash, but it was true to form. From before Usk. He hadn't given her much reason to believe he'd changed. He'd never done anything to make her proud. He wanted to tell her how he was involved in catching the Cardiff Ripper, but he didn't want her to worry about him. He'd tell her everything when it was over, when they'd locked the sick bastard up for good.

Dressed in jeans and a black shirt, reeking of cheap aftershave, Jason donned his jacket and headed back out into the city. The pavement was slippery with wet autumn leaves and he stumbled towards town, going over his plan in his head. He'd seen it on cop shows plenty of times: if he went into the bar and bought Dan a drink, he could then nick the glass and get both DNA and fingerprints off it. He'd taken a couple of freezer bags from his mam's kitchen cupboard and stuffed them in his pocket, ready to safely stow the glass for the detectives. If he could just stop himself from smashing Dan's face in, it would be a successful night.

He took a shortcut down one of the streets that held fancy hotels and few pedestrians – and felt a prickle on the back of his neck, the immediate sense of being followed. He slowed his pace, taking in the shadows and side streets around him. He clocked three of them, kids watching, keeping their distance. Waiting.

Jason risked a look and swore under his breath. He knew these kids – and they ran with Damage. Stuart's gang. He did not have time for this tonight. With a burst of speed, he aimed for the well-populated streets of the city centre, where the kids wouldn't dare touch him under the nose of the cops and the crowd of students roaming the streets for some midweek drinks offers. He was only two minutes from St. Mary's Street – there, he'd be safe from a scuffle and able to find the evidence they needed on Dan.

He was so focused on reaching his goal that he missed kid number four. The boy snagged his jacket, yanking him backwards, and then another ran in, slamming a fist into his gut.

Jason got his fists up and cuffed one aside, but two had hold of his jacket and were trying to wrestle him into an alleyway. Jason would be damned if he gave up on the limelight. He twisted out of the jacket and tried to make a run for it.

'You're not fucking turning your back on me.'

Damage seized his shoulder and pulled him round, smacking him across the jaw. Jason tasted blood but kept his feet, preparing to take down the little shit with a minimum of fuss.

'Stop! Police!'

Damage pushed him away and legged it, the rest of his little gang tearing after him.

Two police officers came up behind him, an older copper clapping him on the shoulder. 'You hurt, mate? Nice fat lip you've got there.'

Jason touched his bleeding mouth and winced. 'Yeah, ruined my good looks.'

He bent down to retrieve his scuffed jacket.

'We'll get you inside to clean up and get a sympathetic pint on the house, eh? Nice story for a barmaid.'

That was how he found himself in a back room at his target bar, nursing a pint of ale and having the DJ's assistant fuss over him with a first aid kit.

'Thanks,' he said. 'Tell the manager I'm grateful, yeah?'

'It's Dan on tonight,' she said, and Jason tried to hide his predatory smile. 'I'll pass it on for you.'

He flashed her his wounded-soldier grin. 'If he's got a minute, I'd like to see him, thank him proper. Tell him what great staff he has here.'

The girl blushed prettily, and if he didn't have things to do, he'd happily encourage her sympathy and smiles. As it was, he was on the hunt for DNA and nothing could sway him tonight. She left him, promising to bring Dan back when she found him, and Jason drank down his lager. He needed something that would make Dan slip up, catch him in a lie.

Jason didn't have to wait long, as Dan joined him ten minutes later. 'Sorry about what happened, mate. Hey – do I know you?'

Squinting up at him, Jason pretended to consider his face. 'Yeah, yeah – didn't I meet you here the other day? I was on a cleaning contract.'

Dan's face lost the confusion and he nodded slowly, the conversation out back returning to him.

'I remember,' he said, with a slightly guarded smile. 'We were... talking about Kate. Can't believe she's dead. And Laurie too. Fuck, it's like someone's out for our girls.'

Jason took another drink, watching Dan closely. 'But the other one – what's her name? Melody, that's it. She didn't work here, did she?'

Dan scratched his head, as if thinking. 'Not now. Don't think we've ever had a Melody – you'd remember a name like that, wouldn't you? But the girls are getting scared. We're trying to walk them home where we can, get their blokes to pick them up. It's not safe for any girl in Cardiff right now.'

Because of you, Jason thought, gritting his teeth against his anger. If he lost his temper with the bastard, he wouldn't get what he came for.

'I'm losing faith in the cops, mate. I don't think the idiots have the first idea what they're doing.'

'You've changed your tune,' Dan said warily. 'You thought they were well set up to catch the guy before.'

'That's before they found three girls dead, weren't it? How hard can it be to find him? It's not London or Manchester, is it?'

'Maybe he's just very good.'

Jason felt his jaw tighten, his hand unwittingly curl into a fist.

'Maybe,' he said, straining to keep his voice even.

'Well, I need to be getting back.' Dan stood up to leave. 'Nice to see you again, mate. Pop to the bar for a drink after.'

Jason realised his quarry was getting away and he was no closer to getting a sample. He picked up his pint glass and stood, as if to shake Dan's hand. Dan clapped his arm and Jason let the glass fall from his hand, shattering on the wooden floor.

'Ah, mate, I'm so sorry. My hand's still shaking, it is.'

Dan pushed him gently back into the chair. 'No worries. It's to be expected, ain't it? Let me get it.'

He bent down to pick up the shards and, to Jason's delight, cut himself on a piece of glass.

'That looks nasty,' he said, removing his handkerchief from his pocket and pressing it into Dan's hand. The man wrapped the cloth

133

round his dripping finger, the blood absorbing into the white before Jason's eager eyes.

'You should get that looked at,' he added. 'You got a first aid kit?'

Dan gestured to the green box on the wall and, with a delicate hand, Jason disinfected the wound and placed a plaster over it, leaving his handkerchief to one side and forcing himself not to look at it, hoping the glee didn't show on his face.

'Look, mate, I'll wash that for you,' Dan said and moved to pick up the handkerchief.

But Jason shrugged and picked it up, with an easy smile. 'My mam always says it'll wash. Don't worry about it – my mistake, anyway.'

'I'll see you around,' Dan said and wandered over to the door, smiling at his new friend.

Jason waved him off before carefully placing the handkerchief in one of his plastic bags and returning it to his pocket.

I know I'll be seeing you, mate. Hopefully fucking soon.

Chapter 28: Blood and Water

When Jason held up the handkerchief stained with Dan Anderson's blood, Bryn could've kissed him.

'Looks like I was wrong about you, son.'

The boy grinned back, looking to Amy for approval. But she was in one of her 'genius recluse' moods today and barely grunted from the computer, flicking through what looked like a catalogue of high-tech machinery.

Jason looked hurt by her lack of interest and Bryn was surprised at how much he wanted to reassure the lad, tell him it was nothing personal. Amy wasn't interested in anything unless it had committed a crime or had a keyboard.

'The machine is the key,' she was saying, and Bryn thought that summed up her attitude to life pretty well. 'If we find the source of the alarm, we find the woman in the hospital.'

'But if we nail Dan for this, we don't need her.'

Jason had folded his arms across his chest and was staring intently over her shoulder at whatever was absorbing her attention on her monitor.

'I want to know who she is. Voice analysis confirms that she isn't any of the victims so far.'

Bryn winced. He hated the way she had no regard for superstition, tempting fate like that. She was too damn logical sometimes.

'I'm running voice analysis on their known friends and associates but I'm not hopeful of a match.'

Amy would make a good detective, Bryn thought – she always wanted answers, needed everything to fit in. Of course, she could barely talk to people and she didn't leave the house, so that part of detecting went a bit awry. But between her and her errand boy, they made a pretty good copper.

'How are you doing that?' Jason asked, interested despite himself. 'You can't go around recording all those voices, can you?'

Amy shot him a bemused look, as if that method hadn't even occurred to her. 'Interrogating voicemail. The default recording is an irritating obstacle, but I have a telesales interface I use as a contingency.'

Jason frowned. 'So, let me get this straight: you pretend to be a telemarketer to get samples of people's voices to analyse?'

Amy cracked her knuckles. 'It's entirely automated but, essentially, yes.'

The boy was having difficulty grasping this idea, Bryn noted with amusement.

'But what if they actually want to buy what you're selling? What do you do then?'

Amy's lips twitched. 'I've never had that problem.'

Bryn's phone buzzed in his pocket and he fished it out, grimacing. Rob Pritchard. 'Rob, what can I do you for?'

'I have some preliminary information from Miss Fox's autopsy.'

Bryn set the phone on the edge of Amy's desk and put it on loudspeaker. 'Go on, Rob.'

'C.O.D. was a massive subarachnoid haemorrhage, as predicted. He must've hit her pretty hard.'

Owain was making notes on his phone. Bryn, not trusting that thing as far as he could throw it, flipped open his notebook.

'But she put up a hell of a fight: bruising over both arms and knuckles, and she definitely scratched him – blood and epithelials under the nails.'

'We have a reference for that,' Bryn said, nodding to Jason, who grinned like it was his birthday. 'Owain will bring it over today.'

'There's also a muddy footprint in the bathroom,' Rob said, continuing as if he hadn't heard. 'Preliminary analysis suggests sediment and calcium carbonate, so I'd place it in the Valleys by a lake or reservoir. Potential dump site, maybe?'

'I knew it had to be a lake,' Jason muttered. Maybe he was more a three-quarter detective.

'Am I on loudspeaker? Where are you, Hesketh? Are you in that girl's house again?'

Rob sounded scandalised at the idea that his findings were being broadcast for an audience. Owain rolled his eyes.

'You're just upset they like me more than you,' Amy said, typing Rob's findings into a text file for future reference.

Jason peered over her shoulder to read her notes, hand resting on her upper arm. Bryn had never casually touched Amy, thought she'd be the type to flinch and back away, but she seemed easy with Jason in a way he'd never seen before.

'If you find the lake,' Rob said sulkily, 'I can match it with eighty-five percent accuracy. We need a soil reference database.'

'We need people to stop dumping things in lakes.' Why did criminals decide the Valleys were an ideal spot for their dodgy dealings? The underworld used them as a dumping ground for everything from stolen TVs to drug cookers. It was worse than the London gangs and the Thames. 'Anything else, Rob?'

'I'll keep you informed. You, Hesketh – not her.'

The line clicked off. Amy didn't look like she'd lose any sleep over Rob's refusal to play nice, and Bryn was glad he could see them on opposite sides of town. Imagining them working in the same building was the stuff of nightmares.

'If I were going to dump a body,' Amy mused, a map of South Wales open on her monitor, 'I would drive up this road here—' she gestured with the end of her pencil, '—until I got to this big lake.' She made a lazy circle around the lake in question: Llwyn-on Reservoir.

'Bit obvious, isn't it? Someone would see you. Maybe he's into rambling and knows one of the smaller lakes, out of the way like.' Owain was obviously pleased with this theory. Over his shoulder, Bryn could see some kind of OS map on his phone screen.

'He's a fan of a punk pop band and active on their fan forum. How much of an outdoorsman can he be?' Amy shook her head. 'He's a nerd. Anyone who can hide their IP address from me is extremely computer literate, bordering on otaku. You don't get that kind of knowledge prancing around in fields.'

'It's not far out of town either.' Jason peered at the map. 'An hour, tops. At night, probably more like half an hour. The lanes are easier with your lights on.'

'We'll do a grid search,' Owain said, with the air of an intellectual amongst morons. 'A systematic approach will ensure accurate results.'

Amy turned her head towards Jason, who smiled. What were those two up to now? At least in the middle of the Valleys, Jason was unlikely to resort to impersonating a police officer. Bryn might have turned a blind eye once but if the boy made it a habit, he'd have to come down on him hard. Just because he liked the boy didn't mean he'd forgotten his dubious past.

Jason's phone started blaring something that sounded like Queen; he looked at the number, ducked his head and hung up. Suspicious that. Jason hurriedly stuffed the phone back in his pocket and looked back at the map, as if it consumed his interest entirely, steadfastly ignoring the look Amy was sending him. The same suspicious look Bryn was sure had crossed his face moments before.

'So, you've got the lakes, Owain, and I'll get this handkerchief over to forensics.' Bryn fixed Jason in his sights. 'Do you need something to keep you out of trouble?'

He was amused at Jason's 'Who, me?' expression, a blush creeping over his face. The boy had the pale Celtic skin that showed even the slightest hint of mortification – or rage.

'I'm sure Amy will keep me busy,' he said cryptically.

The look of gratitude Amy gave him was beautiful, until she hastily looked away. Bryn nodded, accepting that while Amy worked for him, Jason decidedly worked for Amy, and the pair of them would do whatever they felt needed doing without wasting time telling him about it. As long as he didn't have to rescue Jason from the cells, he was fine with that.

'I'll let you get on with it then.'

Taking the golden bloodied handkerchief with him, left his unorthodox detective to work.

What had started as a good idea was rapidly turning into a nightmare.

Jason needed to keep in with Teresa. She was easy on the eye, could hold a decent conversation, and she kissed well even while drunk. These were all fine attributes in a woman, and Teresa was a woman worth holding on to.

He also needed to go to this reservoir to collect evidence and soil samples for Amy, so that she could rub their findings in the face of

Owain's 'systematic approach'. Therefore, genius Carr thought, why not combine the two and take Teresa down to the water?

It had started well. He'd packed some food – crisps and chocolate and stuff – and another half-decent bottle of wine, with glasses and everything. He'd picked Teresa up at her new place after he left Amy's, when the light was dimming but it was still reasonable to be outside and not freeze to death.

Then, they'd got to the reservoir and, even by dusk, it was pretty stunning. The hills rose up around it and the clear waters spread before them with barely a ripple. The trees across the water were showing their autumn colours, except for the pines standing tall and silent, like sentinels. The grass was starting to crisp and crackle with an evening frost, but Jason spread an old tartan blanket over it only a few feet from the water's edge. Apart from the road behind them, there were no signs of civilisation – they were alone with only the wine and each other for company.

It was dead romantic and Jason was pretty chuffed with his choice of date. The wine went down well and Teresa even picked appreciatively at the box of chocolates.

Which was when he surreptitiously tried to collect a sample of mud.

'What are you doing?' She laughed as she caught him digging a spoon into the half-frozen mud between the glittering blades of grass.

'Just messing around.' He carefully filled a plastic cup to the brim with sediment, moving a little closer to the reservoir to find some softer soil.

'You're like a child at the beach,' she said, shaking her head so that her curls bounced around her chin. She was gorgeous and he liked her, and really, couldn't all this soil and murder business wait a bit? He leaned forward and captured her lips with his, kissing across the picnic blanket.

Jason raised his other hand to her cheek – and knocked over the bottle of wine. Teresa giggled and tried to rescue it, as wine flowed in a stream to join the mighty lake and the bottle rolled away down the bank. She chased it, her skirt flapping around her knees, and he leaned back and enjoyed the view.

Teresa screamed.

Instantly, he was on his feet, running after her down the bank. She was standing at the water's edge, the wine bottle floating in the water. And reaching up as if to grasp it was a woman's hand.

Jason pulled Teresa back from the edge and stared. Beneath the surface of the water, the bloated face of Melody Frank stared up at the sky, the dying sun reflected in her eyes. Jason tried to pull Teresa close to comfort her, but she staggered away from him, terror on her face.

'Y-you brought me here,' she said, backing away as he tried to follow her. 'You found me on our street. All you wanted to t-talk about was Mel.'

Jason held up his hands. 'It's not like that, Teresa.'

But she was distraught, frightened, and she ran back to his car, tugging on the door handles, desperately battering the window.

He walked up to her, trying to stay calm and look nonthreatening, but she tore off her shoe and held it like a weapon. 'Stay back!'

Jason did as she asked, watching as she fished out her phone and held it up, looking for reception while keeping her shoe raised in self-defence.

'Teresa, I don't want to hurt you.'

'You brought me to the place where y-you dumped her!' Tears were streaming down her face now, and Jason's heart broke for her.

'Teresa, let me explain—'

'Explain what? How you killed her? How you lured me here? I'm such an idiot! John told me it was dodgy, but I wouldn't listen.' She was rambling to herself now, shoulders shaking with her sobs.

Jason racked his brains on how he could possibly explain to her that he wasn't a murderer. He decided the only way was to come clean.

'Teresa, I didn't kill Melody. And I'm not going to hurt you. But… it's not coincidence that we're here.'

She froze, as if she was expecting him to continue denying it and this new revelation had thrown everything out of whack again.

Jason took a step forward. 'I haven't been entirely honest with you. I didn't just happen by your house the other day. I was coming to find you – to ask you questions about Melody.'

Teresa cautiously lowered the shoe. 'Are you the police?'

Jason grimaced. 'No.' The shoe started to move. 'But I'm working with them to catch Melody's killer. And…I thought you'd have information to help us.'

Teresa's face shifted from fear to anger in the blink of an eye. 'You used me?'

Jason held his hands out, coming forward to placate her.

'Teresa, it wasn't like that. I like you! It started out that way, but that wasn't why we…y'know…'

But she shook her head, face hard and eyes cold. 'Keep the fuck away from me.'

She stalked off to stand by the road, her back to him, defiant.

Jason sighed and plucked his phone from his pocket. Time to call in the cavalry.

Chapter 29: Prime Suspect

Within half an hour, the reservoir was cordoned off and swarming with police and SOCOs. Teresa, wrapped in a blanket, leaned on the bonnet of a police car, giving her statement to a uniform copper and glaring daggers at Jason. For his part, Jason just stood by his car, trying to explain to Bryn exactly how he'd managed to take a girl on a date to a body dump.

'I was trying to find dirt, not a dead body!'

He scowled and stuffed his freezing hands in his pockets. The sun had truly set now, the moon casting an eerie light over the water as a dredge looked for Kate Thomas's body. Melody was already in the back of a van, Rob prodding at her prior to transfer. He'd already had a go at Jason for contaminating his crime scene with a wine bottle.

'I imagine your girlfriend was less than impressed,' Bryn said, glower fixed firmly in place. 'And am I right in thinking the young lady in question is—'

'Melody's housemate, Teresa.'

Owain just shook his head and walked off. Jason had no idea what he had to be smug about when his stupid system was a complete failure, but he could gloat about that later. Right now, he had to explain to the detective how he'd ended up dating the friend of their murder victim.

'Have you completely lost your mind? I guess you didn't tell her what you were doing. How else would you have got in there?'

'I thought I had it under control,' he said, which was clearly bloody naïve. 'I like her.'

'This isn't the bloody playground! She's a person of interest, a witness. You're on Amy's team, which means you're on my team. If you want to continue to play the game, you can't go around sleeping with the witnesses!'

Jason winced. 'Is there any chance you won't tell Amy?'

Bryn gave him a look of pity. 'Is there any chance she doesn't already know?'

Amy knew. Oh boy, did Amy ever know.

'I see you found the bodies,' she said. 'It was too bad your girlfriend was there – Teresa Danvers, former housemate of Melody Frank. She now lives in Roath, in a house you left on the same morning you were late coming to me. What a strange coincidence.'

Jason wisely kept his mouth shut and let the passive-aggressive tirade continue.

'I hear she thought you were the murderer. I suppose it was because you lied to her and then took her to a place with dead bodies in the water. I think that's a turn-off.'

Continuing his dedicated scrubbing of the kitchen floor, Jason resisted the urge to point out, for the hundredth time, that he did not take her to a place with dead bodies. The fact that dead bodies happened to be there was neither here nor there – it was his intention that was important. And his intention was that no one got hurt. Unfortunately, the road to hell was paved with the good intentions of men like Jason Carr, who meant well but were clearly inept and should just go back to stealing cars. He'd been good at stealing cars. Until he got caught and sent to prison. Maybe he was just useless and should hide in his mother's basement until someone invented a cure for that.

Things were also going south with Derek. Everyone and their dog knew about how Jason Carr had found the bodies in the lake, how he was a hardened criminal with priors for assault for which he'd served time. Of course, Derek knew he had a criminal record, but he was having difficulty squaring it with his clients when today's headlines read 'Ex-Con Lures Melody Friend to Watery Grave' with Jason's picture on the front page.

His mam hadn't been best pleased about it either.

'She's not even that pretty,' Amy muttered.

She was never letting this go. He was doomed to hear about how he'd slept with Teresa Danvers from here to eternity. That was if he still had a job by the end of the day.

'It was a stupid mistake,' he said, suddenly snapping and taking up his own defence. 'I shouldn't have done it and I'm sorry. What more do you want from me?'

Amy huffed and sank further into her chair. But she did finally click off Teresa's Facebook page and return to her new crime scene photographs of the lake, taken by a reluctant Owain.

'Cup of tea would be nice.'

Jason smiled to himself and went to fetch the tea. At least some things never changed.

'It's not a bloody match!'

Amy looked up from the keyboard as Bryn marched into the living room, waving a piece of paper.

Jason stirred on the sofa, where he'd caught a few hours' rest following his night by the lake, the seam of the cushion imprinted on his right cheek.

'Doesn't match what?' he said, voice woolly with sleep.

'Dan Anderson's DNA is not a fucking match.'

Amy stared at her monitor. Jason had been so sure. She had been sure.

Jason sat up, completely awake now. 'But…it has to match. He's the one who killed them!'

He scrubbed his hand over his face and Amy read the bitter disappointment in his eyes. They were back to having no suspects, and all the media's attention was now on that terrible man who assaulted the police officer and just happened to find the bodies.

Bryn looked defeated, weary. 'Not the blood under her nails or the rape kit. I liked him for this, son, but he's not our man.'

Jason slumped back on the sofa, bleary-eyed and miserable. Amy struggled to think of something to say that would make him smile, but she didn't know how. She didn't know how to handle people. She didn't know how to make them happy.

'What do we do now?' Jason said finally.

Bryn looked uncomfortable, shifting from foot to foot, and she suspected that what he was going to say wouldn't make Jason happy either.

'I think you should lie low for a while. Just until this thing blows over. You can't help while everyone's pointing fingers.'

Amy expected Jason to shout, to rant and rave and insist that he could help them. But instead he bowed his head, crumpling forward like wet paper.

'All right then,' he said. 'I won't be no bother to you, Detective.'

'I still need you.'

She wasn't losing her assistant just because Bryn had decided it was a good idea. But Bryn was still looking uneasy and Amy had a feeling he was going to try and disrupt her life all the same.

'Maybe it's best if Jason doesn't come here for a while.'

Amy clenched her jaw, preparing for a fight.

But Bryn held up a hand to forestall her. 'If you're working with us, Amy, and everyone with a newspaper is liking Jason for this, what are they going to think when they find out he's here every day? They're gonna cry foul and I'll have to pull you out of this investigation too.' His eyes were pleading with her. 'I need you to catch this guy.'

So, it came down to a choice, then. She could see Jason, her cleaner, her assistant, or she could help the police hunt down a serial killer. She hesitated, inexplicably torn. A few weeks ago, the choice would've been easy, immediate, but now it seemed the hardest thing she'd ever done.

In the end, Jason saved her the agony. He stood up from the sofa and shouldered his bag. Without looking at either of them, he headed for the door. 'See you around, Amy.'

The silence was unforgiving. Amy struggled to remember how to breathe, felt the room going dark. A warm hand squeezed her shoulder and she contained the panic, the rising feeling that she was lost and couldn't handle anything anymore.

'You did the right thing,' she heard Bryn say distantly.

Her head nodded forward. The right thing. Of course.

Then why did she feel so terrible?

They'd found the lake.

He'd been at work when he'd heard and he swallowed down his scream, calmly walked to the bathroom and hid in the cubicle until the shaking stopped.

It was bad enough that he'd left the last one. He'd been so stupid, giving in like that, but she was so beautiful. He was meant to be having

146

an affair, so why not have one? But as he'd lost himself in the scent of her hair and the faint tinge of iron, he'd been discovered. Careless. He'd almost lost everything. He couldn't have his freebird if he was behind bars.

He'd have to lie low for a while. Wait until things calmed down. Then, he'd make his move. No more wasting time with this jealousy game. No more making time with other girls. It was time he took the prize. He'd be with his freebird forever.

Chapter 30: Back to the Start

Derek fired him.

He looked apologetic about it, but Jason knew that he needed him shifted as soon as possible. Despite it being the middle of autumn, the man was sweating in his little office, mopping his brow with his handkerchief, as his assistant's phone kept ringing and ringing and ringing.

'Roath Cleaning Company. No, Mr. Lawrence is not available for comment. No, I won't talk about Jason. Goodbye.' Over and over, the same thing, until the poor woman finally gave up and took the phone off the hook. Jason stared somewhere over Derek's shoulder and waited for the man to pluck up the courage to say the words.

'Look, Jason, you started out well. And getting into Miss Lane's flat – well, no one's been able to do that for months. So…good show on that one, yeah?'

Jason dredged up a small smile.

Derek smiled like a maniac, either trying to pacify the serial killer or just glad to see some flicker of response.

'But you've been late recently. I've had some…concerns from the clients. Now, with all this—' he waved his hands expansively, as if to indicate the collapse of the universe, '—I just don't see how we can carry on with you. You understand, right?'

'You're firing me.'

Jason watched Derek flinch. If he wasn't going to be man enough to say the words, Jason wasn't going to give him an easy out. He'd liked this job, actually enjoyed it – chatting with the clients, getting their places in order. Meeting Amy.

'I'm sorry, Jason. And…we'll need the supplies back. And your uniform.'

At the end of his tether, Jason got up from his seat and pulled the bloody lilac T-shirt over his head, chucking it in the middle of Derek's desk so the sleeve landed in his tea.

'And here are your supplies.' He dumped the holdall on the desk too, sending the pot of pens flying.

'Now there's no need to be like that.'

But Jason was already leaving, pulling his jacket over his bare chest and running out the door, running back to the dole queue.

In times of trial, Amy took refuge in the internet.

The ebb and flow of information was soothing. Tracking down the genesis of a meme or following a complex IP trail through the servers of the world was like playing hide-and-seek in the playground again. No one ever found her hiding places – or perhaps they never looked too hard to begin with.

Today's treasure hunt was for the identity of a serial killer. To her immense frustration, she had lost his IP address reroute somewhere in Eastern Europe, in what was probably a server in some crumbling hole that used to be somebody's home. It wasn't complex, intricate systems that gave her a problem – it was small, shoddy, half-assed attempts at systems that invariably lost any and all information of value.

However, the reroute signature itself was interesting. It looked like it had been custom-made, selecting a series of servers that were alien to the bigger IP address maskers and mirrors. She might not be able to find the end of the path, but she might be able to find other sites and accounts that had been routed similarly. He had to have an internet presence, she was sure of it – no one with this level of technical knowledge could keep away from his own kind.

The key, she decided, was the Eastern European server, which upon further digging turned out to be in Warsaw. It was small and unreliable, but that also made it likely to be his obfuscation point of choice. He was relying on the fact that no one could get beyond it. However, she didn't need to find the next link in the chain – she just wanted to know what other chains it was part of.

The more she looked into it, the more it seemed like a private server, possibly only used by the killer. Perhaps he had some link to Poland, or perhaps he merely knew someone online who could arrange that kind of thing. The selling of overseas servers was a growing trend and easy to arrange, if you knew where to go.

But the idea started to form in her head that, while she had praised the use of a slow, unwieldy system as the perfect concealment, perhaps it was only this awful because that was the limit of the creator's skill. Maybe he made his own server. Amy's server, of course, ran like diamonds and ice, but that was only because she could never bear to make something so horrendous as an unreliable server. The artisan's pride.

If it really was a single-use system, then all the addresses routed to it would be the killer's browsing history on a plate. She'd have to trace them forward, of course, but for an expert in the field, it was mere child's play. She even had a programme that would run it for her, but where was the fun in that?

Amy cracked her knuckles and went to work.

'Back again, are we?'

Jason sat across from Martin and scowled. That was enough to send the man back to his cowering, shaking ways, and Jason got a childish satisfaction out of it. Then he remembered that everyone in town thought he was a murderer and he sobered up fast.

'Lost my job,' he said sullenly.

Martin nodded with a look of pity that gave Jason the urge to shout and storm out, but he reined in his temper and forced himself to stay still. Losing it in here could lead to nothing good.

'I'm sorry about that. As it was still inside the probation period…' Martin shrugged, his smile turning sympathetic.

Jason slumped forward, elbows on the table and hands clasped at the back of his head. 'What do I do now?'

'There's nothing much around at the moment.' Martin tapped on his mouse with one finger while he scratched at a shaving cut on his left cheek. It was amazing Martin had any face at all with the way his hands shook all the time, as if he had a permanent caffeine buzz. Jason must be bored if he was now obsessing over the guy at the job centre.

'I'll take anything,' Jason said, with his best eager, willing smile.

But Martin just shook his head sadly. 'I've got nothing to give you, I'm afraid. Keep looking in the paper and online. Something will turn up.'

The false cheer in Martin's voice was another kick to Jason's confidence and he couldn't even look the man in the eye.

'Can I...' The words caught in his throat, but he had to swallow his pride if he was to pay his own way at home. 'I need to sign on.'

Martin gave him a knowing look, oblivious to his self-disgust. 'Well then. Let's get through the questions, shall we?'

As if that wasn't humiliating enough, he then had to go home and face his mother. The look of disappointment on Gwen's face was worse than Derek firing him, worse than Martin's questions, and worse than Amy doing nothing to stop him leaving.

'Your uncle came round,' she said hollowly. 'Asked me if you killed those girls.'

Jason flinched and looked at the scarred kitchen table, swallowing against the lump in his throat. If his mam thought he was a murderer, he didn't know what he'd do.

'What did you tell him?' he whispered, dreading her response.

Her mug slammed into the table, jerking him out of his misery to stare at his mam's furious face.

'I told him that if he really thought his nephew could do those terrible things, he wasn't welcome in this house no more!'

Gwen's face was flushed with rage and Jason felt a strange sort of pride in his mother, defending her son in the face of the rising tide of suspicion.

'But...' she said, and his heart sank, 'you're going to tell me everything that's been going on this past couple of weeks and why you've been out at all hours of the day and night.'

Reluctantly, he told her how he'd been involved in a murder investigation and watched her face turn ashen at how he'd taken blood from a suspect and pretended to be a copper about town. When he had finished, she was on her second cup of tea and had worried her hair into an Einstein-like tangle.

'Well, that explains why you were bothering so much with that Amy. She didn't sound like your type of girl at all.'

For some reason, that statement stung him, though he had no idea why. True, Amy was nothing like the girls he chose to hang about with, but she wasn't bad and he thought maybe he would've liked to see her, even if he wasn't getting paid.

'What are you going to do now, *bach*?'

Jason had no idea, didn't want to think about what he might do next, how much he wanted to go back to Amy and help her find the bastard who was murdering girls in his city.

But before he could answer, Cerys hurtled through the door, slamming it behind her. She'd been crying and Gwen stood immediately, taking the girl into her arms.

'Whatever's the matter? Hush now, don't cry.'

Jason rose to his feet, torn between terror and anger. 'Did somebody hurt you, Cerys?'

Gwen looked at him over Cerys's shoulder, eyes wide, clutching her little girl tighter to her.

'It's Stuart,' Cerys bit out between sobs. 'H-he's been cheating on me.'

Jason subsided back into his chair. Ah – another loser boyfriend bites the dust. A look of guilty relief passed over Gwen's face, as Cerys continued to cry into her mother's neck.

'Now, do you know that for a fact, *bach*?' Gwen said.

Jason rolled his eyes. Cerys did have a tendency to overreact, but it wasn't like the dumping of the boyfriend was a great loss. He didn't know why his mother couldn't just let things lie.

'He's covered in her…marks! Scratches all over him.'

Alarm bells started ringing in his head, and Jason remembered Laurie's hands, the red beneath her nails – her struggle to take her killer down with her.

'What's his name?' Jason asked. 'Where can I find him?'

Cerys looked up, face blotchy and startled. 'I don't need you to go beating him up. He's bigger than you anyway.'

'I don't want to fight him,' Jason said, slowly uncurling the fist that had formed of its own accord. 'Just get some answers.'

Cerys looked at him strangely, and he saw the realisation in his mother's face.

'You'd better tell him, *bach*,' she said. 'It could be important.'

And Cerys, confused and unknowing, told him everything: 'Stuart Williams. From that Canton lot. You know him, don't you?'

Chapter 31: Rat and Mouse

Bryn had hit a brick wall. The post-mortem findings on Kate and Melody confirmed what they already knew – Kate strangled, likely with her shower curtain, and Melody suffocated, with a match between the fibres in her lungs and the fibres from the hotel pillowcase. The lake had washed away most of the useful trace evidence, but the medical examiner confirmed that neither girl had been raped. That fitted Amy's idea that Laurie's sexual assault had been an escalation, but didn't otherwise help them.

The media were getting bored of the case now, having interviewed everyone they could think of and paying Teresa Danvers a wad of cash to dish dirt on Jason. However, she hadn't given them much of a story, clearly having calmed down enough to realise he wasn't the killer and that the whole thing just made her look bad.

But that meant the whole case was losing momentum. He had three bodies now, three murder scenes, and no excuse as to why he hadn't caught the killer. He didn't even have a convincing suspect. Amy said something about a server in Poland, but he fully expected her to get swallowed whole by the tech or take to her bed any day now. She was already fraying around the edges, and Bryn was starting to regret sending Jason away.

It had been the right decision at the time, every media outlet breathing down their necks, but now that the whole thing had subsided after the weekend, he should be calling the boy up and telling him that Amy needed her assistant back. And yet he didn't, because as much as he liked Amy, it was her decision at the end of the day who she wanted in her house, and she was perfectly capable of fetching him back herself.

Meanwhile, he had nothing to go on. And no idea when the bastard might strike next.

Jason's first idea was to go down to old Tiger Bay and pound the living shit out of Stuart until he talked. But he needed to be smarter than that. The only way he knew to be smart was to call Amy.

But Amy had made it clear that her work with the police was more important than him and he could respect that, knew what was at stake. So he'd have to do this alone. He'd have to find out what Stuart was doing and work out from there whether he was the killer. To do that, he'd have to follow him.

The Nissan Micra was not a car built for stealth, stakeouts or guys over six foot. But for all his complaints, it wasn't a bad car. It had never let him down yet and, despite the tendency for the driver's side window to fall inside the door and the complete inability to climb a hill, it could eat up a Valleys road. He just wished it looked less like a girl's car.

Huddled inside his thickest winter coat, watching his breath mist before him and condensation freezing on the inside of his window screen, Jason peered out at the gloom of a Cardiff night. The Taff lapped up against the bank, swollen by the autumn rain, and a group of lads sat around in the light of their souped-up Puntos, smoking and drinking cheap cider. Jason liked to think he'd had a little more class at that age, but he was probably kidding himself.

He'd been sitting there for two hours and hadn't learned anything remotely useful except that these boys could drink and liked to play pissing games in the Taff. Having asked around all yesterday, he'd found out that Stuart had worked his way round all of Cerys's friends, liked a bit of M-Cat and diazys, and was mixed up in something with his Canton boys but no one really wanted to find out what. It was the older members of the gang he was hanging with now, roughly the same age, same type, and Jason couldn't really see them being up to much.

Of course, no one had thought his friends up to much until they'd tried to rob the gold exchange – a fancy name for little more than a pawn shop. It was a genius plan, really, right up until the point where their getaway driver came off the road. Kid was seventeen, just got his licence – he was no Jay Bird. He landed Lewis in hospital with his arm broken in two places, handcuffed to the trolley in A&E because he was under arrest for armed robbery. And Jason hadn't been there.

Jason was ashamed of the fact that some days he regretted running with those boys, and others he regretted not going down with them. They were fucking musketeers, him and Lewis. It had been their plan, but Jason had only gone and got himself arrested the week before, trying to get hold of the getaway car. But Lewis hadn't rolled on him, just resented him from his prison cell, and set his little brother on him. Jason had known little Dai Jones since he was two years old – he wasn't going to hurt the kid.

Stuart and the Canton boys finally got bored of the riverside, got back in their cars and headed off down the street. Jason started the car, rubbed at the misted-up windows and followed them. Stuart broke away from the others, heading back towards Butetown, and Jason tailed him at a distance, hoping he was doing more than taking a trip to his mam's.

He was paying such close attention to not losing the car in front that, when Stuart finally stopped, it took Jason a moment to realise where they were – outside his house.

Jason got out the car, striding ahead to cut Stuart off before he got anywhere near his front door – and his sister. 'What do you think you're doing?'

Stuart sneered. 'None of your fucking business. This is between me and your sister.'

'It's between you and my fist.'

Jason pulled himself up to his full height, glowering down at this jumped-up little shit who thought he could interfere with Jason's family and get away with it. Stuart just laughed, starting to turn away, then throwing a vicious right hook.

It landed full on Jason's cheek, pain exploding across his face. But he recovered quickly, landing a thump on Stuart's shoulder, grabbing and twisting his arm up and behind his back. Stuart howled, sinking to his knees and crying for release. Pathetic.

'Stay the fuck away from her,' Jason spat. 'Do you hear me?'

Stuart whimpered and Jason pushed him to the pavement. He heard the front door unlock behind him.

'Go inside, Mam. I've got it under control.'

But it was his sister who ran past him to comfort the poor darling on the pavement, looking up at her brother as if he were Satan himself. 'What did you do to him?'

Jason decided he'd had enough of this crap for one night and turned back to the house. Gwen stood in the doorway, taking in the scene with alarm, but Jason easily pushed past her.

'Try to stop her getting killed,' he said and went upstairs to bed.

Amy stared at the monitor, hand poised over F1. Another tense minute passed.

Then, finally, Cerys Carr left her ex-boyfriend on the pavement and went back inside with her mother. Amy breathed a sigh of relief and, moving the feed to another monitor, went back to looking for the serial killer.

It wasn't that she was nosy or interfering. It was just that crime was so easy to prevent. The council had cameras all over the city and, while that was very useful for catching thieves or vandals after they'd committed their crime, if someone would just watch them live, they could nip most trouble in the bud before a crime was even committed. It did sound a bit *Minority Report* but Amy could live with that.

Monitoring the city's criminal hotspots was easy enough, and required a simple nine-by-nine grid of camera feeds to her distant monitor. She had recognition software to detect potential threatening movements and then notified the police accordingly. Of course, now she had added Jason surveillance to her repertoire, but she'd only had to call the police twice. Given his record, she thought that was pretty good going.

In her ongoing quest for the killer's internet history, she'd hit mostly dead ends. A few forums of questionable morality, the type that advocated domestic violence and rape under the term 'spousal discipline,' where one could learn about everything from beaters that left no mark to how to construct your own cell. However, she couldn't find any active threads with his signature, which meant he was consuming, not creating, and that didn't tell her anything specific about him.

However, this current chain was more interesting, as it seemed to lead to a blogging site. Russian-owned, but very American in outlook, it was a hugely popular platform for fandom, bandom and text-based roleplay. Once Amy had navigated their mess of code, she would – ah, there it was. A personal journal with the name 'yearntolove" It had to be him.

The posts were unremarkable, except for some very purple prose, awful even to Amy's school dropout's eye. They were all addressed to someone called 'freebird'. She was the focus of his obsession, Amy realised, the one who drove him to murder those other girls. He was trying to make her jealous, lure her away from her man. It made a sick sort of sense – posting the photographs of supposedly sleeping girls to hint at a series of liaisons, to make the girl of his dreams jealous. The girl who was most likely their woman at the hospital.

But his latest post was different from the others. He'd been following the news reports of their findings and he knew they were on his trail:

I won't let them get to me before I get to you freebird. You know now how far I would go for you, I know you feel the same way. We'll be together soon freebird. I'm coming to save you. Pack a bag and I'll be there.

He was going after the woman in the hospital. She was his next victim.

Chapter 32: What's Your Emergency?

Jason woke with a splitting headache and the urge to punch something.

His left eye was swollen shut and was sending pickaxes of pain into his brain. God, he hated Stuart and he hated his stupid sister for running to him like a moron. That was harsh – he didn't hate her, but he did think she was an idiot.

Levering himself out of bed, he shuffled to the bathroom and inspected his face in the mirror. His eye looked ghastly, red and angry, with a bruise spreading over his cheekbone where Stuart had lamped him one. Jason soaked a flannel in icy water and pressed it to his face until he could prise open his eye. He took a long, hot shower, trying to dissolve some of the tension in his shoulders, before heading back to his bedroom to mope.

His phone was flashing with a new message and he picked it up before considering whether he really cared about who was texting him. But the message brought a smile to his face, stretching the bruised skin.

Out of milk. @

When Jason arrived with the milk and a packet of chocolate digestives, Amy felt her face break into a smile – which swiftly faded when she saw his hideous black eye.

'Bloody hell, what happened to you?' Bryn said from the sofa.

Jason shrugged, taking the milk through to the kitchen. 'I walked into a door.'

'That door's got a good punching arm. You should watch it doesn't catch you again.'

Bryn sounded concerned. Amy knew exactly how he'd got the bruises, but pushed aside her worry and returned to her spreadsheets. She had to work faster.

As Jason set down a mug of tea beside her, Amy placed a hand on his forearm and held up her surprise, printed on her best white paper. 'Sign at the bottom. Bryn has a pen.'

She turned back to her screen but watched him in the reflection, his lips moving soundlessly as he read through the contract. He would be her assistant – a real assistant, for 'anything she deemed necessary'.

'That can't be right.' Jason had reached the line with the stated salary.

Amy looked at the sheet anxiously. 'Isn't that enough money? I did research.'

'Amy, that's more than enough. Really.' Jason looked up and she struggled to hold his gaze. 'Can you afford this?'

'Yes. You're useful,' she mumbled, unable to find the words to convey exactly what it meant to have him there, beside her. Her assistant.

For her ears only, he murmured, 'I missed you too.'

Her cheeks burned hot, but the feeling of the world righting was worth the mortification. He leaned on a clear space on her terminal, signed his name with the borrowed pen and passed the contract back to her. She admired it for a moment before placing it carefully on top of the printer.

'I found the murderer.'

'What?' he said, startled. 'Where?'

She brought up the webpage. 'This is his blog. It's mostly lovesick tripe but it has yielded some useful information.'

'Such as what?' He peered over her chair and rested his hand on her shoulder. The last feelings of unease faded away.

'He's trying to make someone jealous,' she said, 'and she's his next victim.'

'The caller from the hospital?'

'That's what I thought, but where is she?'

'If she was a patient or relative, we'll never find her,' Owain piped up from the sofa. 'It's like looking for a droplet in the tide.'

'She went running at that alarm,' Amy said, thoughtfully. 'That makes me think staff. I've only got a partial list of machines at UHW that have that alarm—'

'We need to start now,' Bryn said, getting to his feet as if he was about to sprint to the hospital right that moment. 'Maybe the machine's on that list and maybe it's not, but we've got to start somewhere. Time's running out for this girl.'

Amy printed a list of machines and where they could be found in the hospital. It was worryingly long – A&E, theatres, intensive care, paediatrics.

'Does that correlate with my list of women?'

Bryn scanned it quickly, but he was already shaking his head. 'It's none of them. I questioned them myself.'

She shot a hurt look in his direction, and he relented.

'One in A&E and two in theatres. We'll start there.'

The two detectives got off the sofa and headed for the door, but Bryn stopped in the corridor. They all looked expectantly at Jason.

'Well?' Bryn said. 'Are you coming?'

Jason looked to Amy. She smiled. 'Sure,' he said. 'I need to get this looked at.'

There wasn't another moment to waste.

He'd been patient long enough, waiting for her to realise, and she still hadn't come to him. How could she be so stupid? He hit himself on the arm, scratched at it. She wasn't stupid, idiot, she was perfect. He was stupid. He hadn't made it plain to her, that he was waiting.

Well, he'd make it obvious now. She wouldn't be able to ignore him any longer. She'd notice him and then they'd be together. That was how it always worked, in the movies, on the telly, in his mind. The girl realised that the boy had been there all along and then she fell into his arms, happy and content.

He felt himself fill with anticipation, a low burning desire forming in his belly. He was at the doors now, his heart hammering in his chest. This was it – he was going to see her again. He was going to make things right.

'Can I help you, sir?' The receptionist smiled at him, a pretty thing with long blond hair – like his lovers, all beautiful and blonde, attracted to him. He remembered how they'd all come to him and smiled, how he'd known they were the ones. Like this one was smiling at him.

But, no, there was no time for that now. Now he had come to finish this for good. He would have his real girlfriend now, the one he'd been waiting for all this time.

'I'm looking for someone,' he said.

They split up in the concourse. 'I'll take A&E,' Bryn said. 'Owain, go to the children's hospital. Jason, start with theatres. They've got a few of them here, so I'll join you once I'm done in A&E.'

Jason nodded, forcing down the little thrill he got when he realised he was part of a police operation now. The Jason of two years ago would've been disgusted with him, but he didn't care – he was making a difference. He was useful.

When Amy had handed him that contract, it was like running with the gang again, his best friend by his side. He hoped Amy knew she didn't have to pay a penny for him to come running if she needed him.

Jason followed the signs to the operating theatres, ignoring the looks he was attracting with his swollen, discoloured face, and rang the bell at reception.

A harried-looking nurse came to greet him, wearing a cap and scrubs that were faintly spattered orange. 'Yes?'

'I'm...' he hesitated. How was he going to play this? He settled on the truth. 'I'm Jason Carr. I'm working with the police on the Cardiff Ripper case. One of your staff may be in danger.'

He certainly got the woman's attention. 'In danger? Who? I'll need to get security down here.'

But Jason held up his hand to halt her panicked rambling. 'It's not that easy. We don't know which of your staff it is. We only know that she's here.'

The woman's face was aghast. 'We've got over fifty staff here. How are we meant to find her?'

'One at a time. We know she called the police. We just need her to admit to it.'

The nurse looked him over. 'Well, you can't come in like that. You'll have to change.'

Jason stared at her blankly. 'Change?'

'Into scrubs.' She grabbed a pair off the nearby trolley, and a large pair of white slip-on shoes. 'Look, change in the office here. I can't let you into Theatres looking like that.'

Jason sighed impatiently, but did as he was told. They couldn't afford to waste any more time.

Amy was following Bryn's progress in A&E, the cameras absurdly easy to remote access, but he didn't seem to be making much progress. He was talking to the woman he'd identified as the most likely of her list – a Melissa Johns. She was tall, willowy, and even through the black-and-white of the camera, Amy could tell her hair was pale.

Amy paused, hand frozen in midair above her mouse. What if they were completely wrong about this woman? If you wanted to drive someone mad with jealousy, you did one of two things – you went with someone who was exactly like them, or you found someone who was the complete opposite and whom they could never hope to be.

They'd been looking for a tall skinny blonde, because that was the type of girl he killed. What if they really should've been looking for a short, curvy brunette?

Amy scanned through her list of women and found her instantly. Carla Dirusso. Dark black-brown curls, rounded face – lived with her boyfriend, who bought her tickets to the Crash and Yearn gig. And she worked in trauma theatre.

AEON chirruped. Amy flicked to another monitor – there was a new blog post, updated two minutes ago:

I'm so close freebird. Can you feel me?

She hit speed-dial #1. He answered on the second ring. 'Hello?'

'Jason, you need to get to the trauma theatre. I've found our woman – she's Carla Dirusso, and the killer's coming for her.'

Chapter 33: Flight

Carla checked over her instruments, made one last swab count, and turned to the theatre sister, who nodded that she was finished for the day.

Gratefully shrugging off the heavy sterile gown and gloves, Carla washed her hands methodically, draining away the tension of her shift. A crash on the M4 had seen three trauma victims through theatre. Though none of them were individually complex, it had been a brutal day at the office.

Carla dried her hands and left the theatre, heading back to the locker room to change. There wasn't a note on her locker, and she breathed a small sigh of relief. The other nurses hadn't told her about any more phone calls for a few days now, but maybe they were just hiding them.

She knew she should report it to someone, but he wasn't really doing anything wrong, just calling to speak to her. He never left a proper message, just said that she knew how to find him. She didn't even know his name.

She'd vaguely remembered a guy who'd approached her at a gig, yammering on about how Crash and Yearn were the twenty-first-century Lynyrd Skynyrd, acting like they were best friends. She'd been polite enough, even taking a scrap of paper off him, until Tom had come back from the bar and made it clear the guy should move on. That was when the phone calls had started. Heavy breathing, the faint strain of music in the background – and always at work. She didn't know whether to be creeped out that he knew where she worked or grateful he didn't know where she lived.

But then the photo of that girl appeared on the forum. Then another, and she'd realised that she recognised them from the paper. The missing girls in her city. While she didn't have the first idea who the guy was, she knew she had to tell the police about the pictures and that she needed to get the hell away from Cardiff.

Tom hadn't understood why she went to stay with her parents. He'd never had much patience to begin with and, with her being jumpy the past few weeks, he'd packed his things and got the hell out. She had no choice but to manage the flat by herself, and bills didn't pay themselves. She'd had to go to work, avoiding Tom in the corridors and dreading the phone calls her colleagues would deflect. And they just wouldn't shut up about the dead girls on the news.

She knew she should ring the police again, but what would she tell them? She couldn't even remember what the guy looked like, wouldn't recognise his face if he passed her in the street. Contacting the police would just make her a target – just look at that couple who had found the bodies. Their lives were all over the papers the next day. No, she just had to keep her head down until her contract ran out at the end of the month and she could move back to Haverfordwest with her family.

Carla blinked, realising she'd been staring at her locker for about five minutes without moving. She really was exhausted. At least there was a bottle of wine at home with her name on it. She took the padlock off her locker and fished out her watch, placing the delicate silver round her wrist. A present from Tom. She ran her fingers over the face. She needed a new watch.

She tugged off her scrub top, throwing it towards the laundry bin. It overshot and landed in the sink. It was not her day. Not really her week, if she was honest. She pulled off her theatre cap and ruffled her cropped dark hair back into place. The small chipped mirror inside her locker showed dark circles under her eyes, chapped lips. She needed a holiday. She needed the police to catch this killer.

The door opened behind her. Carla reached inside her locker for her sweater, surprised the room wasn't already heaving with the end of shift rush. She started to unfold the jumper – and realised someone was standing behind her.

Slowly, she turned – and screamed. There was a man in the changing room.

Carla clutched the jumper to her chest and trembled. She did recognise him after all.

'Hello, freebird.'

168

'Trauma theatre – where is it?'

This bloody place was a maze and everyone stared at him as if he was insane instead of telling him what he needed to know. The man before him now raised his eyebrows and shook off the hand Jason had attached to his arm.

'The last case is over. You sure you're not looking for neuro—'

'I need trauma!' Jason said again, increasingly desperate.

'That way,' he pointed.

Jason took off, running. He'd been racing around for five minutes trying to find this theatre, hitting dead ends and supply cupboards, but no closer to Carla Dirusso. He'd tried to call Bryn for backup but the signal was dodgy as hell – he had no idea how Amy got through.

Out of breath and panting, he pushed through a door and was met with an empty theatre, a single male nurse staring at him.

'You can't come in here. This is a clean area.'

'I'm looking for Carla Dirusso,' Jason said.

The man's reaction was immediate. His eyes hardened and he squared off, marching towards him. Confused by the reaction, Jason held his ground and met the man's eye. He didn't have time for this shit, and he had no qualms about landing the nurse on the floor of his 'clean area'.

'Are you that creep who's been ringing round here? I don't know how you got in—'

'I'm with the police.' Jason's mind was torn between excitement at having found the woman they needed – and fear that they wouldn't find her in time. 'We think Carla's in danger. Where did she go?'

The nurse backed off, a worried frown on his face. 'It's him, isn't it? She went to get changed.'

'Where?' Jason said, already impatient. He couldn't afford another wild-goose chase around theatres.

But the nurse had some sense about him and strode ahead. 'This way. She only left fifteen minutes ago.'

Jason ran after him down the corridor and it was less than a minute before they hit an unmarked locked door. The nurse punched in the code, Jason immediately pushing open the door. The locker room was empty, but there'd been a struggle. A bloody mirror was smashed on the floor, a woman's top beside it, and a nearby locker left wide open with clothes, keys and phone inside.

Jason rounded on the nurse, who was pale as death and leaning on the wall for support.

'How many ways out of here?'

'I d-don't know,' he stammered.' The nearest is the back stairs.'

'Where?' Jason demanded.

The man pointed towards a second door in the locker room.

'Other exits?'

The nurse shook his head, shaking as he tried to think. 'The main entrance, the lift, the delivery door—'

'Too many.' Jason fished his phone out of his pocket and scrolled through his contacts. 'We'll need hospital security. Which doors don't you need a pass for?'

The nurse shook his head. 'None. They're all locked. B-but he might have Carla's badge.'

Jason pressed the phone tightly to his ear, knuckles white. 'Come on, come on—' It connected. 'Bryn, our woman is Carla Dirusso and the killer's got her.' He turned to the nurse and held out his phone. 'Tell him what she looks like.'

The nurse took the phone and Jason sprinted across the locker room, leaping over the blood pool, and headed down the back stairs.

It wasn't meant to be this way.

His freebird was bleeding, the *splash-splash-splash* of red echoing up the stairs as he carried her over his shoulder, making their bid for freedom.

He'd startled her. That was all it was. She didn't recognise him in these clothes and she'd panicked. He hadn't wanted to push her, but she was screaming and people would come for them before they could get away. People wouldn't understand.

But he could bear the burden, carry his sleeping love away down the stairs to their future. He could still get them out. Destiny, fate – his muse wouldn't let them be taken like this. She believed in them. The universe believed in them.

Smiling to himself, he heard the door at the top of the stairwell slam. That was quick – too quick? His smile faded and he quickened his pace. Another plan. He needed another plan.

'It's like an adventure, freebird.'

As long as they were together. Dead or alive, they'd be together.

Bryn glowered at the man behind the security desk. 'A warrant? Are you serious?'

Without waiting for a response, he slammed his badge down on the desk and leaned forward, voice low and furious.

'One of your staff has been abducted by a man who's killed three women. If she dies because you waited for a fucking warrant, I will come for you.'

After that, security became remarkably cooperative, but it was still taking too damn long. There was backup on the way, but he would be long gone before then. Owain was hovering by the main entrance – more like a shopping centre than a hospital. The likelihood of him using that exit was slim to none, not when he had Carla's badge. To raise his blood pressure further, Bryn hadn't heard from Jason and his phone went to voicemail. Bryn tried not to think about that.

His phone buzzed and he read the text. *Nothing on CCTV. Sent pics of victim to phone. Are you with Jason? @*

She hadn't heard from him either. Shit.

'No hits on her badge since thirteen-twenty-four,' the man said finally.

'Call me when there is.' Bryn flicked him his card and walked away.

The killer was going to use a public entrance, hope to get lost in the crowd. Bryn wouldn't allow that to happen.

Jason leapt the last few steps and looked around, his breathing harsh in his ears. Where was the bastard?

The blood trail ended at the bottom of the steps. He'd cleaned up.

What now? Jason forced himself to calm down and look about him, taking in his surroundings. He appeared to be underneath the hospital, dark tunnels full of pipes and poor lighting. It would be easy to miss him down here, with enough towering supply trolleys and dark corners to conceal two people easily, even if he had both Owain and Bryn with him to search.

The tunnel stretched to the right and the left. Jason reached for his phone – and found it missing. He'd left it upstairs with that nurse. Jason slammed his hand against the wall in frustration. He'd lost him.

'Think, you bastard,' he muttered to himself, forcing himself to concentrate.

Carla was injured, probably unconscious, definitely bleeding. You couldn't just walk out of a hospital with a bleeding woman in your arms. He'd have to find something to carry her…

'Oi! Stop right there, mate!'

Jason turned, instinctively held up his hands as a man in uniform approached him.

'I'm with the cops,' he said, earnestly. 'I'm looking for the missing girl.'

The security guy relaxed – clearly, that was still privileged information.

Jason lowered his hands. 'Now, where can I find a wheelchair?'

He walked into the gift shop and glanced over the shelves. Something in green would bring out her eyes. She could wear it again, when they were alone. That would be nice.

His gaze landed on the perfect match, delicate in silk, and he picked it up, running his fingers over the material. She'd love it. She would smile and thank him, and she would understand then why he had to do this, why they had to be together. She would be grateful, so very grateful. He could already see it in her eyes.

Placing her present on the counter, he pulled out his wallet.

'That's lovely,' the shop assistant said, smiling at him with reddened lips. 'For someone special?'

'My girlfriend,' he said, and couldn't help the grin that came to his face.

The pretty assistant nodded and folded it carefully. 'Would you like a bag?'

'Please.' He watched it vanish, concealed. If she was awake, she could unwrap it. He couldn't wait to see the surprise on her face. 'Thank you.'

She took the crisp tenners he handed her without checking them. He must look trustworthy. His mother had taught him to be polite, neat. The change slid into his palm like the touch of a knife, cool metal between their hands. She was lovely, smiling at him like that, but he was taken now. It would've been nice, though.

He walked away with his present and made a beeline for the row of wheelchairs against the wall. Slipping in a pound from his change, he freed a chair and pushed it through the concourse and out into the cool evening air.

Chapter 34: In Plain Sight

Amy chewed on her thumbnail, eyes scanning the security camera feeds from the hospital. She watched Owain hovering nervously beside the jewellery shop, as if the man was about to walk straight past him. For all they knew, he already had.

Bryn had sent an acknowledgement text for the pictures, reported no use of Carla's badge. That didn't mean a lot at this time of day – anyone could walk in or out of the place. It was impossible to impose a lockdown on a hospital, and it would never shut, was always full of people, crowds and crowds. Amy's breath caught in her throat, but she forced herself to calm down, breathe deeply. She couldn't afford to panic now.

There was still nothing from Jason.

It was quarter to six. Carla had been missing for over half an hour. He could be in town by now, back to his bolthole by seven at the latest. Or he could be hiding in a linen cupboard, biding his time. Especially if Carla was dead.

Amy felt a stinging in her eyes, but blinked it away. It was her fault Carla missing. She should've seen it sooner. They could've got to her days ago and kept her safe. As it was, she was in the hands of a serial killer who was obsessed with her. That might make her more likely to be alive, but he was unpredictable, had already escalated. The condition they found her in might be worse than death.

Her phone trilled and she jumped on it. 'Jason?'

The connection was terrible, but she could make out some words.

'Amy…watch out…blood in the…chair…hear me?'

'Move somewhere with signal,' she said, typing one-handed what she had heard him say. Then the line went dead.

Amy sighed with frustration, scanning quickly over the words. Blood – was he hurt? He'd sounded all right, from what she heard, but he was also walking around with a black eye and bruised ribs from his last two street fights. Maybe Carla was bleeding. That would make her more conspicuous, certainly.

Amy nodded, the pieces clicking into place. 'A wheelchair. Good boy.'

She sent a text to alert Bryn and Owain, and sat back, suspiciously singling out everyone in a wheelchair.

Signal really was terrible. Jason stared at the bloody phone, now unable to find a single bar.

'You're better getting out into the main corridor, by a window.'

The theatre nurse still looked pale. He'd been standing exactly where Jason had left him, staring into the pool of blood like it had hypnotised him.

'Thanks. You stay here until the cops arrive. Don't let anyone disturb this.'

Jason remembered Rob Pritchard's glare – he wasn't going to take the blame for another mucked-up crime scene.

The security guys had followed him up from the lower levels. One looked like he was going to throw up all over the evidence. The other was pointedly looking only at Jason, ignoring the chaos around him.

'Cops want us down in the main entrance. You good to go?'

As Jason marched out of theatres, flanked by security and still wearing the ill-fitting blue scrubs and marked white clogs, he tried to think like the killer. If you wanted to smuggle something out, how would you do it?

While he wasn't proud of it, he had some experience in this, days of shoplifting in the city centre and walking past the security guard, bold as brass. They weren't expensive things, they weren't really even things he wanted – it was just the thrill of it, holding something stolen in your hand.

It was best if you could get a girl to go with you. Pregnant teenager didn't even draw a stare these days, and if her bump kept getting bigger, no one really paid that much notice. Of course, you couldn't talk to each other, or seem to be together at all. People were suspicious of teenagers in crowds, gang violence and all that, but if you wandered about on your own, they put you down as some loser not worth bothering with.

Better still if you could nick some clothes out of your dad's wardrobe and dress older. Nobody suspected you if you dressed like you mattered, like you had a job and money. They also handed over their alcohol and cigarettes without question – you were a guy in a jacket, and it would be insulting to ask for ID. As the tallest of all his friends, Jason had often been the one to pull this trick, though he'd borrowed Lewis's dad's suits. He wouldn't disturb the suitcase where his mam kept Dad's things.

He took the steps two at a time, the security boys struggling to keep up, but Jason barely noticed them. So, what if you were trying to steal a person? The wheelchair was obvious – there were so many people in wheelchairs around here that nobody would look twice at you. Yet Carla was young and that would attract attention, pitying looks and curiosity. Everyone would want to know how a young, pretty girl wound up in a chair. It was the gossiping nature of the human mind.

Either the killer would have to make Carla look older or explain her need for the chair – a plaster cast, maybe, or a splint. Or he would have to make himself look respectable. A doctor? No – when was the last time a doctor pushed a wheelchair? A nurse then, or a porter?

The corridor was starting to fill with people and Jason looked at his watch. It was coming up to six o'clock. Why so many people? Did they run evening clinics in this place? He turned to the security guys, who were now trying to coordinate the other men searching across the rambling hospital grounds.

'It's visiting time,' the guy said. 'Gets busy around now, then they all go by eight.'

Damn, that would make it easy for him to blend with the crowd. Jason started scanning the people around him, looking for wheelchairs and porters. He spotted one almost immediately, but they were coming up the corridor from the main entrance and the woman was clearly in her eighties, walking stick held close as her keen eyes looked out from beneath her elaborate blue rinse perm.

Jason gritted his teeth, as the press of people became too great and he was forced to step aside into the Outpatients doorway. Scores of visitors filled the corridor and Jason realised that they'd missed their window of opportunity. The hospital was full of a new set of strangers, and when they left at eight, one more pair of strangers wouldn't go amiss.

He turned to the security guy at his side. 'We need people on the main doors. We need to check everyone who goes out until all the visitors have left.'

The man sucked in air through his teeth. 'That's a lot of people. We're always going to miss some in a crowd like that.'

'We can't afford to.' If they missed him, Carla was as good as dead.

He pushed the wheelchair into the lift and pressed the button for floor 7. Others crowded into the little metal box and it groaned with the effort. By the time the automated voice had said 'Doors closing' in English and Welsh, it was time for them to open again on the first floor, where the floor and the fact the doors were opening was again announced bilingually.

When he reached the seventh floor, he had learned two phrases in Welsh and ground his back molars into dust. The wheelchair moved easily across the polished floor, his passenger weighing nothing at all, and headed onto ward C7.

'Thank you, dear.' The elderly woman got unsteadily to her feet, getting her ornate stick under her hand, and offering him a sincere smile of gratitude. 'It's a great service you offer here. You should be so proud.'

She tottered off to visit her husband and he watched her go, wondering if he'd be married in fifty years' time. Maybe to his freebird. That would be nice. But maybe she wasn't the marrying type. That would be okay too. Anything to be with her.

He wheeled the chair away from the nurses' station, pausing only to liberate a hospital gown from the linen trolley, and headed back to the lift, which was thankfully waiting and empty. He took it down to the upper ground floor and trundled the wheelchair down the deserted corridor. He manoeuvred the chair through the door of a small women's bathroom and parked it by the sinks. Then, entering the empty stall, he climbed on the toilet seat and over to the partition, to where his sleeping girlfriend was waiting for him.

It was concerning that she hadn't woken up yet, but she was still breathing, and her eyes moved ceaselessly behind her lids.

'Sweet dreams, freebird,' he murmured.

He opened the stall door and hefted her over his shoulder to place her comfortably in the wheelchair. She stirred slightly and he was pleased to think she'd soon be laughing with him, commending him on his daring rescue of the princess from the concrete castle.

He moved the old blanket that covered her modesty and put her arms through the hospital gown, careful to conceal her body from prying eyes. Then he replaced the blanket round her shoulders, arranging it to keep her warm.

'It's cold out,' he told her. 'We don't want you catching a chill, do we?'

Finally, he took the carrier bag off the back of the wheelchair and removed the beautiful silk scarf he had chosen for her. He tied it around her head, hiding her short hair and the matted blood at the back of her skull. It was a look his mother had favoured, towards the end, when she spent more time in that Velindre hospital than in their little home. When she'd moved to the hospice, she hadn't taken her scarves with her, as if she'd given up. He'd barely been able to look at her.

Making sure his love was ready for public view, he pushed her back out into the corridor and headed for the exit – and freedom.

Chapter 35: Exit Strategy

Bryn stood with Owain and Jason outside the Heath's automatic doors, eyes fixed on the emerging visitors. It was half-seven, and security informed them that most would wait until the last possible minute of visiting before leaving. That meant there would be a rush at eight, and that would be the most likely time for him to escape.

Bryn had listened to Jason's theory carefully, and agreed the boy was probably right. A porter pushing a wheelchair with a young woman, possibly disguised to look older – that would be least likely to arouse suspicion. Unfortunately, there were lots of porters and younger men pushing wheelchairs with women of the fractured, elderly or pregnant variety. Most wore heavy clothing and hats, but they checked every wheelchair, looking for Carla's distinctive green eyes and cropped black hair. It was harder to hide a pretty woman than an ugly one.

But as it grew closer to eight o'clock, Bryn's doubts started to get hold of him. As soon as the uniforms had arrived at six, he'd had them watching all the exits, armed with Carla's picture and checking every car that left the grounds. They'd caught some flack off disgruntled staff and folks trying to get home to their kids, but Bryn refused to relent. With an incapacitated passenger, a car was the most likely means of escape.

He noticed Jason getting antsy beside him, pacing with a cigarette in one hand and phone in the other. Despite the distraction, his eyes were still glued to the doors.

'You've got the other exits? No, don't bother with the cars – Bryn's got that.' He stopped, barked a short laugh. 'No, I'm not trying to be the boss, boss. I know who pays my wage.'

Jason glanced up to see Bryn watching him and grinned, gesturing at the phone as if to say 'Her indoors has got me on a tight leash.'

Bryn smiled back. He hadn't been surprised when Amy had called Jason back and hired him to be her assistant and hers alone. He had been surprised that they seemed to get on so well, that she deigned to talk to him on the phone. It had taken Bryn two attempts to get in the door, another three months before she'd look him in the eye. And here comes this cocky ex-con, charming his way into her life. Bryn would be lying to himself if he didn't admit he felt a tad envious of the boy, the ease with which he'd accomplished what it had taken Bryn months – years – of grind to achieve.

'I've got to concentrate,' Jason said. 'Yeah, I'll keep you updated. You do the same. Later.'

He hung up and returned his full attention to the door, as the crowd started to increase. Bryn could grudgingly admit that he was at least focused – he wanted this bastard as badly as the rest of them.

Bryn stepped forward immediately, as a wheelchair came towards them. 'Excuse me, sir.'

The elderly man looked up from where he'd been concentrating on pushing, out of breath. 'Can I help you, son?'

The woman in the wheelchair looked up at him, playing with her long red hair as she smiled with innocence younger than her years.

Bryn smiled back. 'Never mind, sir. Thank you.'

He saw the suspicious looks sent his way, as Jason and Owain targeted the wheelchairs, the able-bodied folk around them wondering what kind of operation this was. Bryn didn't envy the PR department's job in the morning.

But he couldn't bring himself to care about the image over the job itself – that was why he'd never make super. Because a woman's life depended on their work tonight, and he'd leave the chair-warmers to figure out the politics.

'Excuse me,' he said, and got on with the work.

It seemed the police were smarter than he'd given them credit for. They had been in the hospital soon after he'd rescued his freebird, and now they fiercely guarded the main entrance. He'd seen them when he'd brought the old lady in from her taxi and now he saw the tailback of visitors into the main corridor, the word passing back through the crowd that there were detectives at the doors and policemen inspecting all the cars.

He turned the chair around and headed back through the corridor. He remembered the route from when he'd last been in this place, when he'd first met his freebird. Smiling at the fond memory – of how she had comforted him so tenderly, how he'd known despite the pain that she was the one – he pushed the chair towards another door.

From the hospital corridor, it was easy to walk into the back of the A&E department. The treatment area required a pass, but he pushed the wheelchair straight past it and into the crowd clustered around A&E's reception. They were waiting for a nurse, a doctor, a taxi home, or just sobering up enough to tell someone exactly how they'd come to bang their head. A porter with a wheelchair went unnoticed.

The smokers who lurked a step away from the doors concealed him with their haze and their bodies, and then he was pushing his freebird past the ambulance bay and out towards the pedestrian bridge across the A48. Ideally, he would've crossed the roaring dual carriageway, but his love was still too weak to climb the stairs of the bridge and he was glad now that he'd planned for her infirmity. Love made women so weak. It was good that he was here for her.

He'd parked by the dental school, all but deserted at this time of night, and he carefully lifted his girlfriend into the front passenger seat, making sure her seat belt was securely fastened. He took the wheelchair down to the nearby bike storage, where it wouldn't be noticed until morning, and returned to the car. Wrapping his warm winter coat around him to cover his porter's shirt, he drove to the least-used exit and was annoyed to find a small queue of cars and two police officers.

Keep calm, he thought. *They don't know anything. They're just guessing you might come this way.* Destiny was with them, he was sure of it. He pulled up to where the police officers stood and wound down the window.

'Has something happened?'

'Nothing to worry about,' the officer said with forced cheerfulness, peering across him and frowning at the way his freebird lay so still. 'Is she all right?'

He looked across at her fondly, before turning back to the policeman.

'The...um, chemotherapy wears her out. She'll be all right when I get her home.'

A look of sympathy flooded the young officer's face and it took all his self-control not to smile in victory.

'Best be on your way then,' the policeman said.

He drove out of the hospital and towards home, their new life together.

Chapter 36: Frogs and Snails and Puppy Dog Tails

Her living room looked like the waiting room at the mortuary. Nobody had slept, and Jason had thrust strong filter coffee into everyone's hands instead of their usual soothing tea.

'How could we miss him?' Bryn growled, voice gravelly and despairing. Jason took his customary place behind Amy's chair, as she continued scanning through the footage from all the exits. From the moment of Carla's abduction to the following morning – when the uniforms had stopped checking cars and hospital security confirmed they'd clapped eyes on every room in the place – Amy had already looked through two hours of footage at ten different exits. They'd found an abandoned wheelchair by the entrance to the dental school and concluded that he must've left it behind as he made his escape. Forensics were all over it, but had already declared they were unlikely to get a print out of the mess of a hundred hands and winter gloves that had gripped the handles.

'We were looking in the wrong place.'

Amy ignored the wounded look Jason sent her way. It was only the truth – she wouldn't lie to save him pain.

'I think...' Owain began slowly. His brain seemed most affected by the lack of sleep. 'We looked in the right place but the killer got wise to it. We caused a queue of people into the hospital – everyone was complaining about it. He might've seen that and tried his luck elsewhere.'

It was a possibility, particularly as Amy's searching had almost brought her up to eight o'clock. If he had chosen another exit at that point, it might well be that he'd been deterred by the information that the police were checking the exits. Then again, he'd managed to drive or carry her out of the hospital grounds without being seen. It was true that the fences around the hospital weren't particularly well maintained, but a man carrying a woman over his shoulder should arouse someone's suspicion.

The hospital closed its more obvious doors earlier in the evening, so he had to know his way around to avoid the main entrance. Perhaps he worked at the hospital – Jason said that Carla was receiving threatening phone calls at work. If they were routed internally, they had no hope of tracing them, but if they came externally, switchboard should have a log, perhaps even a recording.

'There we are,' Jason said quietly, as she cycled back to the main entrance feed. 'We didn't miss anyone, Amy.'

She believed he believed that, but she needed to see it for herself. Still, in deference to his pride, she set the main entrance feed to one side while she examined the others. He was paying just as much attention as she was, determined that his theory was correct, that the killer had planned to get Carla out at the end of visiting. She was just about to give up on the ever-changing crowd of smokers outside A&E and flick back to the concourse when she saw the wheelchair.

'There—there!' Jason pointed over her shoulder as she froze the picture.

It was difficult to make out faces at this angle, particularly with the cigarette smoke in the air, but the woman in the chair appeared unconscious. She had something on her head, a bandana maybe, and the man bending over the handles of her chair wore a porter's uniform. He'd walked out of the hospital and they'd been looking in the opposite direction.

'Fuck,' Jason said, echoing her thoughts perfectly, as Bryn and Owain joined them at the desk. They stared in silence at the image for a moment, and Amy felt the sharp knife of failure cut through her chest.

'There should've been someone on those doors,' Bryn said, a tinge of desperation in his voice. 'Where were the bastards?'

But Owain grimaced. 'We redeployed them to the back entrance. We didn't have enough bodies to do both – Friday night.'

'Fucking drunks.'

Bryn pulled out his mobile and called through to the station. They were meant to be sleeping, taking a couple of hours to rest and recharge before rejoining their colleagues on the case, but they were too wired to sleep – and they'd come to her, looking for answers. She had none.

'We need to look at Carla Dirusso,' Amy said abruptly, pulling up all the pages she'd found after they'd realised she was the woman on the phone. 'He knows her, he's obsessed with her. If we find out everything about her, we can find him.'

'Carla's parents are at the station,' Owain said. 'Her brothers are on their way. She used to live with a boy called Tom Davies, but we're having trouble finding him. They think he went back to his parents, but guess how many Davieses live in Canton.'

'I know that area,' Jason said. 'I can find him.'

Owain shot him a sceptical look, while Amy quietly panicked.

'Be careful,' she blurted. 'You're not Canton's favourite face right now.'

'In trouble again?' Bryn said, hanging up and returning to the huddle around her chair.

Jason flashed him a quick smile, drawing a crease through the purple-yellow bruise of his black eye. 'Nothing I can't handle.'

'They're sending a profiler down from London,' Bryn said. 'I'll need everything you have so far, Amy.'

She nodded, copying her research folder and database to a USB drive before handing it off to him. She grabbed a yellowing Post-it from her desk drawer and wrote out a series of letters and numbers, pausing only once or twice to draw the code from her memory. 'Here – the password to unlock the files.'

Bryn looked at the device and password as if they were going to bite him. 'You don't mind me having this?'

'It changes every two days. AEON will update it now that I've removed files – she's paranoid like that.'

She stroked the edge of the keyboard. AEON had a life and personality all of her own. Amy had no doubt that, when the robot revolution came, AEON would be leading the charge, followed closely by the Googleplex.

Bryn just looked at her as if she'd grown an extra head, and put the USB drive in his pocket. 'When you find anything, call me. My PC is on – just do that remote thing where you put stuff on there.'

Amy nodded, already extending a link to Bryn's clunky old work computer that was somehow still running Windows XP. She always suspected that he'd refused to update, having got used to the OS, and she couldn't say she blamed him. There was a reason she ran Linux.

Bryn and Owain showed themselves out, and Amy felt a wave of tiredness wash over her. She was always tired, the heavy feeling in her limbs just part of life, but this was pushing her beyond the limits of her meagre reserves.

A heavy hand settled on her shoulder. 'You should get some sleep,' Jason said.

Amy made a vague noise of assent and shuffled over to the sofa, curling up at one end.

When Jason went into the kitchen to wash up, she pulled out her iPad and browsed Carla's Facebook again. Welsh mother and Italian father, two older brothers, raised out in Haverfordwest, the wilderness of West Wales. Moved to Swansea, the nearest big town, and qualified as a Registered General Nurse in 2011. Recent breakup with Tom Davies – though she'd tried hard to erase all evidence of said relationship. However, Zuckerberg kept everything, and Amy was soon able to find exactly which Tom Davies she'd been seeing. He didn't go on there much, and he didn't list his relatives or employment details. He did, however, text update and that made her life a lot easier.

An iPad was not designed for this kind of work, but she was comfortable on the sofa, half-listening to Jason's off-key humming in the kitchen. She set up the trace remotely through AEON and rested her eyes for a minute.

Amy woke to AEON's insistent beeping and sat up, belatedly catching her iPad as it slid off her lap. The washing machine was whirring in the kitchen and Jason was dozing in his armchair. Amy glanced at her wristwatch – two o'clock. She'd lost four hours of work time.

Prising herself off the sofa, she padded over to AEON and examined her findings. She'd struggled to find Tom because he'd been moving in and out of dodgy signal areas, but she'd finally narrowed him down to a ten-metre radius in Canton.

Amy glanced over at Jason. She didn't want to wake him, but he'd said he wanted to do this. On the other hand, she could just send it to Bryn and have Owain do it. Jason would never be any the wiser and he wouldn't have to go to Canton, where people hated him and might hurt him. In fact, that sounded like the best plan.

'Have you found him?'

Jason's eyes were open and he was looking at her keenly. A coarse beard coated his cheeks, dark fuzz visible on his shaven head, and his black eye gave him the look of a hard man. He stood up, stretched and wrinkled his nose at the stink of his clothes. He looked at her screen and grinned. 'Yeah, I know that street. I'll change at mine and head over. You need anything?'

'Some bread,' she said, suddenly desperate to stall him. This man could be a killer. She didn't want to send Jason into danger, not to a place with sparse cameras when the police were occupied elsewhere.

'On my way back.'

Amy handed him a picture of Tom's face, Welsh Dragon painted on his cheek, and Jason's fingers brushed hers as he took it. 'He could be dangerous.'

But her words fell on deaf ears, the spark of excitement already alive in his eyes. He missed the thrill of the fight, she realised. Running with his gang, flipping off the police, getting into it with other boys. And, this way, he got to do it with the protection of the law – Amy's protection.

Amy watched him go, sick to her stomach, before heading to the shower to wash away the stench of fear.

Chapter 37: She's a Lady

It seemed like the entire police force was in the detectives' office.

The open-plan office was sterile white and glass, usually haunted only by a few unlucky detectives at this time on a Saturday. Now it was thrumming with activity, a mixture of plainclothes detectives and uniform cops talking and typing and drinking strong coffee. The whiteboards were out, covered in a battered map of Cardiff with the residences, workplaces and murder scenes of the girls spread across them. One of the uniforms was adding Carla to the board.

'Mark her differently,' Bryn said to her. 'She's not like the others.'

The room hushed at his arrival, as his super came over with a look of pity and disappointment. Bryn hated that look.

'What have we got so far?' Roger Ebbings asked, taking in the boards and Bryn's dishevelled appearance.

Bryn held up the little toggle Amy had given him, and one of the boys in tech took it off him with the password and loaded it up on the smartboard. Hundreds of images unfolded – Jason's scene photographs mixed with drunken Facebook snaps and CCTV footage from the Heath. There were spreadsheets, documents of notes in Amy's rambling style, and half a dozen examples of highly illegal data mining that could get Amy sent down for ten-plus years. Thankfully, the super looked more inclined to hug him than prosecute his source.

'This is a good place to start.' Roger dropped his voice, stepped closer to Bryn. 'Is she working on anything else?'

'She's tracking down Tom Davies. I think we'll have him down here by evening.'

Roger stroked his greying beard thoughtfully. 'Take the boys off Tom then. No point covering the same ground twice.'

Bryn was barely listening, his tired eyes scanning the evidence before him. He was out of his depth with a serial killer who was snatching girls out of their houses, from the Cardiff streets by night. He knew where he was with kids like Jason, the lads of the old Tiger

Bay, who wanted to be part of something and nicked cars to prove their devotion.

Bryn was a street copper hauled through the ranks to detective, only to find there were bright young things chasing his tail, with their gas chromatography and their data capture devices. Give him a wiretap and a professional grass any day. That was why he had Amy, to close the gap between a man pushing sixty and a cop like Owain, who could analyse fingerprints on his phone.

'All this and you haven't caught him yet?'

Bryn turned to see an immaculately dressed black woman in her fifties striding into the office. Everything about her screamed 'profiler' and Roger's unease proved it.

'Bryn, Dr. Eleanor Deaver from Scotland Yard. Doctor, this is DI Bryn Hesketh – he's been working the case.'

'Yes, I've been kept apprised of your...efforts.'

Eleanor looked at him with the same pity and disappointment as his colleagues, her silver bob emphasising the sharp cut of her cheekbones and her disapproving frown. Approaching the board, she adopted the attitude of a woman making the best of a bad job. She reminded him of his wife just before their divorce.

'I'm surprised you didn't call me sooner.' She removed her laptop from her briefcase, glancing up at the smartboard. 'Though this is more than I expected. Your tech department should be commended. Though data's all very well, without extrapolation and analysis, it's largely worthless.'

The mood in the office, already strained, took on a hostile air. Strangers were never welcome in a police department, regardless of their supposed skill, but her BBC English accent in a Welsh city added that extra flavour of distaste.

'Our boys did their best,' Roger said. Bryn coughed. 'And our girls, of course.'

Eleanor's expression sobered. 'I'm afraid it wasn't good enough this time, Superintendent. Shall we see where we've got to? I'll need a cup of tea for this.'

Detective Sergeant Owain Jenkins, reduced to teaboy, fetched her a drink while she reviewed Amy's work and Bryn's case notes.

'You have a pet hacker, Detective,' Eleanor said, and Bryn thought she might be impressed, perhaps even envious. 'His information is useful and his conjecture reasonable for an amateur.'

'Her information,' Bryn corrected, more than a little gleeful.

Dr. Deaver just took his sniping in her stride. 'Hers, indeed. From this, we can certainly throw up the basics.'

Owain took up a marker and wrote down Eleanor's profile as she dictated around the plum in her mouth.

Single, white male.

Low socioeconomic class, basic education (exemplar: blog posts).

Linked to Carla Dirusso, possibly romantically, probably marginally.

Likely to have met Kate Thomas, Melody Frank and Laurie Fox in person.

Motive: to make Carla jealous with a type (tall, blonde, slim).

Stalked his victims (exemplar: Melody's night out, Carla's phone calls).

Likely resident in South Cardiff.

Possible university connection.

'The university?' Bryn asked. 'We've already gone up all the alleyways on that one – no lectures in common, shared one or two classmates who they never spoke to. Hell, there was only one day a week when they were both in class.'

'They're all students.' There was a hint of stubbornness in her voice, as if she had gripped this idea with both hands and was unwilling to leave go. 'Humanities students, no less. Maybe they all frequented the same library?'

'They didn't have common friends, common interests,' Bryn said dismissively. 'They spent more time in the pub than anywhere else.'

'It's a connection,' Eleanor said firmly. 'It may only be a trivial thing – he may only have met them once to set his sights on them. Try the libraries, try the bartenders at the student union.'

Owain ran off to scramble some uniforms to start the daunting set of interviews, while Bryn looked at Eleanor with grudging respect. Perhaps he'd set aside the university connection too quickly. These girls weren't found in libraries – they had part-time jobs, wide social circles. They just happened to be at university. But the psychologist had a point – it only took one meeting for a man to fixate on a girl.

'I agree that the reservoir is largely irrelevant – it seems merely convenient, like his choice of murder weapon. Like he never means to kill them until it comes down to the moment.' Eleanor's dark eyes glazed over, her full lips moving soundlessly.

Bryn shivered. Profiling scared him – getting into the killer's head like that. It had to do something to you.

'Melody's murder revealed the most forethought, fetching her from the city centre and booking a hotel. He was no doubt the Mr. Dixon who checked out early, paid cash and never looked at the camera.'

'We checked all the others,' Owain confirmed, returning from his little exercise in management.

He was hanging off Eleanor's every word. Clearly, he'd found someone else to worship. If Owain had his way, they would install Amy and people like Eleanor in a sleek glass office, of which Owain was master, and solve international crime like some kind of James Bond outfit.

'The key to finding this man will be Carla Dirusso,' Eleanor said, echoing what Amy had said about six hours earlier. 'We need to know everything about her – how many boyfriends she's jilted, what she liked to eat, where she shopped.'

Bryn's computer beeped at him. He pushed his chair over to the desk and opened another three pages of notes. Eleanor looked over his shoulder with interest, and Bryn grinned.

Usually Tesco, but M&S as a treat.

'My people are on it,' he said.

Chapter 38: The Birdcage

Her head hurt.

Carla moaned and turned her head away from the sunlight filtering through the blinds. Had it been tequila? Tom would be so angr—

She sat up, suddenly awake, a roll of nausea in her stomach. She'd been at work. That man…he'd hit her. Carla reached for the back of her head, wincing as she probed the lump there. Acceptable level of haematoma, didn't seem to be a fracture. How long had she been out?

She wobbled to her feet and went to the window, her head hammering. Through the blinds, she could see up to the street – a converted basement then. It wasn't too bright outside, maybe early morning? Evening? Had she been asleep for a whole day? She could've died from a concussion that bad.

She scratched at the back of her neck, where a label had started to itch. She was wearing a hospital gown and the scrub trousers she'd worn in theatre. How had he got her out of there? How had no one noticed? She clenched her fists, angry at the world for abandoning her, at Tom for not being at home to notice she was gone. Would anyone even realise she'd disappeared? She had three days off and her mam wouldn't be too bothered if she didn't call until after the weekend. She had no plans, no friends expecting her out – it could be Tuesday, Wednesday before anyone even thought to look for her. She had to escape.

She tried the door – locked, solid oak. She wasn't getting through that. The window was also locked, barred on the outside. Not uncommon in the rougher parts of Cardiff, no one would even blink at it. The room itself was a mausoleum, thick with dust and the lingering scent of lavender. It was sparsely furnished, a bed with a knitted woollen coverlet and a few pictures of a woman and her young son, taken at least twenty years ago.

Carla picked up one of the pictures – was this woman one of his victims? Or had that smiling little boy grown up to be a cold-blooded killer?

There must be something to break down the door, she thought, opening drawers to find anything to help her. But they were full of an older woman's clothes, her makeup and jewellery, now flaking and tarnished. Carla threaded her fingers through the cool links of a thick silver chain. Who was this woman? Why wasn't she here? Was she dead? Had she slept in a dead woman's bed?

She heard someone move upstairs and stilled. A door opened and closed, and then there were footsteps, louder, as if someone was coming down the stairs. Carla shoved the drawers closed and lay back on the bed, finding the still-warm dent her body had left behind. Could this be her chance to escape? Her head still pounded and she felt sick to her stomach. No, she'd have to wait until she was stronger, until she could take him.

The door opened and she struggled to keep her eyes closed, her breathing even. He didn't approach her, just stayed where he was, his breaths coming faster. It took every fibre of control not to tremble, to whimper, to give herself away. After what seemed like hours, but could only have been seconds, the door closed again, the key scraping in the lock.

Carla opened her eyes to stare at the ceiling. She needed a plan.

By the time Jason escaped his mother's insistent need to fuss and feed him, it was four o'clock and already getting dark. He walked into the centre, pulling his jacket around him as his breath came out in dense white clouds.

The frosted leaves turned the pavement into a death trap, but his old trainers gripped well enough to stop him making an arse of himself. Christmas shoppers were already flying away home, the city tense with the spectre of the missing girl. Gwen had begged him to stay, had already banned Cerys from leaving, but Jason insisted he'd be fine, that the man wasn't out for him and he could handle himself.

He texted Amy as he walked, asking her to update him on Tom's location. The bloke wasn't likely to be in the same place as he was two hours before, especially if he was avoiding the cops.

They were assuming this was someone Carla didn't know, but what if she knew about the forum posts because her boyfriend had uploaded them from the sofa beside her? They'd broken up about the same time as the murders started. Sure, there were the heavy breathing calls to her at work, but maybe he just wanted to spook her? And he was a theatre porter – he had the knowledge to get around the place, and the uniform.

Something didn't sit right about it, though, and Jason wondered if there was something else going on with Tom Davies. Maybe he was into something he shouldn't be and was worried at the police sniffing about his life. Maybe he just figured that the abduction of his ex-girlfriend would look bad on him, and he was right. Bryn had wanted to send down a couple of extra cops to Canton, but Jason had put him off. Cops were the fastest way to send the boy underground, with all his friends and family playing dumb about it.

From under the shadow of the Millennium Stadium, he emerged opposite the walled-in greenery of Bute Park before continuing on across the river and into Canton. Here, the pound shops rubbed shoulders with bohemian cafés and Indian restaurants, and Jason caught a whiff of marijuana floating alongside the strong smell of curry.

Jason walked past the turn for Dylan's garage, which was tucked away down a residential street, occupying the place where a couple of terraced houses once stood. One of the first things Jason had done when he got out was help Dylan repaint the shabby signage to reflect a reputable business. A lick of paint could cover a multitude of sins. Jason felt guilty that he hadn't given his mate more time recently. But he'd understand – Dylan had three sisters. He'd get that Jason was trying to keep their streets safe for the girls.

Jason was just the man for this job and he was determined not to let Amy down. He'd been some use, sure, but he'd also blundered upon the bodies in the reservoir with a spectacular media backlash. He'd focused all their efforts on the hospital concourse, leaving the A&E entrance wide open for the killer to escape. He had to make amends.

His phone vibrated in his pocket and he checked it.

Lost him. @

That was just great – defeated by Cardiff's bloody awful phone signal. He was deep inside Canton, deep into Stuart Williams's territory. He needed to find Tom and get out. This wasn't the time for heroics, no matter how much he felt this was on him.

He approached the street where Tom had last been and found not a lot on it, except a couple of closed shops and a café. Making for the café, he stepped inside and immediately sussed out the kind of café it was – local, greasy and hostile. You didn't order a skinny chai latte in a place like this. You didn't stay long if you wanted to leave with your wallet still in your pocket.

The man behind the counter looked at him like he was scum, but with a trace of fear. Jason caught a glimpse of his reflection in the grease-stained window. He looked bloody awful, bruises blossoming and his old fat lip making him look more boxing champion than police lackey.

'We're closing,' the man said.

'I won't keep you. I'm looking for Tom Davies. Heard he came by earlier.'

Jason watched the man carefully, saw from his eyes and the quick look at the two lads sitting at the back that he knew exactly who Tom Davies was and wasn't going to give him up any time soon.

'Doesn't ring a bell. Lot of people come through here.'

Jason doubted that was true, given the state of the tables and the stale Welsh cakes in the glass case, but he didn't let on.

'See, he said I'd see him today. Had something for me. It reflects badly on the boy's mates if he can't pay his way, doesn't it?'

He glanced over at the lads in the corner, who looked scared shitless, much to Jason's satisfaction. However, the man behind the counter held firm, clearly used to this kind of intimidation in his establishment. 'We don't know no Tom Davies.'

'I heard the police are looking for him,' Jason said casually, and noted the sharp inhale from a boy behind him. 'You'd better hope I find him before they do.' Still nothing. Jason had to admire their loyalty, but he needed to find this boy. 'I see how it is. I guess I'd better pay a call to Mrs. Davies then.'

He headed for the door. Had to look like he meant it, he thought, hoping the boy had a mother who gave a damn.

'Round the back of that arts place,' the man said, able to square his betrayal with his conscience now that Jason had invoked poor Mrs. Davies. 'They all go there.'

Jason decided he was definitely out of touch if the kids were going to the arts centre, but nodded and left without another word. To thank the man would be callous and, despite what folk might say, he had no desire to hurt people.

He made his way down the street, planning his next move. He had to persuade Tom it was in his best interests to come with him to the nick – or, as a last resort, to Amy's. There were too many reasons for the boy to be in hiding, but no one had been surprised that Tom owed a man like Jason money, so there was one obvious answer.

The arts centre was a nice modern building completely out of place in the back streets of Canton, but Jason found that a back alley was still a back alley. He peered into the gloom, wishing he'd thought to bring a blade. The best defence was offensive weapons, or something like that.

But it was empty, just old flyers and a couple of stray Coke cans. Bloody hell, he'd been conned. He had to get back to the café before the guy warned—

Jason saw a flicker at the end of the alley. With a crack of pain, the world went black.

Jason hadn't called. Amy needed to instil in him the importance of checking in with one's employer and why it was necessary for said employer's sanity. Particularly when the blockheaded boy was on the hunt for a murder suspect in a dodgy part of town. She should've insisted Owain go with him, but judging by the fact Bryn wasn't answering her texts, she guessed the police might be otherwise occupied.

She'd sent them her information on Carla as she'd found it, but it was mundane, bordering on tedious. Carla's social life had tailed off, most likely due to her breakup and the harassing phone calls rather than a newly discovered passion for World of Warcraft. Though she had spent a lot of time on Candy Crush Saga, which couldn't really be classed as a hobby.

Carla had nothing in common with the other girls. She'd graduated years ago, had no mutual friends, and had been to Koalas once eighteen months ago for a friend's hen do. Bryn had relayed the profiler's suspicion about the university and Amy admitted it had merit, but Carla had no connection to the place.

Of course, the others were chance victims – he happened to encounter them while he was looking for a type. Carla was his main obsession; he might have met her somewhere entirely different. Perhaps at the hospital?

Medical records were notoriously difficult to access, mainly because of the NHS's reluctance to acknowledge the twenty-first century. However, their bookings system was networked, so, while the ins and outs of a patient's diagnosis and treatment were hard to come by, a trip to the Sexual Health clinic was pretty telling.

Amy connected her server through the laptop of a senior professor who shunned the idea of hospital computers and, it seemed, personal firewalls. A lot of people had the wrong idea about hacking. Hacking wasn't about having a skeleton key that opened all the locks. It was finding that small bathroom window round the back that nobody ever remembered to close.

Cross-referencing all admissions to trauma and orthopaedics in the past year with the university employment register was an epic, time-consuming task, but AEON merely beeped indignantly and got to work. The process would run quietly in the background, but Amy suspected it might not complete until the following day. Minutes mattered in this case – the chance of finding a missing person alive after forty-eight hours was slim to none, and when this man realised the woman he idolised didn't love him? The repercussions were likely to be deadly.

Amy shivered, drawing her blanket closer to her. She couldn't remember the last time she'd slept in her bed, washed her hair or eaten something that wasn't toast or biscuit-based. But those thoughts just brought her back to Jason and she looked at her watch: 20:47. He'd last texted her at 16:12, asking for an updated location on Tom Davies, but the signal had vanished. Since then, she'd received nothing as his phone bobbed in and out of the murky signal haze that was central Cardiff.

Suddenly, her phone rang – it was Jason. She hooked him through her tracking system and picked up.

'Where are you?' she said, cursing the anxious tremble in her voice.

'I...I don't know.' He sounded dazed, hurt.

Amy willed the tracker to work, as she clutched her phone to her ear. 'What do you see?'

Another pause, but she could hear something – the rustle of cloth, Jason's low groan.

'Jason!' she said sharply. 'What do you see?'

'He's coming back,' he slurred and there was a harsh scraping sound that forced her to tear the phone away from her ear.

'Jason? Jason, what was that?'

Sound filtered back in and she heard a voice that could be Jason's, but quieter – farther away? *He pushed the phone away*, her numb brain supplied. *He's keeping the connection open so you can find him.*

She'd tell him, when he got home, that he didn't need to take that kind of risk, that she'd already traced him within ten seconds to an area the size of a king-size bed. He was watching too many movies. He was putting his life in danger because of *CSI*.

One voice got louder, louder, louder, until the line went dead with a crunch. Dead tech. Someone had found the phone.

Amy couldn't breathe. The air was close and thick, her pulse pounding in her neck, her hands trembling on the keys. He was dead. He was dying. She was useless. She couldn't help him.

But if she lost control now, if she vanished into this panic attack, he would definitely die. She would have failed him completely and utterly. She couldn't let that happen. Black spots danced across her vision, but she fought to push them away, breathe deeper. She had to keep it together for another thirty seconds.

Amy used her emergency line and calmly, coolly told police control that her assistant had been kidnapped. And then, with the panic running wild in her veins, she waited.

Chapter 39: Run, Baby, Run

The house was still and quiet. He thought it was peaceful, tranquil. It was time to check on his guest.

She had been sleeping for hours, too many hours, and he worried about her head. If she hadn't woken up by morning, he'd have to take her back to the hospital, leave her with them and return for her when she was better. He didn't think he'd hit her that hard. He'd been so nervous about their first proper date, had struck without thinking. He couldn't bear to have hurt her when she didn't deserve it.

He went down the stairs to his mother's room, the only place that was worthy of his freebird until she was better, until her wedding day. It would probably be a small ceremony. Her family would likely disapprove, stay away. It was better that way. They could elope, go to Gretna Green – they didn't need their permission.

The paper thought he'd stolen her, thought she was missing. Maybe it was for the best if they went far away, to France or Ireland. They were Catholic there but that would be okay. He would do anything if it meant he could be with her. He knew she felt the same.

He turned the key in the lock, fingers shaking with excitement. If she was awake, maybe they would share their first kiss. He'd dreamt of it, felt himself grow hard at the thought of it, the way she would taste. How soft she'd be under his hands, how she'd smile as he came inside her, how she'd want to be owned.

He pushed open the door – and she wasn't there. Something heavy landed on his head and he fell, his freebird pushing past him and running up the stairs, away. Slowly, he got to his feet, clutching his bleeding head.

That bitch, that vile little slut. How dare she strike him! How ungrateful could she be? He'd saved her from that poor excuse for a man, that Neanderthal who was always drunk and pawed at her hips like a flasher in the street.

He stumbled up the stairs after her, could hear her shaking the front door, trying to pull it off its hinges. His mother had taught him never to leave the key in the front door – that was how thieves got to it. The best place for it was around your neck, and he'd always kept it there, just like she said.

As he approached the door, she was trying to smash through the glass with a plant pot. She rounded on him, brandishing the pot in his direction, but he just picked up the coat stand and cracked it over her jaw. She screamed, clutching her face and sinking to the floor, all the fight gone out of her. Discipline. Rules. That was the only way she would learn.

He knelt beside her and ran his fingers through her hair. She shook and tried to move away, but he held her close, running soothing hands over her arms.

'I know you didn't mean it, did you? But this is what happens, I'm afraid, when you don't do what's best for us. It's all about us now, freebird.'

Her cries faded to soft whimpers and he picked her up reverently, carrying her back to her room. She needed to rest if they were going to go away. Far away.

'Fuck off, Stuart.'

Jason's head was killing him. If Lewis could see him now, he would be laughing his arse off, telling him what a pansy he was for getting himself knocked out like a girl, held captive in a bloody junkie squat. As it was, Jason was struggling to focus on which Stuart Williams was the real one and keeping his mam's roast pork in his stomach.

Stuart wasn't alone. He'd brought a couple of his mates and, in the corner, the disgusting heap of what had been Tom Davies but now thought he was a Powerpuff Girl. The man was a million miles away from the Facebook picture Amy had handed him, the powerful rugby boy out for a good time. He was pale like sour milk, bright blue veins standing out on his hands and arms. His skin was taut across his bones, gaunt like he'd lost too much weight too quickly. But the twitching alone would've given him away, the way he scratched at his arms as if there was something crawling through them. Jason knew a cokehead when he saw one.

The defiant bastard in the café must've ratted Jason out, sent him to that alley and told the boys where to find him. Of course, Tom bloody

Davies would be under the eye of Stuart. Of course they knew each other. That gave Stuart perfect access to Tom's pretty girlfriend. *Shit.*

Jason scowled up at Stuart, blinking away the trail of blood from above his eye. Scalp wounds bled a lot. He must look like an extra from a horror set.

'What do you want?' he ground out.

His eyes darted to the smashed remains of his phone. Amy was good – Amy had his position. She could probably still trace him with the phone's innards spilled out, though hopefully her cavalry would arrive before his insides were also decorating the floor.

'I want your sister,' Stuart said. Jason resisted the urge to fly at the bastard. He stayed on the ground, kneeling, despite his humiliation. 'She's angry with me right now, but she's a pretty good lay.'

Jason threw a clumsy punch, only to find his arms restrained and his lip stinging. When had they moved? He wasn't paying close enough attention. Damn blood was in his eyes.

'Why'd you come sniffing around our boy Tom anyway?' Stuart said, as Tom pushed himself further into the corner, batting away unseen spirits who ventured too close to his nose. 'What's he ever done to you?'

'Kidnapped his girl, didn't he?' Jason said with a grin, spitting blood on the floor. 'The police are looking for him. Don't you watch the news? Now they'll be looking for you too.'

Stuart looked at him as if he were mad, before casting a nervous glance at Tom. One of the boys holding him wrenched Jason's shoulder back, and Jason bit down on his cry of pain.

'He was with us yesterday, weren't he?' the bloke said. 'Tom don't come down no more, see? Stays in his little party land all day and night.'

If Jason had been in full possession of his wits, he'd have realised that Tom wasn't the killer the minute he laid eyes on him. The boy was whacked out, the kind of whacked out that requires days of dedication to the art. Jason and Lewis had once spent a weekend ripping through whatever money could buy – he didn't remember much about it, but he knew his face had looked just like Tom Davies's in the mirror Monday morning.

There was no way Tom could've been sober enough to smuggle Carla out of the hospital. Even if he'd had the brainpower to do it, he would've drawn too much attention with his twitching and conversations with the fae folk.

But Stuart would have access to his mate's stuff, including his uniform. Including his girl? Jason wanted to beat the information out of the sonuvabitch, but he couldn't even get up off the floor.

'So, you thought you'd come turn our boy Tom in to the coppers, did you? Knew you were a fucking snitch.' Stuart's eyes glittered at the prospect of meting out punishment to a grass.

Shit, there wouldn't be anything for Amy to find. His mam wouldn't be able to identify his remains. And Cerys would probably bring this bastard as a date to his funeral.

'You don't want to do this,' he managed, as the chatty bloke pinned him bodily to the floor. His partner pulled Jason's right arm straight above his head and held him at the wrist.

Stuart sauntered into his field of view, grinning as he swung a length of piping up onto his shoulder. 'Are you ready? No? Too fucking bad.'

He brought the pipe down on Jason's arm with a sickening crack. Jason screamed, the agony of his arm coming apart followed by a wave of nausea that threatened to choke him.

'Listen, listen,' Tom said from the corner, voice full of childish wonder.

'There's no time for your games, Tommy,' Stuart said, frustrated. 'Leave us to do our work, yeah?'

'Nee-naw, nee-naw,' Tom sang to himself.

Stuart rounded on him, screeching: 'Will you shut the fuck up?'

But Jason laughed, a slight edge of hysteria in his voice. 'Can't you hear it, Stuart?' he gasped, tears of pain and mirth in his eyes.

Stuart listened.

'Shit, let's get out of here,' he said.

His boys released Jason but there was already someone banging down the front door. Too late to run.

'Nee-naw,' Jason muttered, fading away to the sound of sirens.

Amy sat immobile on the sofa, staring at her phone, waiting for it to ring.

She'd thought she was dying. Everything was hot and heavy, like a smothering blanket. Blood rushed to her face and neck, and she felt her throat close. This was the end. Heart racing, air thinning – as Jason lay dying, so she would die, a sympathy death.

But it went away, by vague degrees it went away. She blinked away the sparkles and took a deep breath. Another. She was still alive. Jason was still dying.

Once she'd found something like control, her fingers flew over the keys, urging AEON to locate a security camera feed in the area. The nearest was two streets over and told her sweet FA. Frustrated, she slammed her fist down on the desk, before activating the trace on Bryn's mobile. He was moving through the city, but nowhere near Canton.

She sent him a text: *Find Jason. @*

It buzzed back within a minute. Owain must be driving. It said simply: *On way.*

Amy's heart pounded – was no one with him yet? Had no one got to him? People who smashed phones also smashed faces – the escalation of violence, the London Riots, the burning of books. Why wasn't Bryn there yet?

She sent: *Hurry. @*

A reply: *Uniform on scene. Boy lives.*

Amy sank back into her chair, dizzy from the exertion of her heart, the pounding of fear in her arteries. But there were many states between alive or dead. He could be in a coma, head in pieces like Humpty Dumpty, or bleeding internally. He could need surgery. He could need a nursing home. Or he might still make it to the crematorium before he turned twenty-four.

Her thoughts churned round and round her head, barely stopping for a moment. She imagined everything that could happen, a hundred horrible deaths, unable to unsee them. Her leg started to bounce, like it had when Lizzie first left her, an outward sign of her inner turmoil. How could he do this to her? How could he make her hurt so much?

She collapsed on the sofa then, and waited. Her phone stubbornly did not ring, as the minutes ticked by. Was Bryn afraid to tell her the truth? Was he afraid she would take all the pills she kept carefully hidden in the flat? The ones she took when the racing thoughts and pounding heart grew too much and she just had to sleep, if only for a few dreamless hours. She thought to take one now, but her hands were trembling so much, she didn't think she could even unscrew the cap.

The phone burst to life and broke through her haze. She seized it, almost dropped it and finally answered. 'Bryn?'

'He's all right. Banged his head and the paramedics think he's broken his arm, but he's talking to us.'

The words washed over her, soothing like medicine, and she swallowed. 'Okay.'

'Also, we've got Tom Davies.'

Of course they did. Of course Jason would've done as she asked, even if it meant splitting his head in two. She resisted the urge to laugh hysterically. Loyal to a fault.

Amy tore her thoughts away from Jason to remember the missing woman. 'Carla?'

'Nothing.' Bryn's frustration was evident despite the distance between them. 'And Tom doesn't look like he's in any state to tell us. I've got the uniforms tearing the place apart.'

Amy crossed and uncrossed her fingers. *Let this all be for something, please.*

'And I'm not sure if it's the concussion talking, but our boy reckons the guy who battered him could be involved. Stuart Williams.'

'He gave Jason a black eye,' Amy heard herself say. 'Cerys's boyfriend.' She could hear shouting and swearing in the background, the sounds of a disgruntled arrested perp.

'Who's Cerys?'

Amy heard Bryn flicking through his notebook, and put him out of his misery.

'Jason's sister. Eighteen. Left school, no job. String of Facebook relationships. Out a lot. Doesn't drive.'

There was silence at the other end of the phone. 'Do you research all your assistants' sisters so thoroughly?'

She heard a teasing note in his voice, and felt the tension in her shoulders start to ebb away. They had a suspect in custody. Bryn was joking. Jason was going to be okay.

'I want to talk to him,' she said.

Bryn seemed to be wading through a crowd, as it took several noisy seconds before she heard Jason's voice.

'Amy?' He sounded like he was in pain and half-asleep, but he definitely sounded alive.

'What happened?' she said, phone pressed against her ear.

'Pipe,' he bit out and she winced, cradling her own arm to her chest. 'Gotta go to A&E. I'll be back after.'

'All right,' she said.

Bryn took the phone back, said something about the profiler, but she wasn't really listening.

'Keep me in the loop,' she said and hung up, curling up on her side, waiting for Jason to return.

Chapter 40: Four Walls and a Light Bulb

Jason balanced on the edge of a gurney in A&E, contemplating his splinted arm with a sense of shame. He'd seen the pictures of the break, a neat black line through white bone. The A&E doctor had placed him in this contraption, wedged it under his armpit and secured it at his elbow, with more padding than a model's bra.

His head was a mess, throbbing and aching. They'd put him through a CT scanner and told him nothing was bleeding or broken, but that he needed to stay in overnight for observations. When he'd insisted on leaving, they'd asked him who was at home and he'd told them he was going to his boss's house. That was when they'd called for Bryn.

The detective shuffled in, looking like he'd aged twenty years and hadn't slept for a week.

'Shouldn't you do what they say, son?'

But Jason was already sliding off the trolley. 'Amy's expecting me.'

He took a moment to get his feet under him. The splint made him unbalanced, awkward, and he'd lost his dominant hand. He must look bloody awful, because Bryn seemed genuinely concerned.

'Is Amy's really the best place for you? What about your mam? She'll be worried.'

Jason ran a hand over his stubbled head, dislodging flecks of dried blood. He didn't want to look in the mirror.

'What she doesn't know...' he mumbled, shuffling his feet guiltily. They'd offered to call his next of kin, but he'd shaken his head, then stopped when that made him feel like he was about to retch up his stomach. No need to worry his family over this – his mother would just lock him up for a year. As long as he told her before it ended up on the morning news, he'd escape a bollocking. Probably.

Bryn hovered at his side as he made his way out of A&E, stopping only to sign the form that the sour-faced nurse handed him. The one that said he realised that the doctors wanted him to stay but screw them. She also directed her glare at Bryn, as if he were responsible for this foolishness, and Jason shot her a ghastly grin.

211

Over in the corner, he recognised Tom Davies, laid out on a gurney and muttering to himself.

Bryn followed his gaze and smiled. 'Sleeping it off. God only knows what he's taken or whether he knows anything useful.' He hesitated. 'Stuart's down the nick with his mates, denying everything.'

Jason felt his stomach turn, but put it down to his aching head. Not fear. 'Did you find her?'

But he already knew the answer from the dejected slump in the detective's shoulders, the heavy tread of his worn shoes.

'Turned that dump upside down and nothing. The gangs unit is helping us turn over Tom and Stuart's usual haunts but they're not confident of finding more than a couple of bags of smack.'

They stepped out into the night, through the same door that the killer had used to escape with Carla only yesterday. Jason shivered on the threshold, as Bryn guided him towards where Owain was waiting with the car.

'You did all right,' Bryn said grudgingly. 'Next time, wait for backup.'

'They ambushed me!' Jason said defensively. 'I thought I could handle it.'

He shrugged, grimacing when the motion aggravated his broken arm.

'We live and learn.'

Bryn held the door for Jason as he slid slowly into the backseat. Jason was looking forward to lying down on the sofa and not moving for a while. Of course, he'd have to make his own tea, but that was a small price to pay to avoid his mam's fussing and Cerys's worried silence.

Jason jolted awake as the car stopped. When had he closed his eyes? Bryn opened the door and prised him out of the seat. Jason leaned on him more than he'd have liked and just about made it into the lift without his head exploding. When the doors opened, Amy was hovering in the corridor, staring at him as if she hadn't seen him for days.

'You look like an extra in a zombie movie,' she said and retreated into the living room.

Bryn let go of his arm. 'You all right from here, son?'

Jason flashed him a terrible excuse for a smile, and Bryn clapped him on his good arm before retreating back into the lift.

Jason wobbled into the living room and saw the sofa surprisingly free of clutter. There was even a pillow, a red one that wasn't from Amy's bed. A cup of tea was steaming on the end table.

Amy hovered nervously beside the sofa, her fingers twisting around themselves, joints popping as they stretched. 'You need to lie down.'

Jason gratefully sank onto the sofa and obediently lay down.

Amy, instead of returning to her computer, perched on the edge beside him, her fingers playing over the Velcro of the splint.

'Does it hurt?'

''Sfine.' Jason closed his eyes.

'It doesn't look fine.'

He smiled. She couldn't be anything but honest with him. The mug was pressed into his left hand and he held it clumsily, taking a scalding sip before keeping it close for warmth.

'Have you found anything?' he asked sleepily.

Amy explained about cross-referencing medical records with university employment registers. 'It's a shot in the dark. Maybe he didn't meet her at the hospital and maybe he isn't a university employee. Maybe he's one or the other. Or neither.'

'Like shooting fish in a barrel.' His words were slurring together. Had they given him something in the hospital? He didn't remember. 'Except the barrel's an ocean and there might not be a fish.'

'Something like that,' Amy said, and he heard the frown in her voice. 'Go to sleep. I'll wake you in an hour. Every hour.'

He groaned, but sleep pulled at him, dragging him under until there was nothing.

It was midnight when Bryn and Owain sat down with their suspect. Stuart Williams was a surly bastard, with a face on him like a bulldog and that terrible lightning scar bisecting his cheek. Like a hard man's Harry Potter. But Bryn could see the edge of fear in his eyes, and that pleased him. The bastard had taken a pipe to a friend of his and Bryn didn't let a thing like that slide.

'You know why you're here, Mr. Williams?' Owain said.

Bryn scowled. The kid before him was no 'Mr. Williams' – he would've preferred 'Oi scum.'

Stuart shot Owain a look, then kicked at the leg of the desk, exercising his right to remain silent.

'How do you know Tom Davies?' Bryn said, watching the boy shrug. 'What about Carla Dirusso?'

Stuart looked up at that, glancing between them uneasily. Bryn realised that he hadn't thought he was here for Carla – he'd thought he was in the shit for assaulting Jason, not for the kidnapping.

'She's Tom's missing girl,' he said, clearing his throat. 'Get me some water, yeah?'

Bryn ignored him. 'How well did you know Carla?'

Stuart sat up straighter, the seriousness of the situation sliding into place behind his eyes. He'd broken a guy's arm and he could go down for that, but they were talking about serial murder and a missing girl. He would never see the light of day.

'I've seen her around,' he said vaguely. 'She didn't like Tom's mates. Thought us beneath her.'

Bryn nodded. 'So you killed her.'

The effect was instantaneous, Stuart's face paling. 'Carla's dead?'

'You tell me, mate.' Bryn kept his voice even.

There was dawning realisation on Stuart's face – the shit was four feet high and rising.

'I don't know nothing about those dead girls,' Stuart said, panic in his voice. 'And Tom, he was with us all day. Off his face, he was.'

As loathe as Bryn was to admit it, Stuart looked like a floundering man spewing the truth. He needled him further: 'Sure about that, Stuart? We don't want to add perjury to GBH, do we?'

But Stuart nodded vigorously. 'He was there all day. We were trying to keep him from chucking himself out the window, see. High as a kite. My mates can tell you – I was with them all day.'

'We'll look into that. Now, about Jason Carr...'

'I didn't know he was with you,' Stuart said, wide-eyed. 'Honest to God. I was just after his sister, right? And I thought he wanted a piece of Tom, told my old man that Tommy owed him money.'

Bryn chose to set Jason's dodgier investigating methods to one side for the moment. 'So you took a pipe to him.'

'He...he provoked me!' Stuart said.

Owain leaned back in his chair, as if bored.

Bryn laughed. 'That's what you're working with? Oh boy, you do not want to start pointing fingers.'

'Look, I thought it was that guy Tom said about!' Stuart protested, holding out his hands to beg for understanding. 'The one who was creeping around his place.'

Bryn and Owain exchanged looks.

'What guy?' Bryn said slowly.

Stuart, seeing that he'd seized on information that was of value to them, regained some of his control. 'What's it worth—'

'Think very carefully,' Owain snarled, scaring the hell out of Stuart and stunning Bryn a bit. He hadn't heard his mild-mannered partner get angry. 'A young woman is missing. You've just broken a man's arm. Do you want to play games, Mr. Williams?'

Stuart swallowed. 'Tommy said he was just hanging around their place, before he left, like. Tom thought he was part of the gang that get him his stuff, yeah? We didn't pay it any mind though, 'cause Tommy was jumpy all the time, with all the coke and shit.'

'Did you see this man?' Owain asked.

Stuart shook his head. Bryn ground his teeth. Damn.

'But Tommy did,' Stuart put in. 'Said he got a good look at him under the streetlight one night. He thought he might've recognised him, too. From some gig they went to.'

Bryn and Owain stood up, heading immediately for the door.

'Hey, what about me?' Stuart called after them. 'What do I get?'

Bryn turned and smiled. 'Oh, twelve to fifteen years, I'd say. Jason sends his best.'

He left a flabbergasted Stuart in his wake and pulled on his coat. 'Let's get back to the hospital.'

Chapter 41: A Clutch of Mother Hens

Jason was woken early by the doorbell and tried to bury his head further into the sofa. As promised, Amy had woken him every hour for eight hours, before finally letting him get some real sleep. Now there was someone at the door – why couldn't Bryn just let himself in?

'Oh my, look at the state of you!'

Jason's eyes flew open, sitting up in alarm and regretting it as the room started to spin. 'Mam?' he croaked

His mother enveloped him an awkward hug. Cerys was hovering by the living room doorway, pale beneath her hastily applied makeup, while he could hear Amy doing something in the kitchen. Amy never did anything in the kitchen, so she was clearly hiding.

'How did you know I was here?'

Gwen shot him 'the look'. 'Amy texted me. She knew I'd be worried when you didn't come home – as I had every right to be! Look at you!'

'I'm fine, Mam. The doctor said it would be all fine in a couple of months.' He rubbed at the top of his shoulder, willing away the throbbing in his arm and his head.

'A couple of months!' she said, obviously horrified at this injury to her son. 'What happened?'

'Cerys's boyfriend hit me with a pipe.'

The words were out before he'd thought them through, their sibling one-upmanship a silly game compared to what had gone down in Canton. Cerys immediately found her shoes fascinating, gnawing on one ragged fingernail. She hadn't bitten her nails for years.

'Tea.'

Amy placed three cups of passable tea on the table before returning to her computer with her own mug. Jason made a mental note that Amy was perfectly capable of making her own tea and to exploit this in case of future injury.

'Thank you, love,' Gwen said, taking her tea gratefully and sitting beside him on the sofa. 'Why didn't you come home?'

'I didn't want you to worry,' he said honestly, omitting the part where he intended to help Amy with her investigations as soon as his head stopped aching.

'Well, we were worried, weren't we, Cerys?'

Gwen looked up at her daughter but Cerys couldn't tear her eyes away from the floor, hadn't even touched her tea.

'You aren't responsible for him,' Jason said to her, and she looked up at him, face pale and blotchy. 'He's just a cu—no good for you. Anyway, he's banged up now.'

'Did he kill those girls? Have you found that poor nurse?'

Gwen looked to him anxiously for answers, but Jason just shrugged his good arm and looked to Amy.

'We'll find out soon,' Amy said cryptically, but then the lift doors opened, admitting an exhausted but jubilant Bryn and Owain.

'We've got a look at the sonovabit—' Bryn stopped, as he realised that there were strangers in the living room. 'Sorry, didn't know you had…people over.'

'We were just going, weren't we, Jason?' Gwen said, standing and smiling.

Jason looked up at her but didn't move. 'Mam, I'm…staying here for a bit.'

Gwen tried to control her expression, but he could see the sorrow and rejection in her eyes. 'Oh. All right then, bach.'

He reached for her arm. 'Just for a bit,' he said, not believing his own words. 'I…well, I work here now. For Amy.'

Gwen looked to Amy, who was typing away on her keyboard, apparently oblivious to the rest of them. 'Well...I'll leave you to it then. Call me after.'

He promised to call and she left with Cerys, who had recovered from her all-consuming guilt and was eyeing up Owain as if he were all her Christmases come at once. The young detective blushed under the attention, to Bryn's amusement.

Once the door was closed, Bryn brought a piece of paper over to Amy, grinning. 'We've got a sketch of him. Off Tommy Davies, now that he's come back from the Realm of the Fairies.'

Jason levered himself up off the sofa and came to look over Amy's shoulder. It wasn't brilliant, a little uncertain in places and with a

218

baseball cap pulled over the eyes. But it was the same jaw they'd seen on the CCTV, with nose and mouth clearly defined and straggling hair under the hat. Jason had a vague feeling of recognition, something familiar about the face, but he couldn't quite put his finger on it.

'I'll run it against the university employees,' Amy said, breaking his reverie.

'Students too,' Owain said. 'Dr. Deaver thinks the murderer could be a mature student.'

'Who's Dr. Deaver?' Jason asked.

Bryn huffed at the name. 'The mighty London profiler. Though she is impressed with you, Amy. She thinks you're pretty good at this.'

'I am good at this,' Amy said distractedly, already running the search. 'Do you have anything else for me?'

Bryn held up a battered iPhone in a plastic bag, a new model with a purple glittery case. It looked like it had been caught in the rain and a string of weed was clinging to it. Amy regarded it with interest and took it off him.

'We pulled it out of the reservoir with Kate and Melody,' Owain said eagerly. 'The techs said it was unsalvageable, but I thought you could probably do it.'

Jason smothered his grin at Owain's obvious case of hero worship, aware that he himself thought Amy's work was very like magic at times.

'It's Melody's.' Amy handed the bag to Jason. 'Put some rice in with it and put the bag in the airing cupboard. Remind me about it tomorrow.'

Jason clutched it in his clumsy left hand and shuffled towards the kitchen.

'I can do it,' Owain called.

Jason ignored him, getting out the rice he'd added to the weekly shop. Good food, rice. Simple, filling. Seemed a shame to waste it on a mobile phone, but it wasn't expensive and if Amy thought it would work its voodoo magic on the tech, then it was worth it.

'How do you know it's Melody's?' Bryn asked.

'Kate has a Samsung. And, given the state of Melody's laptop, she would cover her phone in something that sparkles. It may not help us – the water in the reservoir is foul.'

'We drink that water,' Bryn said, as Jason bore the phone to its resting place amongst the towels and bed linen. 'You drink that water, Amy. Every day.'

'Jason boils it. That is sufficient for my immune system.' She had that blog open again, but it hadn't been updated since the day of Carla's disappearance. 'He doesn't need to write to her anymore.'

Jason felt a shiver go down his spine. Of course not. He had her right where he wanted her – by his side.

Chapter 42: Goodbye, My Lover

Bryn tried to insist he stay behind and rest, but Jason would be damned if he'd upset his mother just to sit on the sofa. Amy's list of errands would keep him busy most of the day.

His battered little Micra had been standing outside Amy's since he'd returned to her employment, but he was in no fit state to drive it. He started the engine and it turned over first time, proving its worth once again. Jason longed to update it, get something with a bit of speed, but he knew he wouldn't get something half as reliable at the price.

While the engine was warming through, Jason popped open the boot and took a deep breath. He'd hoped he'd never have to use this, but he couldn't defend himself with his fists. He couldn't risk being caught out by the killer. Or Stuart's boys, out to revenge their leader in the nick. Or Damage, looking for someone to blame for his brother winding up in Swansea for ten. Jason decided that his New Year's resolution would be to acquire fewer enemies next year.

Careful that no one was looking, Jason slid his dad's old Beretta out from where it had been concealed in the spare tyre well. He'd never known why his dad owned the gun or how he'd come by it, but his mam had locked it away in the trunk with the rest of his things when he died. Sixteen-year-old Jason had discovered it one day, and him and the lads had shot at tin cans in the park. As he stowed it in the pocket of his messenger bag – one belonging to Amy's sister, with a gothic pony emblazoned on the side – he hoped he never had to use it. The police hadn't found it when he'd crashed that old lady's car, and he had no desire for them to find it now.

Jason headed towards the hospital on foot to fetch the last three months of recordings from the switchboard. The walk tired him out, but he needed time to think. And, on the way, he had to see Teresa.

Owain had been dubious about the sanity of that idea, but Jason had told him that he was on it, ta very much, and Owain had wisely shut up. Jason needed an excuse to go and see her, clear the air between them. He'd lied to her and she'd sold her story to the papers. Jason liked to think that neither of them were innocent in this.

Jason approached Teresa's door and rang the buzzer.

'Who is it?'

He hesitated, but decided that she'd only be angrier if he lied. 'It's Jason.'

There was a long silence and Jason thought she might not let him in. Then he'd have to run back to Owain with his tail between his legs and Teresa would sue him for harassment. But, against all odds, the door opened and he stepped inside, relieved.

The stairs took him longer than usual and by the time he reached the top, she was tapping her foot impatiently. Her expression softened slightly at the fact he looked like a war veteran and she reluctantly let him in.

'You're got a nerve,' she said, coldly.

'I'm here on business,' he said lamely.

She grew hostile again, standing in the middle of her living room and pointedly not offering him a seat. He withdrew his copy of the sketch from his pocket, shaking it out with his left hand.

She took it from him and her face blanched, with high spots of colour on her cheek. 'Is this him?'

'Do you recognise him? He might be someone from uni, or hanging around your house.'

But she shook her head. 'No, I don't. Mel didn't know anyone like this. And the street was okay, no one shady hanging about.' She looked at him pointedly. 'Apart from you.'

Jason winced. It had been a long shot anyway. As he reached for the paper, she touched his hand.

'I'm sorry. For talking to reporters.' She stared at her feet. 'They didn't write anything like what I said. It was embarrassing.'

'I'm sorry I didn't tell you who I was,' Jason returned, feeling a weight lift off his chest. 'But…that's not why we… I didn't sleep with you because of this.' It was his turn to blush, shift uncomfortably. 'I did it because I liked you. Like you.'

Teresa dropped her hand from his, an unreadable expression on her face. 'You'd better get going.'

He folded the page and put it safely back in his pocket. 'See you around,' he said, knowing that he probably wouldn't and that was okay. As long as she didn't hate him. He'd never meant to be the bad guy.

Carla listened to the radio and wondered why no one had found her yet.

She'd found the ancient machine in a bottom drawer under thick winter blankets and was surprised when it hissed to life. The reception in the basement was awful, but if she placed it on the windowsill, she could just about get Radio 1.

They were looking for her. That knowledge alone filled her with hope, and she was determined that she would survive this. They even had a sketch of the guy, so someone would soon recognise him and then she would be rescued. She only had to wait it out.

Her abductor had given her water and sandwiches, but he'd always come down with a hammer and a look in his eye that told her he might just bash her head in. She'd realised then that another escape attempt was futile, that he didn't trust her and that provoking him would only make her situation worse.

She could hear his footsteps on the stairs and she quickly turned off the radio, stuffing it under her pillow. If she didn't have that connection to the outside world, she thought she might go completely insane. And now she'd seen what that looked like.

He opened the door, holding the hammer warily, but then saw her on the bed and relaxed. 'Freebird, I have a surprise for you. We're going on a trip.'

Suddenly, all her resolutions flew out of the window. She wouldn't go anywhere with him. Not to the reservoir where he'd dumped those girls, not to a remote village where no one would know her. Not in the boot of a car on a ferry to vanish to somewhere in Europe where she couldn't find her way home.

Carla flew at him, seizing his wrist and slamming it against the door frame. He yelled, dropping the hammer. She grabbed for it, but he tore at her hair, yanking her up and throwing her against the wall. She was dazed, barely holding her own weight, whimpering like a child.

'After all I've done for you,' he spat – his hand at her throat, thumbs digging in.

She couldn't breathe. Her hands came up to claw at him, but his grip was a vice around her neck, crushing the life from her. *This is how the first girl was killed,* her brain supplied numbly. *This is how he did it.*

Her arms grew weak, cramping, tingling. A black curtain crept across her eyes, like the end of an act, the play half-done. *Don't let it end*, she thought – and then thought nothing at all.

Chapter 43: See No Evil, Hear No Evil

She slept.

He stood over her, clenching and unclenching his fists. She made him so angry! Didn't she know what was best for her? He was her life! Why did she have to provoke him like that? He'd had no choice but to take the matter in hand.

Placing a hand on her chest, gentle, reverent, he felt her heart beat and smiled. Everything was ready for their departure. He'd packed a bag, and he'd bought her some new things to wear. It was like the newspapers were announcing their engagement, placing their pictures together like that. He'd thought of the perfect place, where they could be together without people interfering. They'd be happy there.

They'd be alone.

'You took your time.'

Amy held out her hand for the recordings, not even looking at him. She couldn't afford to be distracted – she was manually reviewing the potential matches from the sketch of the killer. So far, there were three maybes out of 274 possibilities, but she wasn't all that convinced. For a start, one of them was on secondment in Toronto.

'I had to make a stop on the way,' Jason said and she heard him settle into the sofa with a pained sigh. 'Have you got anything for dinner?'

'Isn't that your job?' she shot back.

He grumpily got back off the sofa and went to explore the kitchen.

'There's codeine in the cupboard,' she added. 'Above the washing machine. Don't touch anything else.'

'God, you could start a pharmacy.'

She wondered if he'd comment on some of her more…interesting tablets, but Jason was a man of the world – a few prescription medicines with the wrong label were unlikely to excite him.

The smell of frying onion started drifting through to the living room. In theory, aerated vegetable fat would be bad for AEON's systems, but the scent made her salivate. The rich scents of cooking meat and sweet tomato infused her workspace and she was unable to think of anything beyond the heady aroma and the gnawing emptiness of her stomach. When had she last eaten? Had she had a biscuit today?

'It's ready!' Jason called.

Amy pushed back from the computer, waiting for her food. A long minute passed and nothing appeared. Another minute. She frowned.

Jason stuck his head round the doorway. 'Aren't you coming? It'll get cold.'

'I can't stop to eat. I need to work.'

'You'll spill sauce on Ewan. He won't like that.'

He had a point. Reluctantly, she got out of her chair and made her way into the kitchen, where the rickety little table was set for two. There were two glasses half-full of red wine, and Amy wondered if she'd stepped into an absurd romantic comedy.

'Do we have time for this?' she asked tetchily, the smell stronger in here. 'And her name is AEON – A-E-O-N. Not Ewan.'

Her stomach growled and she had already sat down, completely negating her complaints. It seemed her body would have her eat, ganging up on her with Jason, whether she wanted to or not.

'You'll work better after you've eaten.'

Jason placed a plate of spaghetti bolognaise in front of her. She didn't stop to wait for him, already shovelling it into her mouth, spaghetti hanging from her lips and sauce splattering over Booster Gold's grinning face on her T-shirt.

Jason laughed and she scowled around her spaghetti, but he seemed just as enthusiastic, though slowed by his injured arm. When had she last had a proper meal like this? It was usually whatever she could make with the kettle and the microwave. The oven had stood idle since Lizzie left.

'Vegetables,' Jason said suddenly, 'should be picked by hand. The onions were all half-rotten.'

Amy didn't think they tasted all that rotten, but maybe Jason was a better cook than she'd given him credit for. She didn't think a quick course in prison would lead to any degree of competency but maybe she needed to have more faith in the justice system.

'You need your own credit card. I'll order one for you.'

Jason looked at her as if she'd just turned into an onion.

Amy frowned. 'So you can pick vegetables. And buy me...things.'

She wasn't entirely sure what else she might need that wasn't online, but she had never considered that internet-obtained vegetables would be inferior. There was clearly a lot to learn here.

'You're honestly going to get me a credit card? The bank won't give me one.'

Amy waved her hand dismissively, and washed down her last mouthful of mince with her wine. 'Use my name and address. It's not my real name, and the address is registered as business premises. They never ask many questions with my bank balance.'

Amy stood up, deciding to risk AEON's fate to her glass of wine. Jason finished loading the dishwasher, and then followed her through, watching as she started transferring the switchboard CDs to an external hard drive.

'Amy's not your real name?' He sounded hurt.

She wanted to say that thing to him – what was it? 'A rose by any other name would smell as sweet.' Probably Shakespeare. People used his words a lot, though she had never read or seen his works. Books were boring. So...papery.

'Amy is my name,' she said finally, deciding he could be trusted with that much. 'Lane isn't our surname. I chose it when I made our new identities. It was suitably boring.'

'Yours and...your sister's?' Jason said slowly.

She nodded, deciding she didn't want to talk about it anymore. There was only so much he needed to know right now and she didn't like talking about her past. New Amy, new start.

'Why are some of these entries marked?' she asked, referring to the entry log from the switchboard.

He peered over her shoulder, resting his arm on the back of her chair. She quite liked him standing there, hovering over her while she worked. It was vaguely comforting.

'They're the ones they know for certain are him. Apparently, he's been giving them the creeps for weeks now.' A note of frustrated anger entered his voice. 'Not that they bloody well told anyone.'

She nodded, opening up one of the sound files. '*University Hospital.*'

There was a pause, and then the killer spoke: '*Theatres please.*' Not a local accent. Southern England, perhaps.

'*Who's calling?*' The operator already sounded suspicious. The line went dead. Of course, they would remember the calls where they'd recognised him and hadn't put him through. They needed the calls that switchboard had missed.

'These are all from withheld numbers.' She skimmed over the starred entries. 'We should eliminate the other entries.'

She placed the paper in the scanner, so she could modify it digitally. Striking something through with a pen was absurd – what if she lost the paper? Did she have more than one working pen – and where was it, anyway?

'What if he slipped up?' Jason countered. 'Then we'd miss his number because we ignored them.'

'We have to listen to all of them.'

They couldn't afford the risk if it turned out that the killer was stupid. She despaired of such manual work. Was there no way to condense the data into a manageable workload?

'Do you have…whatsit? Voice recognition?'

Amy pulled up her sound analysis suite. They didn't have enough references to make a profile for his voice, but they could eliminate voices that were nothing like his. High pitch, heavy accents – she could remove those outliers and make their job marginally easier.

AEON scanned the files, groaning under the strain of yet another search. She'd have to treat her to a deep cleanse and defrag after all this. The first build of AEON was getting on for ten years old; Amy was sure there wasn't an original part left now, but the essence of AEON remained. In the world of computing, she was an elderly veteran.

Amy went back to her profiles, looking through the photos of university employees and students. She was getting faster, deciding for or against within seconds. She eliminated a further fifty while Jason made coffee and before AEON announced that her filtering was complete. Amy had added the 'Theatres please' rider to the search on the off-chance AEON did pick him out from the crowd. To her surprise, the computer had marked fifty-three files as possessing that tag.

'That can't be right,' she muttered, listening to the first file, dated August 18.

'*University Hospital.*'

'*Theatres please.*'

'*Theatres – putting you through.*'

His voice sounded exactly the same – same tone, same inflection, perfectly calm and detached. Amy had expected breathy excitement, heady with the anticipation of speaking to his love. Not this precision monotone.

'*Theatres reception.*'

Another pause of around two seconds. '*I would like to speak to Carla Dirusso.*' There was something odd about the voice. There was detached and then there was…robotic.

'*I'll get her for you now – hang on.*' The call was on hold for a minute, without a sound from the other end of the line.

Finally, a woman's voice: '*Hello?*'

The quality of the line changed and Amy registered the buzz of static. Digital to analogue. She could hear someone breathing, the heavy pant that Amy expected, and the sound of something with guitars playing behind him.

'*Hello? Is someone there?*'

Amy recognised the woman now, the same modulated Welsh tone as the Whitchurch police call: Carla Dirusso.

'*Tom, this isn't funny.*' She slammed the phone down – the recording ended.

'He learned his trade at the cinema.'

Amy jumped, not realising that Jason had retaken his place at her back.

'Typical Hollywood horror.'

Amy hummed her agreement, dissembling the sound clip into its composite parts. 'The parts where he speaks are synthesised. Pretty realistic, so high-end software. You can hear the line switch when she answers – that's him breathing, playing music to her. Clever.'

'Too clever?' Jason asked, laying his hand on her shoulder.

Amy looked up at him and smiled. 'I didn't say that.'

Chapter 44: Caerdydd Canolog

Dr. Eleanor Deaver was watching the news. And Bryn was watching her.

Bryn had been stirring his cold cup of coffee for twenty minutes and wondering if she was really looking at the TV or just thinking at it. Bryn used to do that to his ex-wife, working through the finer details of his latest case while she talked at him about her day and the gossip down the chapel. Of course, she'd cottoned on eventually and that was one of many reasons she'd finally called it a day.

'What's she doing?'

Bryn jumped as his boss came up behind him, glad that something work-related was on his computer screen even if he had no idea what. However, Roger was too busy scrutinising the profiler to notice.

'She's been looking at it for almost half an hour.' Roger shot her a look of disapproval. 'She's meant to be working, not watching telly.'

Owain looked round at his raised tone, somehow still looking like he'd just woken up from a good night's sleep. 'She's thinking, isn't she? See that look on her face? She's about to have a revelation, she is.'

Bryn could admit that there was definitely something working behind the woman's eyes, a certain pensive expression on her face that could indicate an upcoming epiphany – or the onset of a seizure. They'd all been up since that ugly Friday night at the hospital, and the woman had to sleep soon or fall into a coma like the rest of them. He had to admire her dedication, even if he worried the robot revolution was upon them.

Bryn shook his head. He'd been paying too much attention to Amy if he was thinking about the robot revolution.

Abruptly, Eleanor jumped to her feet, knocking her paper cup flying. 'He's leaving Cardiff!'

Everyone in the office stared at her. Her hands flapped around her head, her words tripping over themselves as she struggled to get them out in her excitement.

'Give her time to wake up and try to escape. She's feisty, isn't she? She wouldn't take being kidnapped lying down. He realises this isn't quite the happy-ever-after he imagined and he sees his face everywhere. On Monday morning, he'll be missed at work and he can't leave her alone in the house. He has to get out of the city before they're discovered. He has to go tonight.'

'How do you know he works?' Owain asked, and Bryn was pleased to hear a note of scepticism in his voice.

Eleanor waved her hand. 'He only kills on the weekend – no murders on a school night. He has a nine-to-five and he's due in work tomorrow. He has to go now.'

Bryn looked up at the clock. It was 8 p.m. on a Sunday. The main roads could be closed, sure, but what about the lanes? Cordoning off the city would take time, and a local could escape before they'd even got their boots on. He might already be gone for all they knew.

His phone started to ring in his pocket and he fished it out: Amy. 'Look, Amy, can I call you ba—'

'I was looking for his voice emulation software by his download history,' she began and he realised she was completely oblivious to his protests. 'He visited National Rail Enquiries half an hour ago. He's moving, Bryn.'

Suddenly, Eleanor was a genius and Bryn was declaring himself a convert. 'Listen up,' he said, voice carrying across the whole office. 'The killer's looking at train times. We need to get to Central Station.'

Eleanor looked pleased with herself as his detectives scrambled to gather their things and get out. Bryn belatedly realised Amy was talking to him again.

'...no definite destination. Live departures indicate trains to London and Portsmouth leaving within the next hour. North Wales, Shrewsbury, Birmingham – I can't narrow it down.' She sounded frustrated and Bryn could hear Jason's voice in the background. 'Jason's on his way there now. Bryn, how's he going to move Carla without drawing attention? She won't be willing.'

Eleanor was pacing. 'She'll be drunk. Or he'll find another wheelchair, but I think he's too smart for that. Drunk, large coat, hat. We'd never recognise her from a distance.'

'We've got it covered, Amy,' Bryn said. 'Any chance you can find out more?'

He heard her fingers dashing at the keys. 'I can try, but it will take time.'

God knew they didn't have that, but he told her to work on it anyway and fetched Dr. Deaver's coat. 'I think you'd better come out with us,' he said, holding out the elegant thing for her to step into. 'You've got a better idea than the rest of us what to look for.'

Eleanor shot him a winning smile and Bryn decided she wasn't half-bad after all. 'I thought you'd never ask.'

Amy threw a brand-new phone at him as he left the flat and told him to keep the line open. He tried to put the fancy Bluetooth earpiece in place as he marched down the street, but he had to stop under a streetlight to look at it properly before finally shoving it in awkwardly with his left hand.

She called him almost immediately and he picked up, finding it strange to have her mumbling in his ear as he walked through the Cardiff night.

'Are you sure you should be going? The police are on it.'

He danced around icy puddles, his jacket hanging awkwardly over his splinted arm. 'I'm the overseer. Can't expect Cardiff's finest to find their arsehole with both hands.'

Amy giggled and he grinned. He liked that she laughed when he told naff jokes. Honestly, now that he knew a couple of them, the cops weren't that bad – maybe he was just growing up. Moving in different circles. His mam would call it bettering himself, but he didn't think he was better, really. Just less likely to wind up in prison.

He'd had no clue, really, when he'd swaggered around Butetown with Lewis. Prison was what happened to those stupid enough to get caught, and it was so far removed as to be a mythical place where people disappeared for a long holiday at Her Majesty's Pleasure.

In prison, Jason had been anonymous. A cell, a number, another stupid boy. He'd been beaten, sure, but he'd watched men lose their minds in Usk. That was what made him determined to take something away from it, even if it was only a bit of cookery and the passionate resolution to never go back.

He had no idea how he was going to repay Amy for protecting him from going back, giving him a livelihood from her own pocket. He would find a way to show her how much he appreciated what she'd done for him.

He decided to go via the heaving Newport Road and get a train from Queen Street to Central. He tried to tell himself it was because he might catch the killer, but it was mostly because it was bloody freezing and his arm was aching from the cold and the almost-jogging pace he'd set.

'Do you think we can find her?'

'I don't know,' Amy said, with typical honesty. Jason wasn't sure she was capable of being positive. 'You're there, Bryn's there. It's a fair chance.'

Jason grinned, licking at his chapped lips as he spied the lights of Queen Street in the distance.

'I think if I leave your place without getting a broken bone, that'll be an improvement,' he joked, but the long silence on the other end of the line told him that Amy didn't find that one funny.

'You could've died.'

He shrugged one shoulder, even though she wasn't there to see it. 'I didn't,' he said and left it at that.

He veered round to the station entrance and immediately saw two coppers, their civilian clothes doing nothing to disguise the fact they were police.

'I'm at the station. I might lose signal for a bit. Might get noisy.'

'I have your location,' she said.

Jason realised that she would probably track him constantly now. He found the thought oddly comforting. When he entered the building, the barriers were open. There were a couple of tramps hanging out by the ticket machine, reeking of booze, which was more reason to skip the fare and walk through. The screen said it was only three minutes until the next train to Central, so he'd timed that one well.

Jason shifted from foot to foot on the platform, wishing he could rub his hands over his arms to keep warm or stuff them in his armpits. At least his right arm was warm, surrounded by padding, though it hurt like a bitch. To his disgust, the tramps had followed him onto the platform, one holding an open bottle of cheap whisky. He did his best to ignore them, sure they'd start begging him for money any minute.

The train pulled into the station and he deliberately got into a different carriage, thankful to sit for a couple of minutes. It was practically deserted, only a woman and her kid and an elderly man who'd fallen asleep. Jason rested his arm against the window and studied his own reflection. The bruises were fading. Soon, he might look like a decent citizen again.

'Jason?' Amy's voice broke his reverie. 'The profiler thinks Carla will most likely be drunk. It would be the only way to get her through the city unnoticed.' Drunk. Oh fuck. 'Wearing a big coat, maybe. Sounds like bullsh—'

'I've seen them,' Jason said with dawning horror, leaping to his feet and trying to see into the next carriage. 'They're on my train.'

'What? I'll put you through to Bryn – hang on.'

He couldn't see them – why couldn't he see them?

'Amy, wait!' But she'd already gone.

The next carriage was empty. Had they even got on the train? Shit.

'Jason? Where are they?' Bryn's voice came through urgently. The train was already pulling into Cardiff Central and they only had seconds.

'Train from Queen Street. They look homeless, got a bottle on them. But I've lost them – I can't see them!'

He clutched his head, cursing himself for ten kinds of fool. It was a fucking brilliant disguise. Nobody looked at the homeless, went out of their way not to look.

'Bryn, the train's at the station.'

Staring out as the platform came into view, looking for police officers or the platform number, he saw Bryn and Owain, and let out a breath. The elderly man had been woken by his raised voice, and the woman was eyeing him suspiciously, clutching her child close. But he didn't care. He didn't care as long as they caught the bastard.

The doors opened and Jason hurtled out, marching down the train. Only a few people got off, but others were getting on, blocking the doors. Where were they? He was sure they got on this end.

He saw Owain board the train, searching for them inside, and he was heading for Bryn to give him more description when he saw them. They stepped out of the last carriage and made a beeline for the stairs.

'Bryn!' Jason yelled, running after them and pushing past the travellers getting in his way.

The man looked up at his shout and Jason caught sight of a beard, glasses. Joke shop disguise. He disappeared down the stairs and Jason, struggling to get through even this meagre crowd, couldn't get to him quickly enough.

When he hit the top of the stairs, the man was halfway down, Carla slowing him down.

'Stop! Police!' Jason shouted.

The man glanced back. In a split second, he made his call – and threw Carla down the stairs, leaping over her tumbling body to make his escape.

Jason was torn – the victim or the killer – but there were already people on her, more poorly disguised policeman, and he ran after the man towards the Bay exit. He was already out of sight, speed on him now that he'd lost Carla and all the furies of hell were at his heels.

Jason hoped Bryn had a man on this side but as he rounded the corner, he saw one guy on the floor, bleeding from his head, as his friend crouched over him. Divide and conquer. Fuck.

He kept on running, out into the night, eyes darting around to try and find the guy. A police car screeched round the corner, sirens blaring, but it was too late. But wait—there! Movement by the trees and Jason took off, running in front of the police car and forcing it to brake. He would have the bastard if it was the last thing he did.

'Do you have eyes on him?' His earpiece crackled to life with Bryn's voice.

Jason tried to answer between aching breaths. 'He's heading...out for...Penarth Road!'

The car park was badly lit, open ground on Sunday night, but the man was damn fast. Jason tore after him, pumping his arms despite the screeching pain above his right elbow.

'Cars are right behind you,' Bryn said in his ear and Jason could hear the sirens. He didn't have time to look back, as they ran out of the car park.

The man veered right, running down the road, dodging the few cars coming over the river this late. Jason kept to the edge, ignoring the blasted horns, but slower than his quarry. He actually cared if he lived or died – and the killer didn't. He was a dangerous man with nothing to live for.

'What's happening? Where are you?'

Jason didn't have the breath to answer him, all his energy focused on sprinting after the man who was increasing the distance between them.

'Grange...town,' he managed, hoping that Bryn realised that was the direction he was heading, that Amy was feeding his coordinates into the man's other ear.

Suddenly, the suspect shot off to the left, heading down a dark unmarked street. Jason was fifty yards back now and he hoped the man wouldn't vanish down an alleyway before he got there. At the entrance, he spotted a shadow disappearing to the right just ahead and pelted after him. His energy was fading, full stomach threatening to eject its contents. He was never eating spaghetti again.

Jason ran into a narrow alley, dark and filthy, but straight. He ran on, breaths coming harder and faster, as he spotted movement at the end. He was losing ground, tiring too quickly, but he kept on, barely hearing Bryn's words in his ear, demands for his location.

The alley was now just a space between buildings, with random trees and rubbish piled high, and he nearly tripped over a broken pram. He couldn't see, couldn't hear anything beyond his heartbeat roaring in his ears, and he had no idea if he was even on the right track.

He forced himself through the gap between a wall and a hedge, the only way out, and saw open space at last, the moon glittering on water. He was at the river. The path stretched away to either side of him, quiet and shadowed. There was no sign of the killer.

'Bryn...' Jason panted, 'I'm at the riverbank. But...he's gone.' He closed his eyes against the frustration. 'He's gone, Bryn.'

Chapter 45: Down by the Riverside

The police helicopter flew overhead, the sound of its blades cutting through the night sky. Jason watched it fly across the stars, a rare cloudless night for Cardiff in the autumn.

There were uniformed police officers, crime scene technicians and detectives swarming over every inch of the riverbank to the south of the bridge into Grangetown. It reminded Jason of the last time he was down by the water, a little place just off the A470 with a pretty girl and dead bodies floating nearby.

He was cooling off in the back of a police car, his legs trembling from their exertion and the adrenaline still surging through his veins. Bryn was talking to a woman in a long black coat, who was pointing at the river and gesturing towards the bridge. If she thought the man had jumped in, she was clearly not from around here – no one in their right mind went for a dip in the Taff, especially not in November.

Bryn broke away from his lady friend and headed for the car. 'Someone taken your statement?' he asked.

Jason nodded. The police officer had been very patient with him as he'd stuttered over his description and the route they'd taken through the Cardiff back streets.

'Carla's up at the Heath,' Bryn added.

Jason had almost forgotten about her in the chase, but now the sickening tumble came to mind, how she'd been laid out like a rag doll on the bottom step.

'They're keeping an eye on her head injury, but she's mostly sleeping off the gin. She smelled like a distillery.'

'Did she say anything?' Jason croaked, then cleared his throat. That was it – he was giving up the fags for good.

Bryn looked out over the river. 'Nah, she can barely remember her own name. We'll get more sense out of her in the morning. Meanwhile, there's a copper on her door and hospital security is as twitchy as we can make 'em. They'll transfer her to Bristol when she's stable.'

'Do you think we'll find him?'

Jason joined Bryn in staring at the river. There were a lot of alleys on this side of town and it had been an hour since Jason had lost him. Bryn didn't answer and Jason heard what he wasn't saying. They had to look as if they were doing something, even if the likelihood of catching him was pretty much nil.

They had more time now, with Carla out of his hands. Though they also had no idea what he'd do next. Would he try to get her back? Or would he kill more women to lure her back to him? Jason's brain hurt just considering the possibilities, and he was glad he wasn't the profiler Bryn had talked about.

There was a ringing in his left ear and he realised he still had the headset in. He tapped it. 'Amy?'

Bryn smiled and walked away, returning to coordinating their efforts on the riverbank.

'Why did you have to run where there are no cameras?'

'It wasn't exactly my decision,' he reminded her.

Still, she launched into a tirade about better provision of CCTV for the greater good of the city and she would tell Bryn exactly where he could get off unless he made sure she had more eyes in alleyways. Jason leaned back and closed his eyes, letting her voice wash over him as she groused about how the police helicopter didn't even have a camera.

'Are you even listening?' He made a vague response to indicate he was paying attention. 'Don't fall asleep in the police car. They might mistake you for a crook. Come back home.'

'In a minute,' Jason said drowsily, then shook himself awake. 'I'll have a word with Bryn, check he doesn't need me. Then I'll be over, all right?'

'Get a lift or a taxi,' Amy said. 'I mean it.'

Sometimes, she was more like his mother than his boss. Jason disconnected and walked over to where Bryn, Owain and the mysterious woman were discussing the escaped killer.

'If, as you say, there is a path all the way down the river on this side, I imagine he would stick to it,' the woman was saying. 'His disguise is recognisable now, his cover blown. We put it out on the ten o'clock news – your girl works very fast, doesn't she?'

'She does at that,' Bryn said, nodding to Jason as he approached. 'This is her assistant, Jason Carr. He was the one chasing the suspect this far. Jason, meet Dr. Eleanor Deaver, the profiler from London.'

Eleanor held out her left hand to shake his and he smiled as he clasped it with his good hand. 'A fine chase, Mr. Carr. I'm surprised you got so close. He's as slippery as an eel, and only predictable to a point. The best ones always are.'

She sounded tired, more than the fatigue of an all-nighter or two. Jason guessed she'd seen a lot of death, met a lot of killers. It must change a person.

'What do we do now?' Jason asked.

Eleanor and Bryn simply looked at each other, wearing the same dissatisfied expression.

Bryn checked his watch. 'Call it a day at midnight.'

Three and a half hours after the original chase was nearly time enough to get to Newport on foot. It was more likely he'd gone to ground in his own house, relying on Carla being too addled to remember its location.

'Get some rest.' Eleanor looked at Bryn with an almost-fond expression. 'We can start fresh in the morning.' She paused, then added, 'If the searchers don't find him.'

They all nodded, with the tacit understanding that it was all but impossible.

'Detective!'

Rob Pritchard hurried over, looking significantly less grouchy than the last time Jason had seen him, despite the late hour. He was holding up a large paper bag and waved it excitedly. 'He's dumped the disguise!'

Bryn went to take the bag, but Rob held it out of his way like a childish game of keep-away. 'Don't contaminate it, Hesketh! It was under the next bridge down, stuffed in a bag. He probably scrambled the entire distance in five minutes if the state of the bank is anything to go by. And then just wandered down the road, pleased as punch, wearing whatever was under the damn coat.'

'Any clue from the inside of the coat?' Bryn asked.

Rob shot him an indecipherable look. 'Yes, I just did complex fibre analysis with my iPhone and my portable chromatograph.'

241

It took Jason a moment to realise that Rob was being sarcastic and couldn't actually do those things on the move, and from Bryn's scowl it was clear that he had also been taken in.

'Hilarious, Pritchard. Well, get on it then. Owain, tell the searchers that the description is wrong and that he surfaced at…Clarence Road, is it? Probably would've got lost in the south end of Grangetown rather than the Bay?'

He looked to Eleanor for confirmation, but she frowned. 'If he was confident his new appearance would go unnoted, he'd take the most direct route to his safe house. If he had to continue to hide, he would go for the least-populated area with the most opportunities for concealment, and he would look far more suspicious.'

Bryn looked unhappy and Jason could understand why. They didn't know the most direct route to his safe house, because they had no idea where he lived. And now they didn't know what he'd been wearing either.

'Jason,' Bryn said, turning to him, 'ask Amy if she's got eyes on that bridge.'

'She said there weren't many cameras,' Jason said hesitantly, but at the look on Bryn's face, hurriedly nodded. 'I'll ask her. I'm going over there now—'

'I'll give you a lift,' Owain said immediately.

Jason frowned but accepted, catching the look that passed between Bryn and Owain. Maybe they thought they had to look after him after his race through the city streets with his broken arm. He didn't feel quite one hundred percent, it was true. He'd be glad to get back to the stuffy, close environment of Amy's flat.

'I'll call you after,' he said.

Bryn nodded, returning to his worrying and strategising. Once again, Jason was glad he was only an amateur and could walk away. He'd seen more than enough of this night.

Chapter 46: A Murder of Magpies

When Jason walked into her living room, Amy inspected her assistant as thoroughly as a pathologist, tugging off his coat and looking him over with a clinical eye. She distantly heard Jason asking Owain if he wanted a cup of tea, but the young detective declined, returning to the riverbank.

When the door closed, Jason touched her hand. 'I'm all right. Just tired.'

Amy was sceptical to say the least. 'You shouldn't run with your arm like that. You might displace it and need an ORIF.'

Jason laughed, startling her. She didn't see why major orthopaedic surgery was funny. 'Have you been reading about my broken arm on the internet?'

Amy sniffed and returned to AEON, reviewing the CCTV footage of Jason chasing the killer from the station. Instead of lying on the sofa as she expected, Jason came to stand behind her, watching his pursuit through the car park.

'I watched it live,' she said quietly, remembering the acrid taste of fear in her mouth as she'd seen this fool of a man run after a serial killer in the middle of the night with flimsy backup.

'Pritchard reckons that he left the riverbank at the next bridge down. Bryn said to ask you about cameras.'

Amy had already considered the downstream and upstream exit points, and focused in on that bridge and the cameras on the Grange-town side as well as ones in the Bay, which were far more numerous. It always seemed odd to Amy that the more affluent areas had the most cameras, despite being the least likely to host crime. The paranoia of the rich.

'What time did you lose him?' she said.

In the answering silence, she perceived that wasn't the most tactful way of accessing the information, though it was the most direct. She glanced up at him, but he seemed to be thinking, not brooding.

'Um…Bryn can tell you exactly. I'd say it was about five minutes after we left the station, maybe less.'

'I'll take it from the last time we sighted you on camera.' Amy checked the timestamp and moved the footage to the correct point. 'We won't miss him then.'

The lighting was reasonable in this area because of the approach to the Bay, so they had a fairly good chance of seeing his face. It was barely ten minutes after the station departure time that a figure appeared beside the bridge, turning his head left and right, before strolling onto the road. He was dressed smartly, wouldn't be out of place in a restaurant, and walked into Cardiff Bay.

'The glasses are an irritant.'

She cursed their reflection and obfuscation of his face. It was the top half of his face they were missing, at least until Carla could identify him properly in the morning.

She followed him from camera to camera across the entire Bay until he crossed over Lloyd George Avenue, the main road connecting the Bay to Cardiff proper, and she lost him in the expensive housing estate. Cursing him, she picked up the surrounding camera streams but he didn't reappear in a fifteen-minute window on any side where she had eyes.

'I can make a composite.'

She had enough partial glimpses of his face to attempt to reconstruct the whole, and moved to begin the arduous task, when Jason's hand rested over hers on the mouse. She realised he'd come to stand beside her, looking down on her with an indescribable look. Almost affection. Like he cared.

'Why don't we call it a night?' he said. 'Carla's out of trouble, the pictures will still be here in the morning. We've got a hundred leads now and he won't leave without Carla, will he?'

Amy suspected that last statement was more wishful thinking than certain knowledge, but she allowed herself to be drawn into the comforting lie. 'You can't sleep on the sofa,' she heard herself saying. 'Not with your arm.'

His expression held a hint of awkwardness and he stared at the floor. His fingers twitched on hers. 'I can't take your bed.'

This tough ex-con was a bit of a gentleman and she didn't think she'd budge him on that. 'There's another bed. Come on—I'll show you.'

She stood and led him through the flat, past both the bathroom and bedroom doors until she reached a dead end. There was a light switch on the wall and she flicked it.

The wall slid back to reveal a second lift. Jason stared at the lift, then back at her. 'Are you actually a Bond villain? Do you keep a white cat down there?'

'I'm allergic to cats.' Amy got into the lift and Jason followed readily, so she assumed he didn't actually think he was being led to his death. Good to know, she thought, pressing the button for the ground floor.

'There's a button for the top floor too,' Jason said stupidly.

'Lizzie's dining room, kitchen, lounge,' she said, the words coming easier than she'd expected. 'I don't go up there.'

Thankfully, Jason didn't question further, just followed her out of the lift and onto the dim ground floor. The heat and noise of the server hit her immediately and she'd forgotten how soothing that had been for the years she'd slept down here, lulled to sleep by its immensely powerful hum every night.

She turned right into the room immediately below her bedroom. The single bed was stripped down, but it was otherwise as she remembered it – the white rug on the floor with the purple spot where she'd spilled blackcurrant squash, the faded *Firefly* poster on the wall, and the bookcase of outdated Year 9 SATs books and laughable *PC World* magazines.

'This used to be your room.' Jason walked up to the bookcase and pulled a dog-eared copy of *The Hobbit* off the shelf. 'I can't imagine you reading a book.'

'The last one I ever read,' she confessed with a small smile. 'I was thirteen.'

He replaced the book reverently and sat on the small office chair.

Amy waved vaguely towards the door. 'There should be blankets and sheets in the box room next door. They might be musty. They haven't been out for five years. The rubbish skip is outside your window, so that can get unpleasant in summer. I never open the French doors in my bedroom because of the smell. Actually, I don't open any windows...'

She was rambling, but Jason just shrugged with one shoulder, a gesture that was becoming uniquely his.

'I'll be fine. Cheers.' He hesitated, smiled up at her, open and honest. 'You didn't have to show me this. You could've kept me believing you only had the flat. I'd never have known.'

'I don't want to keep things from you. I want you to stay.'

The words tumbled out before she'd thought them through, but he wasn't running away and he didn't think she was a freak. She'd been alone for five years and here was someone who wanted to stay with her – no, who she could pay to stay with her. It was a business relationship. He was replaceable, just like a broken lamp. Not like Lizzie.

'We should get some sleep,' he said and she nodded towards the bed.

'Can you...manage?'

Jason laughed. 'Are you offering to help me? Because I've seen your bed, Amy.'

'You'll do a better job with one arm than I would with two. Lizzie...'

She wouldn't tell him how much Lizzie used to help her. That would make it seem like she was aiming to replace Lizzie, and that was not what was happening here. She had been fine on her own. This just made it easier for her to work, if she didn't have to worry about the washing up or whether the milk was off. He was useful to her work.

She worried about him a little, but she worried about everything. She was one of life's little worriers. That was what her mother had called her. Amy had done her level best to forget that, push everything her mother had ever said to her far out of her mind, but that phrase just kept coming back. 'One of life's little worriers' – it sounded so banal, so harmless. Not so crippling she could no longer walk through the front door.

'Amy?'

She blinked and realised he was standing again, his hand hovering over her arm.

'Are you all right?'

'Just tired,' she lied, wondering if she would sleep, having opened old doors, old wounds. 'I'll let you rest. We'll start at eight tomorrow?'

'Eight's fine. No commute, eh?'

Amy smiled and wished him goodnight, wondering what it would be like to have him always on hand. If constant exposure to her neuroses would wear him away quicker, force him to find somewhere new and away from her. Like Australia.

With too many thoughts crowding her mind, Amy lay on top of her blankets, staring at the ceiling and wondering how she could be better. How to make the world outside safer, to make the world inside warmer. There were too many variables. Too much information. How was she ever to discover the answers?

Like this case. There were too many victims. They had too many facets to their lives, places they might have intersected with the killer and yet none obvious. They had different friends, different courses, different jobs. Kate liked to have a quiet night in with an Indian and a beer; Melody liked to be out and loud with housemates, coursemates, workmates; and Laurie liked to save her pennies for weeks away with her girlfriend where she could form golden memories to carry her through the rest of the miserable, dull year. And then Carla was the anomaly, the chosen one, who had split from a drug-addled boyfriend and had a full-time job that made for crazy, high-stress hours at odd times of the day and night.

Every little thing was a clue, a jewel of information fit for a magpie. But how could she put it all together to make a trail to this killer, this man who knew them all? The most useful thing was the timeline of Laurie's life between Melody's death and her own demise. She must've encountered the killer then and she was sufficiently connected to update her Facebook status, Tweet about it and check in on Foursquare for every active minute of her day.

Unable to rest, Amy returned to AEON and brought up the timeline. Ten days. Ten short days in which so much had happened in Laurie's life. The most striking thing had been the new job at the bar, but she'd met several friends for coffee and cocktails, gone to the cinema with Gina twice, and attended lectures most weekdays. Tomorrow, Amy would send Jason to every one of these contacts and find out if they knew the other girls.

And maybe Carla would wake up with the perfect sketch in her head, maybe the killer's coat would yield some definitive evidence to

Pritchard, and maybe some enterprising member of the public would recognise the killer at the bus stop and call it in. But Amy would still do her bit for these dead girls, her own threading of the jewels left behind, because she needed to be useful. She needed to have a purpose besides hiding in her flat and drinking Jason's tea.

And, for now, catching the Cardiff Ripper was her purpose. Before he came back for more.

He lay on her bed, wrapped in her blanket and surrounded by her gentle musk. Tears warmed his frozen cheeks and he sobbed into her pillow. How could he have been so careless? He'd had no idea they were so close to him, that they would snatch his beloved from under his nose.

They had stolen her, and the nightly news, always so ready to tell tales, had shown new pictures of the two of them in their oversized coats and hats. They'd said only that she was being treated in a 'secret location'. He would find her, though. There was no other option.

He'd barely got away with his life. That man… He shuddered, curling in on himself. He'd chased him down roads he'd barely known until he'd got to the blessed spectre of the river. Down by the bank, he was at home, scrabbling through the soft earth as quickly as he could until he got to the bridge into Grangetown.

Casting off the coat and itchy beard, he'd emerged with a bit of mud on his shoes and a shirt, tie and soft suede jacket. With his trembling hands concealed in his pockets, he wasn't out of place amongst the late diners of Cardiff Bay, strolling along the waterfront as if he belonged there. He wanted to get out of the crowd, back home, but he couldn't bear the thought of being there without his freebird.

He'd walked slowly through Splott, returning to familiar streets and trying not to cringe every time the helicopter flew overhead. They were looking for him. They were casting him as a criminal.

When he'd arrived home, opening up the house he'd never expected to see again, it had seemed wrong without her. The empty bottle of Bombay Sapphire on the table – only the finest for her, all the jewels of the Empire – reminded him of their bold caper, their heroic flight. They would've looked back on it in years to come and smiled fondly at how daring they'd been. But the scum had taken it from them.

And he knew exactly who was to blame. He'd seen that face before, remembered it vividly. Another favourite of the journalists, that one, but he was with the police now. He was the key to finding his freebird.

If he got to Jason Carr, he could have his freebird once more.

Chapter 47: I Don't Like Mondays

'I'm heading back to London.'

Bryn looked up from his desk to look at Eleanor questioningly. She was dressed in another sharp suit, this one in mauve with a frilly white blouse. And his ex-wife said he didn't notice these things.

'Already? You don't want to wait until the thing is done?'

But Eleanor shook her head with a small smile.

'You're doing a good job.' she said with surprising honesty, and Bryn felt his cheeks flush with pride. 'Don't let anyone above tell you otherwise. Besides, you're close to him now and the girl's safe.' Her face settled into an expression of disgust. 'There's word of a copycat in Manchester. I'm going to try to nip it in the bud before the situation escalates.'

Before there are three dead bodies and a hostage, Bryn thought grimly. He'd always be twitchy about missing persons from now on.

'Any last insights before you head off?'

He was genuinely interested in what she had to say. She might be a bit odd and a bit English, but her heart was in the right place, and she was smart in ways he could never hope to be.

She studied the whiteboard carefully before gesturing towards her profile of the killer. 'He'll be in work today. He'll have to be. But he will make a move for Carla, either today or tomorrow. He may have been patient before, played hard to get, but he's had a taste of her now – he'll be back for more.'

A chill crawled down his spine at her words and his hand unconsciously reached for the phone, thinking about adding another officer to Carla's hospital room. Eleanor nodded to him and waved as she left, and Bryn watched her go with a sadness that surprised him.

But then he was back to the work, and she soon faded into the background of his memory, like old marks on a chalkboard.

All around her were dead ends and windows not yet open. It was a miserable day to be alive.

Amy stewed on the sofa, counting down the minutes until Jason came back and made lunch. Then he could get started on the list of places to visit on Laurie's schedule. She'd shaded in the details since she'd handed the copy to Bryn, even going so far as to devise a route through town that would most efficiently cover the places Laurie visited before she died.

But first Jason had some errands of his own – picking up a few things to put in the room downstairs, stopping his benefits, checking in with his mother. Amy liked Gwen because she clearly cared about Jason. She'd stuck by him even after he stole that car, after prison. She was resourceful and she was tough and, if Amy ever grew up out of this shadowed half-life, she wanted to be a woman like Gwen Carr.

Amy had still been working on the CCTV composite when he left, mumbling complaints about the phone signal on the ground floor. She'd barely acknowledged him, putting the finishing touches on the killer's face. It still wasn't perfect and she was uncertain about the width of his eyes, but it was better than nothing. She'd sent it off to Bryn with a deep sense of satisfaction.

However, her productivity had left her with nothing to do. Melody's phone, now slightly less soggy, was still transferring data to AEON but Amy wasn't convinced anything workable would come out of it. And once she'd accessed Jason's police statement and noted the reference to ticket machines, she had started work on accessing their records only to discover their servers were painfully slow and surprisingly resistant to an enterprising hacker. She'd given up on the personal touch and was now throwing her suite of cracking tools at it in the hope that something would penetrate. Meanwhile, Bryn was trying to gain the intel through old-fashioned policing – she had six spring rolls riding on his failure.

AEON beeped at her, then trilled again. Two alerts – almost worth getting off the sofa. Amy made a half-hearted effort to move, then sank back down. In a minute. Maybe when Jason got back.

She pulled her dressing gown closer around her. Jason would have to investigate the heating – it was too damn cold in here. There must be a draught coming in from somewhere, and he would probably know how to do something about that. It was useful having an assistant.

He would be disappointed, though, if she hadn't finished this when he got back. Especially if he found her in exactly the same position on the sofa. He'd started going on about deep vein thrombosis and not drinking enough fluids, and she'd eventually relented and had another cup of tea. It was worse than having a mother. In fact, that particular paranoia had likely originated with Gwen.

Amy prised herself off the sofa cushions and shuffled over to AEON's flashing screen. Melody's phone data, such as it was, was ready for perusal, and the creaky old train ticketing system had finally relented and let her in. Lured by the hope of a man stupid enough to use his credit card, Amy went for the train tickets first and remotely connected to the little machine at Cardiff Queen Street.

AEON beeped again. Amy flicked open the alert – one of the external perimeter wires had tripped. It was the bloody pigeons again. She had been tempted to order a crossbow to rid herself of that menace once and for all.

The alarm beeped again. With a growl of frustration, Amy switched off the feeds from the perimeter sensors. How was she meant to work with all these unnecessary beeps?

While the ticketing machine data slowly loaded, Amy opened Melody's data in a phone emulator and tried to make sense of the files. Some were corrupted beyond all recognition and she might have to go down into the raw data to find anything useful in them. A handful of contacts had both name and number, and a smattering of old text messages were available, but none particularly recent or relevant. Amy made a note of her most frequent text contacts regardless, but didn't expect them to yield much. Bryn and Jason had already exhausted those avenues.

The ticket machine finally connected and Amy trawled Sunday evening for purchases. Twenty-six people had used the machine after eight o'clock that evening and only five of them had used a card. The rest were cash purchases, mostly to local stations, but Amy plotted all the destinations on a map. She also flagged the stops en route, in case he had both brains and means to purchase beyond his true station stop. The five card purchases traced to one woman and four men. Of the men, one was geriatric, so that left three potentials. Amy started an automated background search on the names, looking for addresses, workplaces, social networking, and returned to Melody's phone.

She hoped that Jason would be pleased with how productive she was being. Maybe he would make her more spaghetti, or something different. He'd mentioned sausage and mash the other day, and her mouth had watered at the prospect of onion gravy.

Melody had the usual apps, some games, social networks, a few university-relevant items, and a browser with eight open tabs. Amy flicked through what remained of Melody's notes – books for class, National Insurance number, a postcode, shopping list, university email address. Of all of them, only the NI number and postcode were created in the timeframe between Kate's death and Melody's.

She stuck the postcode into her map search and reviewed the background checks. One unemployed divorcee, one single athletic primary school teacher, and…

Amy stopped. She returned to the map search and zoomed in on the one highlighted building in the city centre.

That was the connection. Of course. How could she have been so stupid? That was what all three of them had in common – it was staring her right in the face. She'd been so bogged down in the *who* and the *why* and the *where* that she'd completely ignored the *what*.

Suddenly, a terrible thought occurred to her. A painful, twisting thought that made her blood run cold. Jason had gone into town this morning. What if the killer knew Jason? What if she'd sent him into the lion's den?

Amy reached for her phone and started texting him. She had to warn him. She had to be subtle, in case the killer was sitting in front of him. *Oh God, please let it not be too late—*

Hands grasped her from behind and hauled her back out of her chair. Amy shrieked and tried to pull away, but he was strong, seeking out the flesh of her neck. He'd strangled those girls. She was next.

Amy twisted and fought, trying to scream against the pressure on her neck. But he was dragging her backwards towards the kitchen, her feet slipping out from under her.

'I'm afraid no one can hear you,' he said, calmly. 'But he'll be home soon, won't he? We'll just wait for him over here.'

This was it – she was going to die. She had to focus, she had to find something strong inside her. She stilled in his arms, dropping her hands from his scrabbling hold on her shoulders.

'Good girl,' he said.

Her fingers tugged at her dressing gown belt and slid free of the heavy robe. She seized the handle of her chair and swung it at him. She saw it collide and then fled, running for the end of the corridor.

She grasped for the light switch and the lift doors shuddered open. Flinging herself inside, she pressed urgently at the ground floor button. At the end of the corridor, she saw a figure lurch into view. She realised she was somehow still holding her phone and, as the doors closed, she pressed Send.

'Please,' she begged. 'Send, please send…'

The lift descended, the sound of banging and shouting coming from the floor above. The doors finally opened and she staggered out, before regaining her mind and shoving her arm in the door. The doors jerked open and she slid down, sitting in the doorway to prevent the lift moving.

She looked at her phone. No signal. She was alone in her house with a serial killer and Jason was walking into a trap.

'Fuck,' she said and banged her head against the door, praying for deliverance.

Chapter 48: When the Man Comes Around

The walk from his mam's to Amy's was brisk and chilly, wet leaves on the pavement and frost in the air. His broken arm hung uselessly under his jacket, fingers changing from white to blue, and Jason figured it was time to invest in some gloves.

He touched the gun in his jacket pocket, the metal cold enough to burn. He hoped the weather didn't affect the mechanism. His dad would never forgive him for letting the weapon go like this, unoiled and unloved. Then again, his dad probably wouldn't have approved of him carrying it through the streets either.

Jason stopped for milk and bread on the way back, wondering if they were running out of tea. It was nice to buy groceries again, not just take what the prison guard gave you or what his mam deemed was good and proper for him to eat. He could get used to this. He juggled the bag, easing it onto his forearm, and clumsily tucked his change into his pocket.

When he was about two streets away, a text came through from Amy. With numb fingers, he struggled to get to his phone to read it. It made no sense.

Don't go to job cen

It ended abruptly without her usual @, and he guessed she'd sent it by accident. He waited for the rest of the message to come through, dodging left and right to get a better signal, to no gain.

Anyway, he was only five minutes away now. If she needed him to fetch something, he could always go back out – after he'd had a cup of tea and some toast. Wishing he could stuff his freezing hands in his pockets, he continued on his way, whistling 'Eye of the Tiger' under his breath. He needed to watch those movies again – they'd been his dad's favourites. Maybe he could talk Amy into a marathon? Though she might make him watch some shit like *AI* or *Gattaca* and those did not have nearly enough explosions or fight scenes for his taste.

As he approached Amy's house, the door remained closed. She obviously hadn't moved from the sofa since he'd left. He'd have to give

257

her the thrombosis lecture again. Jason spoke gibberish at the intercom, waiting for it to recognise his voice, and the door clicked open.

The lift doors opened and Jason started planning lunch in his head. Maybe sandwiches? He was sure he'd got some cheese in—

There was blood in the hallway.

Jason paused, every nerve in his body screaming at how wrong the sight was. His mind flashed back to Laurie and Gina's house, the dead girl stretched out on the bed, staring eyes and dripping blood. He abandoned the groceries, and the gun slid into his hand like it belonged there, his unsteady left hand suddenly sure.

He inched down the corridor to the first patch of blood, inky dark. It seemed someone had staggered down the hallway to the very end, retreating into the darkness. Suppressing his instinct to follow the blood, Jason edged closer to the living room doorway and peered round.

The office chair was on its side on the floor, blood spattered on the wall, and the end table upended on the sofa. He crept through the living room, his heartbeat steady, his breathing quiet. He had stalked people on the street for money. He could do it again for Amy.

Jason studied the kitchen from his vantage point by the sofa. No breathing carried through, no motion disturbed the air. He looked inside – empty, untouched. He turned and retreated back the way he came, finally able to follow the blood trail through Amy's flat. He both hoped and feared to find her at the end of it.

As he got closer, he could see that the blood led to the concealed lift, red smears on the wall that made up its hiding place. Had she made it inside? Was the lack of body in the corridor due to the fact that she had escaped in the lift? Had she shut the killer on the outside?

Was he still here, waiting to finish her?

The bathroom door was closed. Bracing himself beside the door frame, he counted to three and then kicked it open. Clear. The sound echoed, loud and sharp, and Jason was aware he'd given away his position. Shit, this wasn't *Call of Duty*. People could die if he fucked this up. There were no extra lives. There were no second chances.

Only the bedroom left to search before he went for the lift. It was slightly ajar and, as Jason inched closer, he noticed a smear of blood on the door handle. It didn't make sense. If she'd run for the lift, why hadn't she used it? If he'd caught her there, he would've cornered her – there would've been no escape. It made no sense for there to be blood on the bedroom door handle.

He didn't have time for a logic puzzle. He only had time for Amy, to find her and get them both out alive. Jason stepped forward, raising the gun to head height and pushing open the door with the back of his hand.

The bed was in its usual disarray, but the heavy curtains were flung open, daylight streaming into the room through the floor-to-ceiling windows. The low wintery sun was blinding and Jason squinted against the light. He belatedly realised that they weren't windows at all but doors, flung wide to the tiny balcony beyond.

A rope was tied to the balcony rail. There was blood on the tile. Jason could only think the worst, a vision of Amy sprawled on the ground below, neck at an impossible angle. Like that photograph of Melody, forever seared into his mind.

He hurried forward, crossing the room with great strides until he reached the edge of the balcony, and dared to look down. No Amy. Just a rope tied to the balcony, hanging to the ground.

She wasn't dead.

A savage blow against his back sent him crashing forward into the railings, his ribs and shattered arm screeching their agonised protest at the impact. Jason twisted and tried to get the gun up, but it was knocked out of his hand, skittering across the tile. He met his attacker face-to-face and, for a split second, froze completely. But he knew this man. He'd seen him only this morning – at the job centre.

'Martin?' he said, disbelieving, before ducking a punch, pulled back into the struggle for his life. The man clawed at his neck, trying to strangle him, but Jason shouldered him back, giving himself some space. If he could stop Martin from herding him against the rails, he had a chance. If Amy had called the police, he might survive this.

But where was Amy? The thought distracted him enough for Martin to grab his broken arm and twist. Jason screamed, fire and lightning tearing through his arm and shoulder. He wrenched his arm away from the man's death grip and kicked out at his shin.

Martin was faster, smarter, and wrapped his arm around Jason's neck, wringing the life from him. Jason kicked out, but his efforts were futile, the agony from his arm rendering him useless. He was going to be victim number five. Dead body number four. His struggles were weakening, his vision greying as his windpipe fought to suck in air past the pressure of Martin's arm.

Then, out of the corner of his eye, Jason saw her. Her pale, pyjama-clad figure hovered by the open door, blinking into the sunlight as if she'd never seen it before. Jason wanted to tell her to run, to get the hell out, but she was in a trance, one foot in front of the other like a tightrope walker until her last step hovered over the door frame.

Jason wanted to cheer her on, but he could barely hold his own weight. His eyes focused on the arch of her foot, the long slender line as the ball sank down onto the tile, and Amy took her first step outside for ten years.

She released a long, slow breath. She stretched out her arm and picked up the gun.

Martin saw her. 'What are you doing?' he said softly, menacing. 'Put it down. You'll only hurt him, won't you?'

But she held it steady, pointing it levelly at Martin's head. He loosened his grip, nervously readjusting his hold enough for Jason to hook his fingers over the arm and give himself a centimetre to breathe.

Jason studied the line of Amy's body, surveying the fragile tension, deciding how likely it was he was about to get a bullet in his skull.

'You don't know how to use that,' Martin said. 'You can't shoot me. Put it away.'

Amy showed no sign of moving, as still as a sentry, waiting.

Jason wouldn't let her wait any longer. He jumped, hanging off Martin's arm with his full weight, a bolt of agony through his broken arm. The killer cried out as he bowed forward, before yanking his arm out of Jason's grip and holding his hand up to strike.

A gunshot sliced through the air and Martin, surprise painted on his face, tipped over the balcony. There came the crash of metal and breaking glass. Jason struggled to his feet to peer over.

Martin lay dazed in Amy's skip, blood blossoming over his left shoulder. Jason watched him struggle feebly for a moment before he passed out. With an expression of grim satisfaction, Jason turned back to Amy.

She held the gun at arm's length, staring at it like it was possessed, and slowly slid down to the patio tile. 'I shot him,' she whispered. 'I shot him.'

Jason stumbled over to kneel on the ground before her, holding out his hand.

'Amy, I need you to give me the gun.' His voice was a rasp, as if he'd been gargling with knives, and he felt the burn in his throat from where Martin had gripped him.

Amy handed over the gun mutely, obedient like a child, and Jason wiped it on his T-shirt before setting it carefully on the tile away from them. The tremor in her hand spread to her arm and soon she was shaking, body racked with silent sobs, the enormity of what had just occurred hitting her all at once.

Jason drew her close with his left arm, and she tucked her face into his neck, trembling against him, clinging.

'Outside, outside…no…please…' she muttered to him, but he shushed her, letting go for a minute to fish out his phone.

'Bryn, the killer's at Amy's.' He took a breath. 'I shot him.'

Chapter 49: Nothing But the Truth

Bryn arrived at the scene of the crime and, for the first time, hated his job.

The cordon around the house had already drawn gawkers from the general public and press alike, and the ambulance stationed outside with its muted flashing light didn't help. As he passed the back of the ambulance, he saw a protesting figure on the trolley, connected to a drip on one side and handcuffs the other, with two uniforms on the door. *Alive, then. More's the pity.*

He approached the door wearily. He should be thrilled with this arrest, the end to so much heartache, but all he could think about were the implications for a young man he'd grown fond of. Ex-cons who shot people went down for a very long time. Could they make an argument for self-defence? Shooting anyone who wasn't waving a rocket launcher was considered disproportionate these days. And who exactly brought an illegal handgun to the party?

Bryn didn't even want to consider what this would do to Amy. He had finally started to see a change in her, letting someone in to take care of those things she just couldn't keep hold of, like cleaning her clothes and eating regular meals. If Jason went back to prison...

Amy's flat was crawling with police officers, evidence markers highlighting a trail of blood down the corridor. As he entered, Bryn heard the unmistakeable sound of Jason's raised voice and sighed. He'd hoped to avoid this kind of confrontation.

'She's not going anywhere! I don't care if it's a crime scene. She's going to stay here and drink her bloody tea,' Jason growled at the poor uniformed officers over his shoulder, his left hand wearing a metal bracelet and the officer dithering over what to do with its right counterpart.

'He's not going to do a runner.' Bryn drew all eyes in the room. 'Are you?'

Jason raised his chin, defiant to the last – and revealing the red raw scrapes and developing bruises tattooing his neck. *Self-defence then.*

'Amy isn't going anywhere,' Jason rasped, voice broken but fierce in its intensity. 'She wasn't even there!'

He jerked his head towards the sofa and Bryn finally noticed her there, ensconced in a nest of blankets with a mug of tea in her hands.

She was staring into space, a fine tremor running through her. But then she looked up at him, eyes wide as she reached out a hand to cling to the hem of Jason's shirt. 'Don't take him. It was—'

'A struggle. On the balcony. The gun went off.'

The words were short and clipped, and every good policeman's instinct in Bryn's body flared, telling him the boy was a liar. But then he saw the way Amy looked at him, lost and yet painfully grateful, and Bryn understood. He understood all too well what lengths Jason would go to for Amy, and confronting a serial killer was barely the start of it.

'You need to come down the station to answer a few questions,' Bryn said reluctantly.

'Amy stays,' Jason said, hard steel in his voice that reminded Bryn that this boy had run with a gang, done time, taken down a murderer with a broken arm – whether he'd struck the final blow or not.

'She'll need to give a statement.'

Bryn was unwilling to relent on that, at least. If they did this by the book, they would all be above scrutiny. But that would mean psychiatrists and assessments and the disruption of this fragile shell of a life that was all that was holding Amy together.

Amy looked up at him with imploring eyes. 'You will take care of him.'

Bryn hesitated. But Jason saved him, suddenly switching to calm, even tones to soothe the wounded animal on the sofa.

'Amy, I'm under arrest. I've gotta go explain myself, haven't I?'

She slowly nodded but continued to stare at Bryn as if he'd just taken a hammer to her beloved computer.

'When you're done with your questions, he's coming back here,' she said, apparently oblivious to the potential consequences of being arrested. Jason merely smiled. Bryn nodded to the uniform officer, who awkwardly removed the handcuffs and shuffled round to look up at Jason.

'Jason Carr, you are under arrest for illegal possession of a firearm, illegal discharge of a firearm, and unlawfully and maliciously inflicting grievous bodily harm.' The charges were drawn from the officer's lips like the solution to a particularly challenging puzzle. It wasn't every day you arrested a man for shooting a serial killer in Cardiff.

However, as he moved on to the familiar right to remain silent, he picked up speed and confidence. 'You do not have to say anything. But you may harm your defence if you do not mention, when questioned, something which you later rely on in court. Anything you do say may be given in evidence.'

At the end of his spiel, the officer looked at Bryn like a child ready for a lollipop. Bryn shot him a withering look.

But Jason was smiling at him, despite his bruises and the way he gingerly held his right arm, with lines of tension through his body. Bryn should get him to A&E sooner rather than later, though he'd be damned before he let him share an ambulance with the bastard outside.

'Go on,' Jason said, grinning. 'I know you want to.'

It took Bryn a moment to work out what the kid was saying, before he rolled his eyes with a put-upon sigh.

'Take him away, boys.'

Jason was the most-photographed man in Wales. While the Job Centre Creep hid behind the ambulance doors, Jason had to face a dozen flashbulbs outside Amy's house and again at the cop shop.

At least he didn't have to wait long for his interview. Owain entered the room, a man beside him who Jason didn't know. Jason was immediately uneasy – where was Bryn? Despite his strained relationship with the older detective, he'd been relying on his level head when dealing with this situation. And Bryn knew Amy, knew she had to be kept away from the world of cells and interview rooms and grim unsmiling detectives.

The unfamiliar man sat across from Jason, Owain leaning forward to start the recording device against the wall. No tapes – Amy would be impressed. No doubt she'd have acquired the file before he got home.

'Interview commenced at 19:40 on 25th November 2013. Detective Superintendent Roger Ebbings and Detective Sergeant Owain Jenkins present,' Owain rattled off. A super? Jason was moving up in the world.

'You've waived your right to counsel, son – is that right?' Roger had a soft Swansea accent, but there was a hard edge lurking beneath.

Jason shrugged his left shoulder. 'Don't need it, do I?'

His tone was easy, but his heart started to beat a tattoo in his chest. Shit, was he being a moron here? Or did demanding a lawyer look suspicious? He couldn't afford his own, and he never entirely trusted appointed lawyers to be on his side. Bored jobsworths, most of them.

Roger nodded. 'Your choice. Tell us what happened.'

Jason carefully laid out how he'd come to Amy's house, how he'd followed the trail of blood, and how he'd been jumped on the balcony.

'And then he pulled a gun,' he said, voice steady. 'I tried to grab for it. It went off, see. Then he fell over the edge.'

'Why would he start using a gun now?' Owain said, sounding more curious than concerned.

Jason resisted the urge to jump across the table and shake him. 'I don't know.'

But then he thought of Amy, curled up in his arms and shaking, because she'd dared to cross a line to save his miserable life.

Jason took a breath. 'Maybe he knew we were after him. Maybe he got desperate.'

Owain leaned forward, poised to ask another, when Roger interrupted.

'We might never know,' Roger said.

Jason resisted the urge to laugh in relief.

They believed him. Thank fuck, they believed him.

Chapter 50: Hearth

'I worked it out,' Amy said, with a note of triumph. 'Before he arrived.'

She hadn't moved from the sofa, tucked against Jason's side as he rested his good arm over her shoulder. Bryn and Owain had to make their own tea.

'Martin,' Jason spat, as if the name left a bad taste in his mouth.

Bryn frowned. 'You know him?'

'It was the job centre,' Amy said, savouring the feeling of all the pieces sliding into place. 'We were so concerned with where they worked and who they knew there that we overlooked the fact that they all had new jobs. Melody had the postcode for the place on her phone. The credit card on the ticket machine confirmed it.'

'What about Carla Dirusso?' Owain asked.

Amy shrugged, blanket sliding off her shoulder. 'The hospital? It would be easy enough to find out.'

She would run the data when she had time. When Bryn needed it for court. When Jason wasn't just back from the police station and A&E (again) and she could stop checking he was really here.

'He matches the sketches and the profile. He came after Jason when he recognised him at the train station.' Her voice shook on the words, and Jason squeezed her arm, silently supporting her.

'He was worried that you'd recognised him, like he'd recognised you,' Owain said, nodding to himself.

But Amy shook her head, still turning over the facts in her mind. 'He knew he didn't, because we didn't come after him. Jason went to the job centre this morning and didn't say anything to him. There must be another reason for it.'

Amy frowned, struggling to connect the dots. She was tired. Fighting for your life would do that to a person.

'Maybe he wanted to use me to get to Carla,' Jason said.

Amy looked up at Jason questioningly. 'Why would he seek out Carla? She rejected him. She never knew he existed.'

Jason smiled at her. 'Because he loves her. Or he thinks he does, which is as good as. People do stupid shit for people they love. Including killing a bunch of girls and coming after tough ex-cons.' He removed his arm from her shoulder to flex it, showing off an impressive bicep.

Amy giggled, slightly hysterical.

He was real. He was here.

Jason measured the last segment of hallway for the new carpet and noted it down on his bit of paper. Amy had offered her iPad for the task, but he liked the feel of pencil on paper when measuring. It was reassuringly familiar, and right now he needed some of that.

The news reports had been as dramatic as expected, describing the confrontation at the home of the 'private investigator' as if it had been a high-speed car chase through the city centre. However, his mother had dutifully framed the front page of the *Echo* to put up in the kitchen, and Jason was resigned to it being dinner table conversation for the next year.

He'd called Teresa, and she had listened in silence to his story, with only a few telltale hitches in her breathing. She'd thanked him for what he'd done and tentatively wondered if they might get a drink some time. He'd told her no, that he was still caught up in this investigation and it wouldn't be fair on her, and she said she understood. He liked to think they'd parted friends, but they'd never really been friends before and he couldn't see them keeping in touch.

Jason was both relieved and saddened that the gun was gone. Bryn had taken him to one side and reminded him that this wasn't an episode of *The Wire*, and if he ever found him carrying a concealed firearm, there would be hell to pay. Also, he didn't think that any sort of weapon around Amy was a good idea. Jason had agreed with his eyes, despite his nonchalant denial.

Amy wasn't yet back to her usual self. She had been avoiding going to bed, catching naps on the sofa instead, and burying herself in lines of code. Jason had managed to feed her, but only if the food was placed directly in front of her with hints that it was getting cold at regular intervals.

At least she didn't have to testify in court. Jason had identified himself as principle witness and Amy would only be required to submit a written statement. Bryn had declared her a victim who required the protection of anonymity, and the judge had agreed.

Jason had never known anyone like Amy. It seemed that most of the time she just didn't care what happened to her. Meals, sleep, changing clothes – it could all be happening to someone else, a remote person who she didn't particularly like.

He returned to the living room, where she was sitting in front of Ewan, busily typing away. The rhythm of her keystrokes was almost soothing, a tapping lullaby, and he sat on the sofa to watch her for a while. Amy was never still, but she was never entirely in motion. It was as if her energy was all constrained inside her, only released for dire need or the thrill of the case or an exciting piece of coding. She was otherwise inert, uncaring, a lifeless doll.

Well, that wasn't entirely fair. Amy did care – he saw that in the way her eyes strayed to his arm, how she wanted him to sit down with her and take tea to make sure he rested. He'd soon learned that he didn't really have working hours and he was still seeing just as little of his mother and sister as he had been at the height of their investigation. He missed sitting across from his mam in their little kitchen, talking over the day with a cup of tea. He'd have to sound out how Amy felt about her coming over for dinner.

'What are you thinking about?'

Jason looked up, startled to see Amy's chair turned towards him as she studied his face.

'Nothing much,' he said, hurriedly dredging up a neutral subject. 'Dylan thinks the bike will be ready for the road soon.'

'You're not ready for the bike,' she reminded him, looking pointedly at his arm.

The surgeon had decided he wouldn't need an operation, but his struggle with Martin had undone all the healing accomplished so far and he had to start the wait from scratch. Another five weeks before he could ride his beauty down the street. He could hardly contain his excitement and earned another look from Amy.

'What are you up to?' He tried to peer around her to look at the monitor.

She gestured vaguely at the lines of code. 'Trying to commandeer our killer's private server. He's not using it and I can run it better than he ever could.'

'Back to the wrong side of the law, eh?' It wasn't that he disapproved; he just had a hard time picturing Amy as a career criminal.

Amy laughed at him, a small puff of air over lips, before returning to her work.

'Tea?' he asked.

'Please,' she said, and he went to make another round of toast.

About the Author

Rosie Claverton grew up in Devon to a Sri Lankan father and a Norfolk mother. She studied medicine in Cardiff and quickly turned Wales into her home. When she is not writing or working in medicine, she blogs about psychiatry and psychology for writers in her Freudian Script series. Her aim is to help writers accurately portray individuals with mental health problems in fiction.

Other books in The Amy Lane Mysteries series:

Binary Witness (Book 1)
Code Runner (Book 2)
Captcha Thief (Book 3)
Terror 404 (Book 4)

Dear Reader,

Welcome to the new edition of *Binary Witness*! One or two changes throughout, including, crucially, ensuring that the month doesn't abruptly change on the first page (oops).

Please let me know what you thought of the book. You can email me at rosie@rosieclaverton.com or find me on Twitter as @rosieclaverton.

The rest of this letter contains minor spoilers for *Binary Witness*, so I suggest you read the story before venturing further.

I started writing this book when I was living in a little terraced house in Wrexham – the house that the opening scene takes place in. My housemate and I were terrified of the dark alley and taking out the rubbish became a weekly ordeal. Adding a fictional serial killer to this nightmare scenario did not make me any braver!

I am terrible at creating buildings for stories. Characters and plots come naturally to mind, but designing a space is a chore. Amy's flat was drafted and redrafted several times, with one early rewrite dedicated to changing the number of floors and how the lifts work. I know, I know – I'm a nerd.

Most of the other locations are based on places I know well. Number 22 with the blue door was my Cardiff student house, and Teresa's quirky flat once belonged to a close friend.

Cardiff's train stations also play a starring role. Who knew waiting endlessly on a platform in the drizzle was actually research? I also put five years of medical school to good use in depicting the University Hospital of Wales – and in beating up poor Jason!

The next book in The Amy Lane Mysteries is *Code Runner*, where Jason is framed for murder and Amy must prove his innocence before the killers move in.

And not one building was harmed in the making of these books.

Best wishes,
Rosie Claverton
amylanemysteries.com